CASS TELL

THE
COOKBOOK

a novel

The Cookbook - a novel
Cass Tell

Published by Destinée Media   www.destineemedia.com
Written by Cass Tell   www.casstell.com

Cover image courtesy of The General Mills Archives

ISBN: 978-1-938367-22-9

"No one cooks alone. Even at her most solitary, a cook in the kitchen is surrounded by generations of cooks past, the advice and menus of cooks present, the wisdom of cookbook writers."

Laurie Colwin

CHAPTER 1

She opened the front door of her apartment, stared into the living room and shuddered as a flash of horror moved through her spine. The room had been trashed. More than that, it was half empty. The handle of her overnight bag slipped from her hand, swung forward and hit the floor with a loud *whomp*.

She stood in the doorway wanting to scream. Instead, paralysis clutched her throat. With a slow movement she slipped the strap of her computer bag from her shoulder and lowered it.

After forcing a deep breath she took a slow step over her bags and into the room. Everything was out of place. The couch was turned over. Someone had moved a bedroom cupboard into the living room and thrown it on its side. Magazines and papers were strewn everywhere.

Her grandmother had once given her an antique wooden dresser and a walnut bookshelf. They were gone, as well as her books from university.

A crystal vase with yellow daisies was on its side, its water darkening the carpet. The flowers were a gift from Chandler, and now they lay wilted like ragged weeds.

She felt like vomiting, but even that was impossible as unbelief and numbness set into her being.

She moved into her bedroom and found more of the same. The bed was there, but another dresser was missing. Most of her clothing was gone, along with her family photo album, the one with pictures of her parents and of her as a child. It was like someone had ripped out her identity and left an empty void. Her parents were deceased and those photos were the only memories she had of them.

Her only thought was to call the police, so she walked back to the living room, took her cell phone from the computer bag and dialed 911.

A male voice answered. "Nine-one-one. What is your emergency?"

"I've . . . I've been robbed," she blurted out.

"Can you describe it?"

"What do you mean describe it? Someone broke into my apartment and stole my things!"

"Can you tell me what you see? What is missing?" His voice was calm, almost hypnotic, like he had repeated these lines a thousand times.

She looked about frantically. "I just . . . I just got home. Everything is a mess. Everything is missing! I don't know why anyone would . . . They took my furniture! How did they? And my books! Why would they take my books?

"Please give me your name and address. A police officer will be there as quickly as possible."

"My name is Kate Miller," she uttered, then giving her address.

"Just stay there and keep the front door open. Don't touch or move anything."

A numbness filled her as she thought about his words, repulsed by what she saw, knowing it would be a major effort to touch or move anything. "Okay," was all she could say.

He asked a few more questions before the phone call ended, and as she hung up she struggled to find her breath. Never in her life did she imagine she'd have to use 911. Things like this always happened to *other* people. In fact, she couldn't believe she had even thought to call the police, since doing so went against everything her grandmother had taught her, never to seek help or trust anyone from the government, including the police.

She walked past the breakfast bar and then had to tiptoe around her kitchen, utensils scattered randomly across the tiles. The cupboards doors were open, revealing bare shelves where food boxes had once rested. Their gaping emptiness begged to be filled with cereal and cookies that now lay strewn about the kitchen floor dusted with ash-like white flour. Her jaw became tight with anger when she realized her coffee maker and mixer were gone.

Above the sink, to the side, were two open shelves. On one she had placed a small ceramic bowl she brought back from Paris, where she kept garlic. It was no longer there.

The second shelf had held her cookbooks, but it too was now empty. This upset her more than everything else, and a wave of sorrow welled up within her as she fought back tears.

The cookbooks had special meaning because they had been a gift from her grandmother, but there was something more. During the past two weeks she had received two cryptic emails from her grandmother, unsettling because her grandmother had died three years ago. It was as though Kate had received messages from the grave.

The emails were not long, both promising more information to come. It was a shock to receive them and she wondered if someone was playing tricks on her. In the second message her grandmother had said,

"Whatever you do, preciously guard the Betty Crocker Cookbook." Initially that seemed odd and confusing. Why make such an obscure request to preciously guard a cookbook? It took several days of reflection and the only answer was that this perfectly fit her grandmother. She had always been an eccentric and mystifying woman.

Even before receiving the emails she had been treating the old Betty Crocker Cookbook as special, keeping it on a distinct place on the bookshelf. It had been a link to her grandmother for the last three years, holding many precious memories of their happy times together in the kitchen. Now that link was missing.

Dazed, Kate looked at the destroyed room with a sudden realization that she now had no possessions connecting her to her family. Nothing. She turned a chair upright and sat down, ignoring the dispatcher's command not to touch anything. She took a deep breath as tears formed in her eyes, yet she felt her body tighten with a resolve to retrieve her stolen things and punish the people who had done this. The question was how?

CHAPTER 2

Fifteen minutes after the 911 call, a police car pulled up outside and two uniformed police officers walked up to her apartment. Kate guessed they were in their mid-twenties, about her age.

"Thank you for coming," she said.

"No problem, ma'am," one of them replied. "We're just here to see that you're okay. A detective is on his way."

"A detective?" She asked.

"Yes, Miami-Dade has a team that specializes with breaking and entering. Someone will be here shortly."

They maneuvered around her bags into the living room, surveyed the room and then asked her questions, almost a repeat of what the 911 guy had asked. Then they went outside and waited.

Ten minutes later a charcoal gray Ford Taurus pulled in behind the police car and a man got out and walked toward the apartment. He seemed to be about fifty years old, was stocky and wore a crumpled suit about the same color as the car.

People from the other apartments were now opening their doors and watching the activity. A group of curious onlookers was gathering on the other side of the street.

The two uniformed police officers went out on the lawn and with quiet voices spoke with the man, who nodded his head several times and then the officers walked across the street to question the crowd for witnesses.

The man then sauntered up to Kate's apartment and said, "I'm Detective McGill. Are you Kate Miller?"

"Yes," she replied.

"I understand your home was broken into."

She nodded her head, fighting back tears, again sensing the irrationality of what had happened.

"May I look around?"

"Yes, please." It was agonizing to have someone see her place like this, as she always kept it in perfect order.

Detective McGill walked into the living room, made a quick survey and stepped into the bedroom.

He came back into the living room and asked, "Is this exactly how you found it?"

"Yes, except for the chair. I needed something to sit on."

He nodded then stared at her bags by the front door. "Were you away?"

"I was in New York for two days at a company training event."

"What was the event?" He asked.

"It was about stocks and bonds. I'm a portfolio analyst at Wesson Securities. Why is that important?" She didn't tell him she was a junior portfolio analyst having been in the job for less than a year.

"Who'd know you were away?"

"Just people in my company."

"This has to be the work of more than one person, seeing they took furniture and heavier things. We've been tracking several gangs doing this sort of thing. One gang seems to know exactly when people are away from their homes."

"But why me?" She questioned.

"Good question. Mainly they're hitting more expensive homes." He said it matter-of-factly, without judgment. "Do you have anything of exceptional value?"

"No. They took my antique furniture and everything that was personal. It doesn't make sense."

McGill paused for a moment while his eyes scanned the room. "I think you're right. Normally thieves just grab whatever valuables they can. Often it's to feed a drug habit. But, in your case it seems they were looking for something."

"Like what?" She asked.

"At this point, who knows? You see all the papers on the floor and the empty boxes in the kitchen? It appears they were thorough, leaving nothing un-turned. They may have been trying to find something specific. Did you have money or jewelry hidden away?"

"No. Not really. My jewelry was in a wooden box on top of the antique dresser in the bedroom. The jewelry box and the dresser are both missing."

Detective McGill scanned the room and pointed to the telephone. "It's been taken apart."

"Why would they do that?" She asked, realizing she had not noticed the phone.

"They might have been monitoring your calls."

"What? That's crazy," she exclaimed, her voice rising with disbelief.

Expressionless, Detective McGill stated, "Anything's possible."

"It just sounds ludicrous. Why would anyone violate my personal life?"

"Good question."

She took a breath and asked, "What about my stolen things? How can I recover them?"

"That's hard to say. Who knows what they'll do with them. For valuable goods, thieves usually give them to a fence or sell directly to private individuals."

"What about my books?" She sensed all she was doing was asking the same questions.

"For thieves, books are usually a hassle. They often end up in a dumpster, unless they're antique. We have to ask why they'd make the effort to take them in the first place."

"No, I can't have my books in a dumpster," she exclaimed. "Everything must still be all together. Where might I search for them?"

"Ms. Miller, that's the last thing you should do. Some of these thieves are part of dangerous criminal organizations. You've got to let the police do their work."

"So, what will you do?" She asked, her voice quivering, wondering if she could really trust the police to do their work.

"We'll do our best, but it may take time. Currently we're understaffed, so just give me a few days and I'll get back to you."

The thought of waiting was unbearable, knowing her precious possessions could end up in a trash heap. "I can't wait a few days," she declared.

He slightly raised his eyebrows. "Listen, stand down and let us do our job. We're focusing on cases we believe to be associated with organized crime, and from the look of things here, it may fit. But, we've got a backlog to work through."

"Backlog?" She asked. "You mean all the wealthy homes you mentioned?"

He nodded.

"So I'm guessing I take second priority?"

He shrugged. "We'll do our best."

"It's not good enough."

His tired eyes stared at her. "It'll make things worse if you take on the work of the police, so please stay out of it. You could be harmed if you encountered one of those gangs."

Annoyed, she stared back at him, "I'll wait for your call."

One of the uniformed policemen walked up to the detective and announced, "A call just came in. You're needed urgently at another scene."

Detective McGill handed Kate his card and said, "Call me in a few days." He walked outside to his car and drove away.

Kate went to her couch, turned it upright and sat down. She thought about her missing possessions and about the wealthy homes that had been burgled. Surely her case would not be taken as seriously as those. Her apartment was in shambles and the break-in felt personal. *She* had been violated, not just her home, yet it seemed the police had more demanding priorities.

She looked around at the mess and reality sunk in. With no one around to help she felt alone and powerless. Putting her head in her hands, she began to weep, as a slow-growing anger mixed with the tears running through her fingers.

CHAPTER 3

After Detective McGill left, Kate composed herself and began to make order, putting furniture back in place, trying to remember where things went and what was missing. It was slow going; every object she touched filled her with deep angst.

She finally sat on the couch, used her cell phone to call her boss at Wesson Securities and told him about the break-in, adding that she needed time off to clean up the mess and work things out with the insurance company and the police. While he sounded understanding, she sensed displeasure. The work load at the office was building up, but he reluctantly agreed she could take off a day or two.

Then she called Chandler.

After several rings he answered, "Chandler Harrington."

"Hey, it's me," she said, hearing her voice quiver as she said it.

Several seconds of silence hung before Chandler asked, "Is there something wrong?"

"Yes, I've been robbed." She felt a release knowing she had someone to share this with.

"What? What happened?"

She trembled. "My apartment is a mess and things are missing, and . . . the police are working on it."

"Unbelievable. You mean someone broke in?"

"Yes, but they didn't take everything."

She could almost hear Chandler thinking on the other end of the line. He then spoke in a soft voice. "This is so unexpected. I don't know what to say other than I wish I were there with you."

"Thank you. That means a lot to me," she replied.

"I never want anything bad to happen to you." He paused, and then asked, "It's weird. What would they gain from it? Was there something special to steal?"

"The police detective asked me the same thing. I don't know. There was nothing of great monetary value. The whole thing is absurd."

"But, think hard," he responded. "Is there something of importance, maybe something you didn't reveal to the detective?"

She felt frustration rising at Chandler's questioning and having to repeat herself. "No, there's nothing."

"Maybe you'll think of something. In the meantime, is there anything I can do?" His voice was empathetic, reassuring.

"I don't think so."

"I'll come to Miami as soon as I can, just to be with you. And call me any time you need to talk or if you think of anything."

"It would be so nice to see you, but don't put yourself out because of this."

"Kate, it's no imposition. I need to get down there anyway to visit my office and even if I didn't I'd come for you. You know how I feel about you."

"Thank you . . . and, I feel the same."

They said good-bye, hung up and then she felt embarrassed about what she had just said. At the beginning of the week when she was in New York he had confessed that he loved her. Now, she had just said she felt the same, that she loved him. She was sure that he was what she had always dreamed of and she was falling for him. But, did she say it because her emotions were shattered from the break-in, or was it true?

She had met Chandler three months earlier at a business social and had been seeing him ever since. Financial firms from Miami had brought in a Harvard Business School professor for a lecture followed by drinks and appetizers. It had been a chance for the financial community to socialize.

She remembered bumping into Chandler at the drinks table. "Excuse me," she said, not knowing who had made the body contact. She turned, and their eyes met.

"It's on me," he said with a laugh. His smile was confident, reassuring, fun.

They fell easily into conversation and within minutes she felt as though they were the only two people in the room. After exchanging business cards he said goodbye and promised to call, which he did.

Several days later they met for drinks and she learned that he managed an investment firm with offices in New York, San Francisco and Miami. He was unmarried and forty years old, fourteen years older than her. He was fit and handsome, wearing a perfectly tailored suit and a colorful silk tie.

The age difference didn't bother her as they had a certain chemistry, and that's all that mattered. He was a good listener, which made communication easy because he didn't seem consumed with himself.

They went out for dinner when he came to town, which was often, and he sent flowers regularly to her apartment.

She had always been cautious around men, a trait due to her upbringing, but gradually she had relaxed around him and began to open up. More and more she found herself thinking about him.

After a training event in New York they met and over a candlelit dinner Chandler had carefully shared his feelings. He was falling in love with her.

The flight back from New York had been a mix of euphoria and doubts. Never had a man been so respectful with her. She had sensed it was not easy for him to express his emotions in this way. But he had taken the step. This was new ground and she wasn't sure how to tread. She wished she had someone to talk with about this, like her grandmother.

Opening the door to her trashed apartment had shattered her state of mind, but speaking to Chandler had given reassurance. Now she couldn't wait to see him again. She understood that their relationship was still relatively new and they needed to spend more time together until she was fully convinced it was the right thing, but it was going in the right direction. Definitely all she needed now was his presence.

She sat on the couch, her back tense. As she peered across the room her confidence faded. Someone had violated her personal space. She began to consider a plan to put order back into her disrupted life.

CHAPTER 4

Axel Bjorg leaned back in his chair with his bare feet up on his wooden desk. He held a half-eaten sandwich in his left hand and in front of him on the desk was a thick book on European history. He was starting a chapter on the Industrial Revolution in England. Next to the book was a cup coffee getting colder by the minute.

Having just successfully completed a three-week, nonstop assignment, he had decided today he would relax, maybe even catch up on some paperwork. He needed a vacation, so he hoped no new jobs would pop up. The plan was to read a little, finish the sandwich and, most importantly, spend the rest of the day researching holiday places. Two or three weeks on a quiet Caribbean island would suit him just fine.

There was a knock on the door and before he could say anything the door opened and a young woman walked in.

"Is this Dr. Bjorg, Private Investigators?" She asked.

"Ah . . . Yes it is." He swung his feet to the floor and quickly put the sandwich in a top drawer, slipping his feet into his flip-flops.

"May I speak with Dr. Bjorg?"

"This is him." He smiled, aiming a finger at his chest.

He observed her lips slightly tighten and eyebrows narrow as she said, "On your website it says you've been in business for twenty years. You don't seem that old."

"I'm older than I look," he said with a grin. He didn't tell her he did his first detective job at ten years old, when he had tracked down a neighbor's cat. The job had paid fifty cents, but ever since then private investigating had become a passion and a way of paying the bills.

"Strange," she stated.

"What do you mean?"

"You don't look like a doctor."

"You mean like a brain surgeon?"

"No. I guess I expected something different."

"I have a PhD from the University of Miami. See, over there." He waved his hand in the direction of a wall where several diplomas were hanging.

She glanced at the diplomas, then back at him.

"Please, have a seat." He gestured back and forth to the two empty chairs in front of his desk.

She hesitated and then sat down in one of them.

His quickly observed her. She was tall, maybe five-nine or five-ten, with a slender figure. She wore a dark blue pants suit and a white blouse buttoned to the top. He prided himself on profiling people, which was forbidden in the police world but standard procedure for a private investigator.

A quick guess put her in her early to mid-twenties. She had blond hair that flowed just below her shoulders. What struck him was her face and eyes. Her eyes were a wonderful, light green and her skin was cream-colored, like translucent silk. For a moment he pegged her as Scandinavian, but somehow that didn't fit. Her eyes were slightly slanted toward her eyebrows, so perhaps she from Russia or some surrounding area. He wondered if she was a fashion model; something about her was almost feline. *That's it*, he thought, *a Russian fashion model.*

"How might I help you?" He asked.

"Your website states that you specialize in recovering missing objects," she said.

"That's one of my services, along with matrimonial discovery, forensic accounting and a bunch of other stuff."

"Matrimonial discovery?"

"Finding information about your spouse."

"Like infidelities?"

He chuckled. "Yes and no. I've done some of that, but no, I have partner agencies that tail wives and husbands to secret hotel rendezvous. I don't like sitting for hours on stakeouts in hot stuffy cars. Instead, I focus more on finding hidden assets, like a husband hiding bank accounts from his wife." Axel paused and looked deep into her eyes. "Is that what you need?"

"Not at all."

"Then how can I help?"

She paused, glanced at the cup of coffee on the desk, and surveyed the computers and electronic equipment on a table against one wall. And then her eyes met Axel's. "I need to find some personal possessions."

Axel cocked his head. "Why don't you tell me about it?"

Her folded hands nervously rubbed against each other. She took a deep breath and began, "Yesterday, I found that my home had been robbed." She continued, describing the state of her apartment and the missing items. She told him about her conversation with the detective, describing the possible phone tap and the fact that the thieves may have been searching for something specific.

Axel saw her eyes water and become distant as she talked as though she was reliving the experience. He also sensed strength in her as she rationally described what happened.

Finally she stopped and asked, "Can you help me find my belongings?"

"Why do you want them?"

"What do you mean? They belong to me."

"Sorry, I'm just asking if they have any value."

"There's some antique furniture that my grandmother brought back from Europe. It may be worth something."

That caught his attention. His PhD was in history, more specifically the economic history of the Reformation, an obscure subject to put on one's resume unless one wanted to get into academics, which he did not. Still, that's where his curious brain centered whenever he wasn't working a case. "Which part of Europe did they come from?" He asked.

With questioning eyes she asked, "What in the world does that have to do with finding my stolen goods?"

He realized his academic inquisitiveness may have led them off track, so he covered by saying, "Maybe nothing and maybe everything. It depends on how these objects are valued in the event they are resold. We may get a lead because of the description."

She nodded. "I think they came from the Czech Republic or maybe Hungary. I spent summers in Europe with my grandmother and aunt and they always brought back something."

"What else besides the furniture? Anything valued with significant worth?"

She stopped and took a deep breath. "Everyone is asking me that question. Honestly, most of it is of sentimental value, like a family photo album and some cookbooks. But, I want everything back."

"Cookbooks?"

"My grandmother and her older sister loved to cook, and they often included me. I have many happy memories of them making things from those cookbooks. They were of the opinion that a well-made meal goes deeper than nourishment; it touches the soul. So they were always experimenting."

"Huh. Okay, I guess I understand," Axel said, scratching the side of his head. Sentimental value often had more importance to people than financial properties. "I think I can help. I've had lots of cases involving stolen objects, like jewelry and art. But are you willing to pay the price for that?"

"What's your price?"

"My fee is a thousand dollars a day, plus expenses. Are you willing to pay that just to recover some furniture, a photo album and books? It might take many days." He had quoted her his base price. If he were to investigate more expensive financial assets the charges would be much more. Sometimes he employed associates and they weren't cheap.

"A thousand dollars a day?" She gasped, her eyes widening.

"That's my bottom price."

She remained quiet for a moment then said, "These stolen belongs are very important to me. Can we try it for a few days?"

"I need to warn you that a few days may not be enough," he said. "I need to think about this. It's likely the furniture would end up in pawn shops and antique shops, so I'd start there. On the other hand, the books might appear in used bookstores. Do you know how many bookstores there are in Miami, let alone in the state of Florida?"

"A lot I suppose, but I still want them back."

"You'll need to give me an inventory of the stuff."

"Please don't refer to it as *stuff*," she stated.

"Okay, an inventory of your *purloined possessions*," he said with a slight grin.

She slightly shook her head. "Very funny. I'll email it to you."

He reached into a desk drawer, moved his half eaten sandwich to one side, dug through some papers and pulled out a business card. He handed it to her and said, "So now you have all my information, but I still don't know your name."

"Oh, of course. I'm Kate Miller." She took a business card from a pocket and handed it to him.

Kate Miller, he thought to himself. *There is nothing more Anglo-Saxon than that. So much for the Eastern European theory.* He glanced at her card and saw that she worked for a financial services company as a portfolio analyst. *So much for the fashion model theory. So much for the brilliant private investigator getting things right.*

They both stood, shook hands and she turned and walked to the door. He observed her posture and movement, athletic and confident; although, experience told him that her life had been shaken. After an event like she had just suffered, it always took time to recalibrate. That's what he did for his clients. His service of finding their *stuff*, for lack of a better word, enabled them to reestablish their equilibrium. And that gave satisfaction to his work.

There was something else in her movement that captured his attention. She was downright attractive, but he had to be careful. He had learned in the past to maintain a strictly professional relationship with clients.

Two years before, one of his cases had turned messy. A woman had asked him to investigate her brother because of a conflict over their inheritance. Instead of focusing on his client's case, he got sidetracked with a romantic relationship with her. It gave her brother's lawyers an opening, which almost blew the case. In the end, and lucky for him, everything was settled out of court.

He had learned his lesson and wouldn't let that happen again.

Once Kate shut the door to his office he sat down and thought about her request. He thought about the sentiment she carried for a few personal items. It seemed odd that she would pay so much for his services when she could go out and buy new books and clothing and furniture. But something told him this might be one of those strange cases that made his job interesting.

He took a sheet of paper from a drawer in his desk and began to brainstorm, jotting down the few facts he had:

Young woman.

Tapped telephone.

Breaking and entry.

Thieves searching apartment.

Taking all personal possessions.

Potentially a gang?

Now, paying significant money to find goods only of sentimental value?

Indeed there was something weird here and an internal voice was telling him to proceed with caution. He stared at her business card and wondered about Kate Miller. Who was she? She could be a nutcase for all he knew. He had come across plenty of those. Did he really want to take this on? The thought of a sandy white beach in the Caribbean sounded quite attractive, but something in him urged him not to dismiss Kate Miller quite yet.

CHAPTER 5

K ate went back to her apartment and turned on her laptop. While it was booting up she looked around and sighed. Anger and resolve soon replaced her sadness. *Whatever it takes,* she thought, *I'm going to get my possessions back. More than that, I want to know who did this and why. If these people think they can get away with this, I'll prove them wrong.*

She clicked on the document file where she had started an inventory of the stolen items. Both Detective McGill and Dr. Axel Bjorg needed this.

It felt good to know that she had both men working her case. Finding her apartment in such a condition left a lingering shock. She was glad it was Friday. The weekend would give her the chance to clean up the place. Making order was something she took pleasure in, but the state of her apartment took away that joy. Hopefully the police detective and the private investigator would make progress. The sooner the better so she could get her life back to normal.

The problem was, lately she wasn't sure what *normal* meant. Typically on weekends she did things with her two best friends and university roommates, Sarah and Rebecca. Sarah's parents had a yacht, and the three young women had sailed most of the Florida coastline together. When they weren't sailing they went to movies and hung out. But Rebecca had recently taken a job in Chicago to be close to her fiancé. Likewise, Sarah had moved to Greece for several months to participate in an archeological dig. The absence of her friends now meant that *normal* had changed to lonely weekends filled with unnecessary hours in the office combined with Pilates classes on Saturday mornings.

When she thought about her meeting with the private investigator, doubts filled her mind. He seemed too young to be a doctor, and she wondered if he was telling the truth about being in business for twenty years. If he was stretching the truth here, how else would he prove to be misleading?

He seemed to be in his late twenties or perhaps early thirties. Did he have the experience she needed or would this be an expensive endeavor leading to nothing?

He was not what she expected in a private investigator. He wore jeans and a black t-shirt with a peculiar logo on it, *Nordmenn.* That was unfamiliar to her. When he stood up to say goodbye, she noticed how tall he was, maybe six-foot-three or four, with a muscular build, not like a weightlifter but more like a basketball player. His face had high, rounded cheekbones, a square jaw and cleft chin. And he had a killer smile. With his blue eyes and blondish brown hair he could be a poster boy. The bare feet on the desk and the flip-flops were anything but professional. Could she trust someone like that to help her, to be competent in his profession?

Kate completed her inventory and then emailed it to Detective McGill and to Axel Bjorg. Then she called Detective McGill.

After five rings, he answered, "McGill."

"Hello Detective McGill, this is Kate Miller."

"Who?" He asked.

"Kate Miller. We met yesterday afternoon when you came to my apartment, the breaking and entering."

Silence hung in the air for a few seconds. "Oh yeah," he said.

"I'm calling to see if you've made any progress."

"When was it again?"

"Yesterday. You were at my apartment."

"Sure, yes," he said.

"How are you coming on recovering my possessions?" She asked.

"Look, a lot has been happening. We're working on it, like I said. Didn't I say to wait a few days?"

"Yes, but I thought you might already have some information."

"I'm in the middle of a crime scene. Can we talk tomorrow?"

"Okay, I'll call you tomorrow, but I wanted to let you know something else."

"What's that?" He asked.

"I hired a private investigator to help me."

There was a pause on the line. "Why'd you do that? I told you not to get involved, and to let the police do their work."

"I want to find out what happened and need all the help I can get."

There was another pause. "Legally you can do anything you want, but I'd advise against it. You don't know how far you'll get in touching the underbelly of the criminal world. For your own safety, you should let the police deal with this."

"I understand, but I feel better by getting some independent help."

"That's your right, but it should be stated again," he said in a low serious voice, "Stolen goods are connected to criminals. You don't know what you're stepping into. Who's the private investigator?"

"Dr. Axel Bjorg."

"Who?"

"Dr. Axel Bjorg. He's been a private investigator for twenty years."

"Don't know him, but I'll ask around. You have to be careful. A lot of these guys are charlatans. How'd you pick him?"

"Pick him?"

"Yeah, who recommended him?"

"Ah . . . I found him on the internet."

There was another pause. "Oh my goodness."

She felt defensive and repeated, "He has twenty years of experience."

"I've been around for more than twenty years, so why haven't I heard of him?"

"Because . . . ah."

"Right. Just be careful, and let the police do their work. I've got to go. Call me tomorrow afternoon."

He hung up before she had a chance to say anything.

Kate went to her couch and sat down feeling a sense of hopelessness. The phone call with Detective McGill made her feel stupid. He was right. She had acted too quickly. Her home had been robbed, and the following morning she was searching private investigators on the internet, picking one based on the fact that he had 'doctor' in front of his name and, supposedly, twenty years of experience. The website had said, 'Experts in Finding Things.' How lame was that?

In reality this Dr. Axel Bjorg appeared to be anything like a private investigator. He was muscular and athletic, more like someone you'd find in a singles' bar. She had once gone to a pick-up bar with some girlfriends from work, and once was enough. She felt highly uncomfortable with all the superficial, but admittedly good-looking men hitting on her. Was he one of those?

Had she made the right choice in hiring a private investigator and if yes, had she hired the right one?

She had a couple of weeks of vacation time due, so she decided to call her boss to see if she could extend the few days he had given her. Maybe he'd give her a full week.

She needed to get control of this. She needed to know if it was the right thing to hire this Dr. Axel Bjorg . . . and what kind of a crazy name was that?

A disturbing thought crept through her mind. What if this so called *doctor-detective* was nothing more than a con-artist aiming to take her money? If that was true, it might take a long time to get her life back to normal.

She needed advice. After some hesitation, she called Chandler in New

York. His administrative assistant answered and asked her to wait.

Three minutes later she heard his voice. "I'm sorry Kate. I was just finishing up with a client. How are you doing?"

She suddenly felt bad about interrupting his day. "I'm sorry for calling, but I just needed someone to talk to."

"You can call me anytime. What's going on?"

She replied by telling him about the lack of progress with the police and that she was thinking to hire a private investigator, not wanting to sound foolish that she had actually hired one, especially after what Detective McGill had said. When she was finished she asked, "Any thoughts?"

A tense pause hovered between them before Chandler said, "You're going through a very difficult time and your emotions have been shaken. Maybe it will help to think this through again. There has to be a reason for what happened. Do you know now if the thieves were after anything in particular?"

"I have no idea."

"Then maybe you want to hold off on hiring a private investigator. If you really need one, I have plenty of contacts."

"You're right. Let me think about it," she said. "I'm grateful. Your advice is comforting."

"Anytime. You know I'm here for you, so call me day or night. And please keep me up to date on how it's going. I'll try and get to Miami as soon as possible."

"Thank you, Chandler. That means a lot to me."

She hung up and sighed dejectedly. Now she had even more doubts about hiring Dr. Axel Bjorg, but firing him after one day would be a waste of money. No, she was already committed, so now she just needed to set her mind at rest.

She had to make sure he did his job. The only way to do that was to supervise the guy.

CHAPTER 6

The following morning, Saturday at nine o'clock, Axel Bjorg took the elevator to his office. His hair was wet, as he had just showered at the gym down the street. He worked out five mornings a week. For three days he did weights and cardio. The other two he filled with Krav Maga, a street savvy martial arts system made up of efficient and brutal counter attacks. His previous boss and mentor, Harry Raintree, had insisted he master self-defense, "in order to be respected in a bar fight."

Axel carried a cup of coffee in his right hand. He wore a dark blue, Hawaiian tiki shirt with a print of white flowers and palm trees. He had replaced his flip-flops with green and gold-colored cross trainers. As the elevator climbed to the second floor, he began to consider the Kate Miller case. Compared with the other cases he had worked on, this one seemed simple, and he hoped to complete it as quickly as possible in order to get on with his much needed vacation.

He enjoyed the independence his occupation provided. He liked to work alone, as this enabled flexibility and speed.

His office was located in a two-story building shared with five other companies. It was modern, with a marble exterior and large glass windows. Axel owned the building, an opportunistic purchase resulting from the failed romantic relationship he had with a previous client. While the client and her brother came to a mutual agreement on the split of most of their assets, this building became a relational battleground with neither side giving in. Finally, in a moment of desperation, they dumped it on Axel at half its market value. He got a mortgage and now the rent from the other companies covered the bills.

The building was close to Interstates 95 and 195, giving him easy access to all of Miami. Most of his clients came from Miami Beach, as well as from Fisher Island and Bay Harbor Islands with their large concentration of millionaires. They required discretion, and Axel kept a low profile.

As he came out of the elevator he saw Kate Miller standing by the front door of his office. Even though she was a lovely sight with her flowering pastel blouse and nicely fitting beige slacks, he felt irritated by her presence. He had work to do and didn't need interference.

He forced a smile and said, "Fancy seeing you here."

She frowned and said, "Its nine o'clock. I expected you to be at work."

He grinned and replied, "Maybe I should hang a clock out next to the front door to punch in my time?"

He walked to the door, unlocked it and motioned his hand toward the room. With her back stiff, she walked past him, taking the same seat as the previous day.

With twinkling eyes he asked, "And what gives me the pleasure of welcoming you here today?"

She looked at him, her face tight. "I'm not sure I did the right thing by hiring a private investigator. That is, I'm not sure if you are the right person for the job."

At least she was blunt and to the point. "Why's that?" He asked, wondering what had changed from the previous day.

"I spoke with Detective McGill from the Miami-Dade Police Department and he said that I should let the police handle it. He might be right."

"Maybe. Sometimes the police can be smart."

"Do you know him?" Kate asked.

"I've heard of him."

"Well, he doesn't know you."

"I hope not." Axel stated.

Kate frowned. "And why's that?" She shook her head. "He warned me about hiring private investigators, saying some are charlatans."

Axel laughed. "I suppose some are. He doesn't know me because I stay clear of the police. For sure I have a few contacts among them, but I work independently."

"You don't collaborate with the police?"

"I try not to." He paused. "Mainly it has to do with methodologies. Sometimes I need to cross gray lines. The police are more restricted." He neglected to say that he often went considerably beyond the gray lines.

"But, shouldn't they be handling this case?"

Axel waited a few seconds and asked, "Are they?"

"What do you mean?"

"Are they handling your case? I bet anything that Detective McGill is working on dozens of burglary cases and most of them are for high value properties. Where do you fit in the hierarchy?"

Kate's lips tightened. "They are working on it."

"Right. And what's your feeling so far on how they're handling things?"

Kate stared at the desk. "Well, maybe not so well. But he said to give him a few days."

"What you have to understand is that they have dozens of cases and most of the time they are trying to identify major crime syndicates behind the high-end robberies. We don't know who broke into your place or why. While they work on many, I'll focus on only one case. Yours. But it's up to you to make your choice."

Kate took a deep breath and looked across at him. "How old are you?"

He smiled. "Just turned thirty."

"How can you have twenty years of experience?"

Axel laughed. "Okay, it might be stretching things, but it's the truth, in a way."

Her eyes tightened. "What do you mean, *in a way?*"

"Honestly, I got my first taste of this profession when I was ten years old. There were a lot of people with pets in my neighborhood, and some were always going missing. I was good at finding them and that gave me a fascination for this kind of work."

"And that's it, finding cats?" She questioned.

He laughed. "No, there was a bit more. I did security work during high school, and that's where I met Harry Raintree, one of the most experienced private investigators in Florida. He took me under his wing and I worked for him during university. In fact, it was Harry who recommended that I major in accounting, saying it was important for private investigators to know about the numbers. You need to know how to spot details on anything from bank statements to phone records. I then worked for him fulltime after I got my degree. Five years ago he retired and I took over the business, and I did my PhD studies on the side."

Axel didn't tell her about the countless hours he had spent learning analytic skills, spotting discrepancies in banking transactions and developing strategies to question people. Then there was learning about weapons and how to shoot a gun, and the years of perfecting martial arts.

"So, there's your twenty years," he said.

She hesitated, and then frowned. "Well okay, I suppose we can give it a try. Where do we start?"

"I already started," he said. "I sent your inventory to someone and am meeting with him at ten o'clock."

"Already?"

"He may have some leads. How can I put it? He knows the network for your kind of stolen stuff."

"Okay, then let's go. And again, please don't refer to my possessions as *stuff.*"

"What do you mean, *let's?* I work on my own and some of my contacts will be more forthcoming if strangers aren't there." He looked at her clothing and knew she would be out of place in some of the places he needed to visit. The only description of her attire was 'prissy'.

Kate eyes shifted to him. "Mister Bjorg, I absolutely insist that I go with you. I am the client and I need to look out for my investment. How do I know you will be working on this unless I go with you?"

Axel grinned. "It's *Doctor* Bjorg. See the paper on the wall? What's the matter, you don't trust me?"

"I didn't say that. I just need to know you are doing the right things."

"And you know the right things?"

Her jaw tightened. "You may need someone to talk with, to bounce ideas back and forth."

Axel shook his head. He had been involved in the search and recovery of art worth millions of dollars, and those clients gave him complete freedom to do his work. Now this eye-candy blond was demanding to micro-manage his investigation over, what, a few pieces of antique furniture, some photos and cookbooks? Something was definitely weird here; most likely she was unhinged. All he needed was another goofy woman in his life, tagging along to slow him down.

He realized his mind was going in the wrong direction and told himself to settle down. After all, he understood how the robbery would make her high-strung. Actually, wasn't this just a mini-case? To have the company of an attractive woman for a few hours might be pleasant, if he could just get her to loosen up.

He reached into the bottom drawer of his desk and pulled out a small .22 caliber pistol with a holster. He unfastened his belt and wound it through the holster, positioning the weapon so it remained on his back hip, hidden behind his Hawaiian shirt.

Kate's eyes were wide open.

"Okay," he said, "Let's go."

CHAPTER 7

They rode in Axel's car, a recent model red Corvette, the top down. Kate felt uneasy. This was suddenly far out of her comfort zone and she wondered if she was doing the right thing. Were the furniture and books really that important? An inner voice told her they were and that somehow this was all about respecting the wishes of her grandmother.

"Your gun makes me nervous," she said with a slow, irritated voice.

Axel said, "Don't worry. I've got a permit."

"Even so, I'd prefer if you left the gun in your office."

"Not a chance," he stated. "Harry Raintree would disown me if I wasn't packing."

Silly answer, she thought to herself. It still didn't make sense to carry the gun. "Where are we going?" she asked.

"Huh?"

"I asked, where . . . are . . . we . . . go-ing?" She punched every word, slow and deliberate.

"To a warehouse."

"What for?"

"To see someone."

"You mean to see someone who knows about stolen *stuff*, to use your limited vocabulary?"

"Yeah." He turned to her and smiled.

He was holding back information from her, and that raised her frustration level. It was like he was mocking her. She was his employer and expected him not to give curt little answers like "yeah" and "huh" followed by a goofy grin.

Axel smiled and said, "A client gave me this car."

"What?"

"I recovered some very expensive jewelry for him. Maybe you can buy me a car like this once we recover your books."

He definitely was taunting her. She frowned, knowing she would quickly get fed up with his moronic humor. Or, was she already? Instead of making wisecracks, he needed to focus on finding her things. And if he believed that behavior would stop her from accompanying him, he was dead wrong.

Kate's long blonde hair blew in the breeze, and she struggled to keep it in place.

Axel reached into the glove compartment, took out two Miami Marlins baseball hats, put one on and handed the other to her.

"Here, try this," he said.

She took the hat, shrugged and put it on.

Axel glanced at her and grinned.

She suspected she looked foolish in the hat. Growing up, other girls had worn baseball hats as fashion statements, but Kate had never done so. Her grandmother and Aunt Clara were old school, coming from a different world. That influenced Kate's tastes.

Her grandmother and aunt had emigrated from Poland, having fled when it was still under communism. Then they came to the United States, where her grandmother married John Miller, her grandfather.

Axel brought the car to a stop at a red light and pressed, "I still don't get it. Why are these things so important to you?"

Kate paused, wondering how much she should disclose. "Like I told you, they belonged to my grandmother. She and her sister, my Aunt Clara, raised me. Clara was older than my grandmother and died five years ago and my grandmother died two years after that. These are the only things I have that link to them."

"And what about your parents, if I might ask?"

Kate took a deep breath as the light turned from red to green. The Corvette accelerated. "They died when I was three, along with my grandfather. They were killed in a private airplane crash in the Everglades. The airplane was never found."

"Wow, that's tough. What about your mother's side of the family?"

"My maternal grandparents are deceased and my mother was an only child."

"So, you're alone. No family. I see how these stolen things are important. They're your connection with them."

Kate glanced away and held back tears. Yes, they were important, especially since receiving the two unexpected emails from her grandmother.

She reflected on the first one. It came on her twenty-sixth birthday, two Mondays ago. It was short and said,

Dear Kate,

I realize this email is unexpected, but knowing of my oncoming death I set it up in an email system for future delivery. I hope this is not too much of a shock, but I want to wish you a happy birthday.

I suspect that you will have graduated with your degree in finance and have found employment. When you were a child I saw your interest in art. I know I steered you in a different direction. This was for a purpose.

During summers I tried to make up for this by taking you to Europe to visit art galleries. Many children would see this as a punishment, but you were different in that you would spend hours in front of famous works of art.

There will be more to come, but I just wanted to send this to you and tell you that I love you more than anything.

Grandma Emma

Indeed Kate had been deeply shocked when she received it, but after some reflection she understood. Her grandmother was eccentric and, much of the time, a mystery. She smiled when she thought about her.

There was also a warm and loving side to her grandmother; much of this was expressed during their times in the kitchen. Her grandmother had shared much with Kate, as they spent many hours making meals. In fact, cooking was Emma's hobby. The smells and the laughter they shared provided endearing memories. And Kate had become a fabulous cook.

Her grandmother sometimes said, "The way to a man's heart is through his stomach," and Kate countered by asking why there were no men around. Emma loved to laugh and would respond, "Don't worry. Some day you will need these skills."

Yet there was something unknown and secretive about the woman, like an impenetrable shroud. She consistently did the unexpected, and the email perfectly fit her character. Once she was over the initial surprise of receiving it, Kate didn't know whether to laugh or cry.

That email had caused Kate to reflect on how her grandmother and Aunt Clara communicated, sharing opinions with black and white definiteness: "This is good, this is bad, you mustn't do that, etc."

Sometimes it was a heavy load to bear, being raised and homeschooled by two older women who spoke with heavy foreign accents. They dressed in an old-fashioned, yet elegant, style, with dainty white lace collars enhanced by necklaces of light pink pearls.

Though the two women could be overbearing, Kate developed a mind of her own. The result was not conflict, but honest dialogue. Emma and Clara appreciated internal strength, knowing there were moments in life when you needed to be strong-willed.

The few friends she had were often mystified when they came to her home, a large house in Palm Beach on the Florida seaside. The house was full of old oil paintings and dark furniture collected by her grandmother during their summer trips to Europe. Most of the works of art were reproductions from famous painters.

Indeed Kate had visited a lot of art museums and enjoyed them immensely, often reading history books and fictional novels about the painters she saw. In a way, this provided an escape to other worlds.

Aunt Clara was a constant chaperon on those trips and watched over Kate while her grandmother disappeared for a day or two at a time. When Kate was a teenager and began to have an interest in boys, Aunt Clara became hyper protective, like a mother bear caring for her cub.

During those trips Kate saw how boys and men looked at her, and several times European boys had introduced themselves. She was flattered by this, yet there was never an opportunity to get to know them. Aunt Clara had a hidden radar. If a boy showed interest, somehow he ended up drifting away. Clara had a way of putting fear in the soul.

Because of this, Kate had never been comfortable around men; she grew up in a woman's world. At times she had resented Emma and Clara for imposing such strong restrictions, but now understood this had been a protective shield motivated by their love for her.

Kate grew up in an expensive home in a wealthy neighborhood and there were not many other children around. During Kate's senior year at university Grandmother Emma became terminally ill, and they had quickly sold the house. One weekend Kate came home from university and learned that everything in the house had been liquidated.

Even though Kate had come to expect Emma's impulsiveness, she was devastated by the sudden loss of her home.

Her grandmother then moved into a fancy clinic for the final months of her life. Just after Kate graduated with a Bachelor of Science degree in Economics and a minor in Art History, Emma died.

Her grandmother's death had been the saddest time of her life and she and she had spent the summer in mourning. From the sale of the house her grandmother had set up a trust fund that paid Kate a monthly stipend, just enough for her to get by. Kate thought there should have been more funds available, but the medical expenses were high, and she understood that assets had been depleted.

Before her death, Emma insisted that Kate promise to continue with her studies and get a Master's degree in Finance and then work a few years in a financial company.

It had been a struggle. Her heart told her to go into art, maybe to work for an art gallery or art auction house, but she had made a commitment. Yet, the stubborn attitude of her grandmother bewildered her.

Kate honored the dying wishes of her grandmother. She did two more years of study, got the Master's degree and was now working for Wesson Securities. She didn't know if this would be long-term, but there were interesting aspects to the job and she hoped to at least move up from 'junior portfolio analyst' to 'portfolio analyst', or maybe even 'senior'. Although sometimes she questioned how important it was to climb the corporate ladder.

Wasn't there more to life than that? Had Emma directed her into a meaningless, materialistic existence?

Kate felt the Corvette come to a stop and the engine was switched off. She turned and saw Axel staring at her.

"Lost in thought?" He asked.

She had been daydreaming. "Ah, yes, just thinking."

"Anything you want to share?"

"Nothing important," she stated, not wanting to reveal her personal life to this stranger.

"It seems you were in a deep zone," he grinned.

"That's none of your business."

His smirk was getting on her nerves. She turned her head and saw they were parked at the entrance of a dingy warehouse surrounded by a high fence with barbed wire at the top. In faded letters on the side of the warehouse was written, "Buck Bryer's Elegant Antiques: We Buy, Sell and Move Antique Furniture."

A large dog, something like a pit-bull, was roaming in the parking area behind the fence. It barked as it ran to the fence. Like a buzz saw, it began to gnaw at the metal links while emitting a crazed growl.

"Is this is where your contact works?" she asked.

Axel nodded and pointed at a door next to a loading dock beyond the dog. "That's where we're going, and the dog's crazy. How fast can you run?"

CHAPTER 8

They got out of the car as Axel took off his hat and flipped it onto his seat, still feeling uncomfortable that Kate was with him. He needed flexibility at each step of his investigation, and Kate only slowed him down. He had thought his inane responses to her questions would dissuade her from accompanying him, but that didn't seem to be working.

There was one thing he needed to work around. Buck Bryer didn't like visitors. He was a tough southern boy who had an established network of suppliers and re-sellers, some from the shadier side of life. Trust and discretion were primary to his operations and he didn't want strangers entering his domain.

Axel assumed that petty thieves had broken into Kate Miller's apartment. With Buck's help it should be easy to find them, but he might not be forthcoming with Kate there.

In any case, today he'd let her tag along to pacify her curiosity and then hopefully she'd get bored and leave him free to do his thing. The quicker he finished this case, the quicker he could get on with his vacation.

He looked at her and saw her eyes focused on the growling dog. It was now displaying vicious   fangs dripping with drool.

Standing back from the fence she asked, "How do we get past that thing? And by the way, your comment about running fast wasn't funny."

"Here's the magic key," He said, pulling out his cell phone and dialing a number. After a few rings Buck answered.

Axel said, "Hey, Buck. I'm outside. Can you turn off the mutt?"

Two minutes later Buck opened a door next to a loading dock and yelled out, "Dog, come over here." He was wearing overalls, a stained white t-shirt and worn work boots.

The dog continued to charge the fence but after several threatening commands from Buck, it reluctantly went to him and sat by his side, its lungs heaving and saliva dripping from its mouth.

"You can come in, but don't make any sudden movements," Buck yelled.

"Is it safe?" Kate whispered, still staring at the dog.

Axel smiled. "So far the dog hasn't killed anyone. Although… once or twice he came close."

Her eyes darted from the dog to Axel and she hissed, "Didn't I just tell you that your imbecilic comments are not funny?"

Axel shrugged, opened the front gate and slightly bowed. "After you. I'm not sure the dog's been fed."

"After *you*," she said.

Axel went first and as they approached Buck, Axel said, "This is Kate Miller, my client, the owner of the things on the list I sent. Ms. Miller, this is Mr. Buck Bryer, the owner of this establishment."

Kate positioned herself between Axel and the dog.

Buck's eyes scanned from her head to her feet, his eyes blatantly pausing at various parts of her anatomy.

"She packin'?" Buck asked, and then he laughed. "She's got to be okay cuz she's a Marlins fan." He pointed toward her head and said, "I bet she's appealin' even without the hat, or anythin' else."

Kate stared into his eyes as she gave a sarcastic grin. She reached up and touched the hat and said, "Maybe I better switch teams so as not to be associated with certain fans."

Buck cracked a toothless smile and said, "Come on, don't get huffy on me. Let's go inside."

Axel held back a laugh thinking that the girl had backbone standing up like that. Buck would only respect her for doing it.

They walked through the door into a large warehouse full of antique furniture: chairs, tables, dressers, beds and cupboards. It had an odd smell of varnish and mold.

Axel had been here many times. One of his first cases was to help Buck find missing furniture, which had turned out to be an inside job. Ever since, Buck had been a valuable source of information about stolen goods, as he knew most furniture thieves and re-sellers in the Florida peninsula.

Buck led them to an office and they sat down on two worn couches facing each other. Stacks of paper and envelopes littered a desk in the corner.

Buck glanced at the desk and said, "Paperwork. I can't never keep up." He peered at Kate and asked, "Interested in a sec-a-tary job?"

She rolled her eyes and shook her head. "I'd love to . . . when hell freezes over."

Buck beamed from ear to ear and his body convulsed as he released a sound that was half way between a cackle and howl. "Little lady, you sure made my day!"

Kate smirked, shifting her weight on the couch. Axel didn't know if she was relaxing or getting ready to move into the crouching-tiger attack position.

Eying the mounds of paper on the desk, Axel knew they had another purpose. If legal authorities ever raided the place to do an audit they'd spend years searching through useless information. Messy filing systems are a first line of defense.

Axel asked, "Did you look at the list I sent?"

Buck said, "Printed it off this morning. Not much there."

"Do you have any thoughts on where we could find these goods?" Axel asked.

"This mornin' I made calls to a few folks, distant acquaintances if you know what I mean? Nobody knows anything about the stuff. In fact, when I told um what's on the list they laughed."

"Why's that?" Axel asked.

"It's obvious. This stuff ain't worth nothing. Why bother?"

Kate took a deep breath. "Mister Buck. Does it matter what they are worth to others? They mean something to me and that's why I've hired Axel. So, I'm wondering if you even know what you are talking about."

"Look young lady. I sure don't know a lot of things, but for the items on that there list you better believe I know a lot. Retail on those two dressers might be five or six hun-erd dollars, but the thieves would be sellin' um to a fence for maybe a hun-erd each. They'd get fifty bucks for the bookshelves, and pennies on the dollar for the books and clothes and other stuff. Why go through the risk of that burglary for such little return?"

With a demanding voice, Kate said, "So, why would they take those things if they weren't worth anything?"

Buck stopped for a moment, raised his eyes to the ceiling and laughed. "Well, you got me on that one, but I ain't the one to answer that question.

It just appears all goofy to me. What'da-ya think Axel?"

"Sure, but the stolen items are important for Ms. Miller, so we'll try and find them." Axel knew Buck was right. There was something that didn't add up. Was it really the work of petty thieves? He changed the conversation. "Could it be the work of organized crime?"

"Anything's possible," Buck replied. "But why mess around for peanuts?"

"I understand, but let's take that angle for a minute. If its organized crime, do you have any thoughts on who it might be?"

Buck paused and took a deep breath. He lowered his voice. "What I'm gunna say is all spec-a-lation, but in Miami there are two main groups, each with different ethnics. For simplicity, the people in my profession call um the Cubans and the Albanians, but it's a whole lot more complicated than that. The Cubans work with the Venezuelan and Colombian drug cartels. The Albanians are connected with the Eastern European Mafias and there are a bunch of um depending on the country. These are dangerous folks, and I stay far away."

Axel had dealt with the Colombians in a previous case and indeed they were treacherous. He knew of the Albanians but had never directly encountered them. "Would there be anything of interest on that list to either of those gangs?"

"You never know," Buck replied, "Although it seems someone went through a lot of trouble for a small bounty. Honestly I suspect it was some independent misfits needing money to feed their drug habit."

Kate asked, "If it was organized crime, where should we look for my possessions?"

Buck peered at the list again and said, "I wouldn't go looking. Do like me. Stay clear."

"In any case," she said, "Where would these things likely turn up?"

"It's your neck, but here goes. They all have organized sales networks. For expensive stuff like fine art, you'd never see your possessions again. They're sold by word of mouth and often are shipped out of the country, but Axel, you already know about this. It's all the piddly stuff on your list that raises questions. They'd probably end up in a used furniture shop or used bookstore owned by the gangs."

Buck stood up and walked over to his massive stack of papers, dug through it and pulled out a couple of sheets. He came back and handed the sheets to Axel.

Buck said, "One is a list of bookstores and the other is a list of used furniture shops. All those shops are controlled by the two crime organizations. I keep the lists as a reminder of who not to deal with. As far as your family photo album and jewelry, I got no idea where to begin. Maybe you could sneak into their warehouses, but they're guarded and you'd probably get shot to hell, as a manner of speakin'. Wouldn't recommend it."

"We'll start with the shops on your list," Axel said. "Anything else you can think of?"

"Not really, but somehow this don't make sense. It smells fishy. But, if something comes up I'll give you a call." Buck's eyes shifted to Kate and he said, "By the way, if you need that secretary job I'd take you. With or without the hat."

She gave him a dagger-like stare then grinned and said, "That may be your unlucky day."

CHAPTER 9

Back in the car Axel reflected on Buck's warning about the two crime organizations. Even if the thieves were only doing this for drug money, some of Kate's belongs were likely to end up in the second-hand shops controlled by crime syndicates. Warning bells went off in his head. They needed to be careful.

Buck also said something smelled fishy. This confirmed what he was already feeling. There had to be more to this case than the recovery of sentimental possessions.

Kate tagging along for the day would give him a good chance to gain more background on the importance of these goods to her. What was her real motivation? Harry Raintree always advised him to patiently coax information from a client, and that's what he planned to do.

Axel started the car, drove down the street, and then handed Buck's lists to Kate. He asked, "What do you think? Should we start looking for books or furniture?"

"Maybe the books," she replied.

"Why's that?"

"They mean a lot to me." She turned away from him and gazed toward the street.

The question was a way to test her, to understand her priorities and anything behind them. "Why do you choose the books over the furniture?"

"Everything is important to me, but let's start with the books."

"How often have you read your old university books?"

"It doesn't matter if I read them or not. I said they're important to me," she responded.

"Most people put their school books on a shelf and never open them again. If they're so important why not buy new ones rather than spend more money for my services? Sentimental value has its limits."

Her lips tightened. "Listen, it's not for you to question my intentions. I'm paying you to do a job. Find my stolen possessions."

"You're avoiding my question. Please tell me why thieves would take your possessions? Surely the goods from a home in Fisher Island would be much more profitable."

"Obviously they were petty thieves needing money to feed their drug habit. You said so yourself."

"Only as a supposition. Think about it. You told me that your telephone may have been bugged. How many drug addicts would do that?"

"It's possible some might," she stated. "The police are investigating this."

"Do you have any special information that the thieves might need?"

"How could that be?" She questioned.

He felt she was deflecting every question, and he was getting frustrated. "Tell me what they were looking for!"

"How should I know? Anyway, you keep repeating the same questions and this isn't going anywhere."

"There's got to be something about your work at Wesson Securities," he declared. "Is there anything going on there that you haven't considered, someone spying on you, maybe even a competitor company wanting to find out something?"

"I swear there's nothing." She shook her head. "And it seems absurd that someone at Wesson Securities would go to all the trouble of raiding my apartment."

"But there's a reason, whether drug money or something else. Otherwise this wouldn't have happened." His voice level was increasing and he wondered if he was pushing too hard. "We'll start with the used furniture stores on the list."

She turned toward him, her face firm, full of resolve. "The furniture stores? No. I said the books are most important."

"And why?"

"Because of personal reasons."

"What are they? You're not being open with me."

"It's personal. Don't you understand? Personal is personal," she snapped. "I don't see why you..."

He interrupted, "Which books are the most important?"

She paused. "All of them, but that's beside the point. I've hired you to recover my possessions, period."

"That's not good enough. We'll start with the furniture."

"No, I want the books." He saw her right hand tighten into a fist.

He shifted his body weight to the left, wondering if she was going to strike him. He said, "Wow. Now I fully understand your warm and fuzzy reasons for wanting the books."

With light green laser eyes focused on him, she commanded, "Don't mock me. I expect you to use your skills to complete the task I've given you. Why the books may or may not be important is irrelevant to you."

"So then, I'll complete the task I was hired for and I'll do it my way. We start with the furniture stores."

"No. We do it the other way around."

"Ms. Miller, you have to understand something. The thieves will get more money for the furniture and those items are easier to identify. We can trace the books after we find the furniture."

"Oh yeah, you make it sound easy. So let's see you do it."

He took a deep breath and groaned. "Hopefully you might attempt to comprehend the strategy here. We don't want to reveal that the books are your priority. If we look for the furniture first it will misguide the thieves, in case you are wondering."

A feeling of defeat overwhelmed him. He had failed in his tactic to patiently coax information from his client. In fact, it had now become a full-blown war between two stubborn people.

"All I can say is that I want the books," she affirmed.

"Oh brother," he sighed in exasperation. "At some point I hope you start shooting straight with me, because it might immensely help this investigation."

A heavy silence settled upon them, like being in an empty morgue.

★ ★ ★

Kate turned her head away from Axel. He had rattled her emotions, and that's something she didn't need. She had hoped that a hired private detective would give her reassurance, yet she felt anything but that. The encounter with the wretched Buck Bryer was beyond excruciating.

When she thought about it, she didn't want to leave everything to the police, since she was so engrained with a lack of trust for them. Now, in light of the obstinate and patronizing nature of Axel Bjorg, she questioned if it is was possible to continue working with him. Should she find another private investigator or just leave it all to Detective McGill? Maybe Chandler could help?

The morning had not gone well. The visit to Buck Bryer's warehouse had not been that productive and Buck turned out to be nothing more than a chauvinist redneck. *Who did he think he was with those ludicrous offers to be his secretary?*

But, she did feel some satisfaction in how she responded to his comments and a quick bolt of good humor flashed through her.

In spite of his comments, Buck had triggered her thinking. He suggested that organized crime might be behind the break-in. If that was true, could it be that the thieves were searching for information, rather than just stealing possessions for resale? Could this in some way be connected to the emails from Emma? This was a remote possibility but one she needed to ponder.

Based on their last exchange, she now had more doubts about Axel's professionalism. It wasn't normal for a professional to raise his voice and make accusations at a client.

As unpleasant as it was, she would give him a chance since they were barely into the investigation. But, if he didn't make progress, and if he maintained the same attitude toward her, she would cancel their contract.

When she thought about it, the photo album and cookbooks were most important because they linked her to her family. Particularly, the Betty Crocker Cookbook because her grandmother had given special attention to it in one of her emails. Why was that?

How could she get Axel to make this a priority without letting him know about Emma's emails? She remembered something Emma had taught her. "Only give away information with interest. You should always get something in return for anything you disclose." She wasn't sure how much she should tell him or what she wanted in return, so she would proceed cautiously.

CHAPTER 10

There was no conversation until they arrived at the first store on the list, a run-down strip mall. Buck had not specified which store was associated with which crime organization, so Axel knew he would just have to guess.

They walked into the store packed with beds, dressers, lamps, dusty old reproductions of famous paintings, electrical appliances, radios and a host of other things. Most of the furniture was cracked and broken.

Axel knew that crime organizations used these kinds of stores not only as a conduit for stolen goods, but also to distribute drugs and launder money.

Soon after entering, a woman came out from a back room. She wore a heavy layer of mascara and an overdose of red lipstick. She looked to be around forty years old.

"May I help you?" she asked with an artificial smile and heavy Eastern European accent.

Axel said, "My fiancée and I are looking for some unique furniture for our living room. We want a solid wood dresser and bookshelves, something to enjoy through the years. Would you happen to have a walnut bookshelf about this big?" He asked, raising his hands to the level of his chin and then spreading them wide to the approximate dimensions Kate had given him.

The woman reflected for a moment and said, "I am sorry, but that is not here. Let me make call."

She went to a phone behind a counter, made a call, speaking in a foreign language. Axel noticed Kate becoming attentive.

When the woman came back she said, "We do not have what you want, but if it comes into warehouse I let you know. Do you have telephone number?"

Axel gave her his cell phone number, thanked the woman and left the store with Kate.

Kate glared at him and said, "Fiancée. Where did that come from?"

Axel smiled. "What else do you want me to say, that we are after stolen goods and are you selling them in your store?"

"Okay, I guess that make sense," she said with a glimmer of a smile.

"What do you think of the shop and the woman?"

"It wasn't promising. It might be a waste of time running around town visiting all those stores. Isn't there a better way?"

He sensed her impatience. "That's what detective work is all about: dead ends. But then you discover something that opens a door that opens another door."

"I'm simply asking if there's a better way?"

He sighed. "You didn't answer about the woman."

"What about her?"

"What did you think of her? Might she be connected to a criminal gang and if so which one?"

"Just because someone speaks with a foreign accent doesn't mean you should jump to conclusions, but if you want to go down that line of reasoning it was most likely from somewhere in Eastern Europe."

"That's what I'm thinking." He paused a moment. "I noticed you became attentive when she was talking on the phone. What language was she was speaking? Was it Russian?"

Kate smiled. "She definitely wasn't from Cuba."

He noticed that she deflected his question. It was like she was avoiding something, or was holding back information. He let it pass and said, "Let's move on to the next place."

★ ★ ★

The rest of the day they visited other used furniture shops, not coming any closer to finding Kate's stolen furniture. Finally they decided to stop for the day and a moment later Kate's cell phone rang. She saw the caller ID and answered, "Hello, Chandler."

"Kate, I'm on my way to Miami, taking a detour on my way to San Francisco. Can you meet me at Opa-Locka Airport? I'll be there in thirty minutes."

"Thirty minutes. That's a wonderful surprise," she exclaimed.

"I wanted to see you, to know you're alright and to hear how you're doing. I'm coming in on our company jet and can't stay long. You know where we park the plane."

She took a deep breath. "Yes, I'll be there. It will be so nice to see you." The thought of seeing Chandler gave her a wave of warm relief. She needed someone with an objective view of her situation. She needed support. She needed comfort.

"I miss you," he said.

"I miss you, too," she replied with a big smile.

"See you soon," he said.

They hung up and Kate turned to Axel and said, "Can you take me to Opa-Locka Airport?"

"Where?"

"Opa-Locka Airport, about twenty minutes north of Miami."

"Yeah, yeah, I know where it is. What for?"

"To meet my friend."

CHAPTER 11

They watched the airplane taxi to an area where other corporate jets were parked and as soon as the engines were shut down the door opened. Kate saw Chandler descend the stairs and desired to run to him, but something held her back. Axel was next to her.

Chandler saw her, waved and walked briskly toward her. She couldn't contain herself any longer and she ran to him and hugged him. He hugged back and kissed her on the cheek.

"I'm so glad you are here," she uttered.

"I needed to see you," he said. His eyes locked onto Axel.

"Let me introduce you. Chandler, this is Axel Bjorg. He is . . . ah . . . helping me recover my possessions."

They shook hands, Chandler stretching out his arm to stay back from Axel, his eyes stern. "I thought the police were working on that," Chandler said.

Kate hesitated. "Yes, they are, but I needed additional help and I ended up hiring a private detective after all," she admitted guiltily.

"I see. How's it going? Can I help?"

"Well, it was awful to find my apartment trashed and to see so many things missing. Now we've spent the day visiting dusty furniture shops, which has been another stressful experience."

"That's strange. Why are you visiting dusty stores?" He asked.

She turned to Axel and then back to Chandler. "Because Dr. Bjorg feels it's what we should be doing."

Chandler stiffened. "It sounds like a waste of time."

Axel's eyes narrowed. "And maybe not."

Chandler raised the palms of his hands. "So, what have you discovered?" He moved slightly forward.

Kate saw Axel shift his weight, legs apart, relaxed. Something about him reminded her of a feral cat. She said, "We just started the investigation." Turning to Axel she said, "Could you please give us a moment?"

Axel nodded, turned and headed back toward one of the airport buildings.

"Where did you find this guy?" Chandler asked.

"He's an experienced private detective," she stated.

"Something about him seems wrong. Are you sure he's legitimate?"

She hesitated. "I think so."

He peered deep into her eyes and said, "Kate, I care for you and want to support you. People in my office here in Miami can find somebody reliable. We've worked with private detectives in the past, those with large networks of offices across the country. This guy seems like a bumbling amateur. Consider what he's wearing. Why don't you let me help you, or at least leave it up to the police?"

Kate turned and peered back at Axel standing next to the building in his sneakers, jeans and dark blue Hawaiian tiki shirt, the white flowers and palm trees shining under an exterior light. Then she looked at Chandler in his expensive business suit, colorful tie and polished shoes. Behind him was his corporate jet. For sure Chandler was a professional and he knew what he was talking about.

"Let me think about it," she said.

"I'd highly encourage you to allow me to find a qualified agency. It's not that I'm questioning your judgment. It's because I care for you and want the best for you."

Those were the words Kate needed to hear. She needed Chandler's comfort, his strength, his advice. How she wanted to be with him, to get in that airplane and fly away from her troubles.

They talked more and Kate updated Chandler on the break-in.

"I just don't understand it," he said. "You claim there was nothing, so why would thieves have done this?"

"Honestly, I don't know."

"You've mentioned your grandmother. Was she wealthy?"

Kate shook her head. "She had nothing at the end of her life. She only left me a monthly insurance annuity. It just doesn't make sense why thieves would rob my apartment."

Chandler shook his head. "Yes, it's a mystery." His eyes glanced at the airplane. "I'm sorry, but I need to be in San Francisco. Honestly, I'll get back here as soon as I can."

"You don't need to do that," Kate said.

"I do, because I want to be with you and help you. You know how I feel Kate. I love you."

"Thank you Chandler. I feel the same about you. You are such a support." She agonized that she couldn't tell him she loved him, almost impossible words to say. More than anything she wanted to be loved and to express love but something held her back. What was the origin of that reluctance, or was it fear?

He stepped to her and she relaxed in the embrace of his strong arms. Just as she glanced to see if Axel was watching, he bent down to her. Chandler's kiss awkwardly missed her lips and rested on her cheek.

He released his hug and said, "Keep me up to date, and I'll see you in a few days." He strode away and bounded up the steps of the corporate jet. At the top he turned, waved and stepped inside. The engines started and in a few minutes the plane grew smaller in the distance.

CHAPTER 12

Axel watched Chandler hug Kate and laughed when he saw the misplaced kiss. The guy was all over her. Could he blame him? She was stunning.

Still, He wondered why Chandler flew all the way to Miami just to meet with Kate for a few minutes. He attributed it to lust and the fact that extremely wealthy people sometimes did erratic things. With his corporate jet and fancy tailor-made suit, it was obvious someone like Chandler could afford anything he wanted.

Axel didn't like Chandler questioning his strategy, yet he questioned it himself. He was unhappy that he hadn't made more progress, but it had only been one day of work.

From now on he'd operate on his own, knowing the pace would quicken without her. Her reluctance to share information wasn't helpful, so there was no need to bring her along.

During the drive back to his office he asked about Chandler and her relationship with him, but she didn't divulge anything. After that, they spent the rest of the trip in silence. When they reached the office he parked in his reserved place close to the front door of the building. Kate's car was in one of the visitor's spots.

Before getting out Axel asked, "How do you feel about the day?"

Kate replied, "It was not very promising, and I'm tired."

"I'll continue on my own," he stated.

Her face was tight. "I need to think about it."

"Just let me do the ground work and I'll bring you in when there's a hot lead."

"No."

"Look, I'm sure you're tired. I can work faster without you."

"I said I want to think about it."

Axel took a deep breath, stared at her and said, "Frankly, it's not going to work that well with you tagging along." He almost slipped by adding, 'like a puppy dog'.

"Who's tagging? I'm the client."

He shook his head and pointed a hand at her. "This is crazy. Please understand that I need to operate on my own."

"We'll see," she said.

"It's your money," he stated.

"I know. Speaking of my money, I'm becoming uneasy about this expenditure. As far as I'm concerned today was a waste. Chandler was right."

"Maybe not," Axel stated. He had never met such a stubborn woman in his life.

They sat for a moment and he asked, "Of all the stores we visited were there any that caught your attention? Did any people seem strange or suspicious?"

She paused a moment. "Well, I'd never guess any of the stores were connected to crime syndicates, unless your disgusting friend, Buck Bryer hadn't told us. But, maybe the woman at the first store was odd."

"Was it the phone call? Was she speaking Russian?"

Kate paused again. "Yes, the phone call was weird."

"Did you understand it?"

She nodded. "Some words."

"How do you know Russian?"

Kate hesitated. "My grandmother and her sister Clara were from Poland and they spoke Russian, which everyone in the old Soviet Union had to learn. Sometimes they spoke phrases with me. My level is basic."

Axel was surprised he hadn't learned this sooner, but she wasn't the greatest giver of information. It also confirmed his first observation of Kate that she had this Eastern European look. Maybe his detective skills weren't so bad after all. "So what did she say?"

"She was asking someone about new things or incoming merchandise, or something like that. That's all I understood."

"Why didn't you tell me that you knew some Russian?" He was perplexed that she wasn't forthcoming with him.

"I didn't think it was relevant."

Axel turned in the car seat and stared into her eyes. "If you want to find your stuff then everything is relevant, even your personal life. There might be something that provides a clue."

"My life is none of your business. I hired you to find my possessions. They simply have meaning to me. And to be honest, I feel that today was a misappropriation of my finances, a thousand dollars spent on visiting a bunch of dusty rundown stores."

She was defensive, which led him to believe made him think she might be concealing more. It was frustrating. In the end her obstinate behavior might kill the investigation. Did she really want him to solve this case? He coldly said, "Alright, if you feel the day was a waste, we can bring an end to our contract if you want."

Kate gazed through the windscreen for a moment and then looked at Axel. "That might be a good idea. Maybe I should just let the police do their thing."

That was unexpected, but he was the one who made the proposition. "You mean I'm fired?"

"Whatever you want to call it. I prefer to explore other avenues. Chandler said he could help and I'd like to consider that."

He grinned. "That's a first."

"It's the best thing," she stated.

"It's your prerogative," he replied. "It's been a pleasure to make your acquaintance." Actually in some strange way he was relieved. The day had been full of tension between them and her reluctance to share information meant the investigation might last forever. Yet, he was disappointed he wouldn't be completing the assignment, and of course there was the humbling experience of being fired by this unreasonable, hardheaded woman.

As they got out of the car, he walked around to her side, stuck out his hand and said, "Well, I wish you luck."

"Thank you," she replied, stiffly shaking his hand.

He felt her hand, a wonderful combination of softness and firmness, and then he let it go. "If you need any help, give me a call."

"Thank you, but I think the police can handle it from here." She turned and headed to her car.

He took a few steps, reached the front door of his building and then glanced back at Kate. She moved gracefully, but her shoulders seemed tight.

Then something across the street caught his eye. Two men sitting in a dark blue SUV were watching Kate. Of course it was normal that a beautiful woman like Kate would have men checking her out, but there was something sinister in their faces. They had stern eyes fixed on her like hunters watching their prey.

Kate got into her car, started it and drove out onto the street. At that moment the driver started the SUV, did a U-turn and drove in the same direction as Kate.

Axel sprinted out of the building toward his Corvette.

CHAPTER 13

Axel stayed a long distance back from Kate and the dark SUV. A sick feeling arose from his stomach knowing she was in danger. Or, was she? Perhaps they were hired to protect her. Maybe Chandler, with all his money, had done this.

He wondered if he had been too flippant with this case, not adequately considering the potential threats. What were these men up to? If they meant harm, could he save Kate from an oncoming disaster?

At one point he managed to get close enough to memorize the license plate number of the SUV and then he pulled back, creating distance again. He hoped the men would focus on Kate and not notice him.

He wondered how they had found her at his office. He realized he had given his telephone number to the shopkeepers at the furniture stores. Perhaps one of them had tracked him down.

He regretted that he was driving the Corvette; it stood out like a fire truck. His Honda Civic would be better suited for the job.

He ran a red light to keep up with the SUV. Far ahead he could see Kate's car. He knew her address, having found it on the internet, so if they got separated he would head there. *But was that where she was going? And what if the two men tried to do something before she arrived home?*

In seeing the two men in the SUV, the main question in his mind was stronger than ever. What were they looking for? Was Kate telling the truth that there had been nothing of great financial value in the apartment? There had to be a reason for the robbery.

A million questions raced through his mind. Kate had not disclosed that she spoke some Russian even when he asked what language the woman in the furniture store had been speaking. *What else was she not telling him? Did her grandmother and Aunt Clara have something to do with this? Was there something from her job at Wesson Securities? Did she have secret information on a client? Did she know about a crime that was committed and she didn't tell him? Why was she reluctant to share information?*

He realized how little he had to go on, other than the immediate reality of a dark SUV following her. Even though she had fired him from the job, he could not walk away. If those men meant harm, he had to protect her.

Up ahead, Axel watched the SUV follow Kate as she turned onto her street. Axel parked a block away, keeping his car out of sight.

The night had turned dark so he carefully walked down the street staying behind cars and trees, moving cautiously forward. The SUV was parked at the opposite end of the street.

He observed Kate walk to the door of her apartment. She inserted a key and went inside. The apartment was on the ground floor and he saw a small alley on one side of the building. He crouched behind some bushes and then made his way down the alley.

At the back door of her apartment, he knocked.

A minute later Kate came to the door, peeked through a small window and then opened it.

"What are you doing here?" she exclaimed.

Axel put a finger to his lips. "You're being followed, all the way from my office building."

"What?"

"There are two men in a dark SUV out on the street."

"I don't believe you."

"Turn the lights off in your living room and then look outside."

He entered her apartment and followed her down a small hallway, through the kitchen and then into the living room. He saw that she had reordered the living room and removed any lingering signs of a break-in.

She turned off the living room light and they walked to one side of the window and peered outside.

"Down the street. Do you see the SUV?" He asked.

She gasped. "They're getting out of the car and are coming this way."

Axel got a glimpse of them as they walked under a streetlight. They were both big and bulky, like professional wrestlers, one taller than the other.

"We need to go," he exclaimed. If there was only one man, Axel wouldn't hesitate to confront him, but with two he didn't want to take any chances. There was no telling what weapons they might be carrying and having Kate with him added more risk.

Kate grabbed her computer bag off the couch as they went through the apartment, out through the back door and into the alley.

They ran down the alley in the opposite direction Axel had originally come from and onto a street, and then doubled back to his Corvette. In the car Kate frantically grabbed her seat belt and clicked it as Axel started the engine, shifted into gear and spun the car around. In the rear view mirror he saw the two men running toward the SUV.

Gripping the steering wheel, he pushed his foot to the gas pedal. The tires of the Corvette burned rubber on the street.

CHAPTER 14

Kate shivered, thinking of the two men. They seemed so serious and intent, evil emanating from their faces. In spite of their situation, for some odd reason she had a flashback to her childhood. Her grandmother Emma had often given her lessons about life and one came to her mind.

She remembered when she was seven years old laying on her bed, her grandmother beside her. As per their usual evening ritual before Kate went to sleep, her grandmother told her a story. This was the wonderful time of the day when Emma or Aunt Clara came into her room. Before turning out the light they'd read from the Bible or tell tales from Slavic folklore.

"Can you tell the story about the frog princess?" Kate asked.

"Tonight you will hear something different. It is a story called *Baba Yaga's Son.*"

A chill went through Kate and filled her with excitement and anticipation. There were many stories about Baba Yaga, an evil sorceress who lived deep in the forest in a turning house that sat on chicken legs. A particular smell emitted from her and she had special powers. Sometimes Kate had difficulty sleeping after hearing these stories.

"I think *The Frog Princess* is better," Kate murmured.

"Yes, *The Frog Princess* is a good story, but this one about Baby Yaga's son is special. Like all our folk stories it has truths."

"Truths?"

"Ideas. Maybe you would call them lessons about life."

"Why is that?" Kate asked.

"First let me tell you the story and then we can talk." Emma didn't need to read it from a book. She had heard it many times herself as a child. She began:

Once upon a time in a far-away land there lived a wicked woman, Baba Yaga. From her dank, moss covered hut deep in the woods she envied the prosperous villages around her. The villagers were happy and had food to eat and nice homes to live in. But, Baba Yaga desired everything they had. Even more than that, she wanted the villagers to submit to her as their ruler.

In an evil trickery, Baba Yaga had gained supremacy over the King of Winter and the Queen of Summer, so one day she commanded them to come to her hut.

They bowed before her and she said to them, "I want you to go from village to village and use your power to bring the people under my control. You will serve them the harshest winter and the hottest summer."

"But that's terrible. The people will suffer," the King of Winter said.

Baba Yaga wrinkled her long pointed nose and said, "What matters is that they submit to me."

The King of Winter and the Queen of Summer were forced to carry out Baba Yaga's commands, even though they didn't want to. The King of Winter reluctantly went to the first village and brought a freezing north wind, so much so that all water turned to ice and the people could not heat their homes. Children and the elderly became sick and died.

Then the Queen of Summer unwillingly brought a stifling heat so that the crops dried up and many people died of thirst and hunger.

Finally, Baba Yaga sent her beloved son to the village to tell all inhabitants that they must bow to her as their ultimate ruler.

Baba Yaga's son was an extremely wicked person, even more evil than his mother. In the village he took all remaining food and ate it while the villagers were forced to kneel before him and watch. Much of the time he lived in drunkenness, consuming several liters of vodka every day. And, in his drunken state he beat and abused people.

So, one by one Baba Yaga gained control of every village around her and the lives of everyone became extremely miserable.

Eventually the King of Winter came to a lovely small cottage surrounded by green pasturelands. He knocked on the door and a young girl opened it.

"Who lives here?" The King of Winter asked.

"Just me," the young girl answered. "My grandfather left me this cottage."

"Do you know me?" The King of Winter asked.

She gently answered. "Be welcome King of Winter. I hope our heavenly Lord sent you for my sinful soul."

He began to talk with her and realized she was kind and innocent. Then he remembered the command of Baba Yaga to bring cold to the "villages". This was not a village, but a stand-alone cottage in pasturelands, so Baba Yaga's order would not apply.

So, the King of Winter took pity on the young girl and he decided to treat her differently than the others, so he placed on her shoulders a warm blue coat covered with pearls and precious jewels. He also gave her a chest full of silk garments, diamonds and gold. And then he went away.

The young girl was wise. With the diamonds and gold, she bought all the land around her and even more, and put cattle and sheep on the land,

and hired workers to tend to her grain fields and gardens.

Then, the Queen of Summer visited her and asked, "Do you know who I am?"

The young girl answered, "Be welcome Queen of Summer. I hope the heavenly Lord sent you for my sinful soul."

The Queen of Summer talked with her and realized the young girl was kind and innocent. Then the Queen of Summer remembered the command of Baba Yaga to bring the heat of summer to the "villages". This was not a village, but a stand-alone cottage in pasturelands, so Baba Yaga's order would not apply.

So, the Queen of Summer took pity on the young girl and decided to treat her differently than the others by sending regular rains and warm sunshine on the young girl's fields.

After that, the young girl gained in prosperity and with her wealth she helped feed the people in the villages.

When Baba Yaga heard about the young girl and her riches she was filled with rage. First, she sent servants to find the King of Winter and the Queen of Summer, but they had hidden themselves from her wrath. Then she ordered her son to visit the young girl and take away all her wealth.

When Baba Yaga's son arrived at the young girl's cottage he asked, "Do you know who I am?"

The young girl answered, "Be welcome Son of Baba Yaga. I hope our heavenly Lord sent you for my sinful soul. I knew you were coming so I've prepared a feast for you."

The Son of Baba Yaga was pleasantly surprised and decided to wait until the meal was finished before he took away all the young girl's possessions. He had traveled a long way and was hungry and thirsty.

The young girl knew about the gluttonous habits of the Son of Baba Yaga, so she served a fabulous meal of borscht, and of sashlik, which is Russian lamb kebabs with tomato-prune paste, and golubtsi, which is ground beef and rice wrapped in cabbage leaves. And throughout the meal she poured him glass after glass of hard-grain vodka.

Of course we all know the deadly dangers of hard-grain vodka.

Eventually the son of Baba Yaga drank himself into a stupor and as the vodka ate into his brain he became delirious, crashing to the ground, hitting his head on the stone fireplace . . . and he died.

Baba Yaga's servants brought her son home, and overcome with grief, she kissed his cold, hard swollen lips. She cried and cried, but there was no one to help. Then she became filled with rage and hated her son for his uncontrollable gluttony and drunkenness. So, she carried his pale blue body to the top of a tall mountain with a cliff overlooking Hades and threw him in. But, at that moment the King of Winter and Queen of Summer came out of hiding and sneaked up behind Baba Yaga. They blew with all their force and Baba Yaga resisted them. Then she lost her footing on the loose rocks and tumbled forward, her hands flailing into the air seeking in vain something to grab as she flew downward, screaming forever, finally landing into the molten, eternal fires of hell.

With Baba Yaga and her son gone, the villagers regained their mild winters and warm summers of bountiful crops. And, at night they sat around their kitchen tables to eat piroshki and apple sharlotka and tell stories of how the wise young girl had overcame the evil Baba Yaga and her son.

The End.

Kate sat for a minute in silence, and then said, "Grandmother, that story is scary. I think I prefer *The Frog Princess*."

Emma reached across and held Kate's soft hand. "My little one, you must listen carefully to these stories from the old country. They contain lessons because they deal with truth. In fact, when I was a little girl these stories about Baba Yaga and the frog princess were not allowed."

"Not allowed? Why not?"

"Because they were seen to hold ideas that were against the propaganda of the Soviet State. Today they would say the stories are not politically correct."

"The Soviet State? What is that?"

"They were government leaders who were like Baba Yaga."

"Why is that?" Kate asked.

"The leaders made themselves rich, while everyone else became very poor. So, of course they did not like stories that made them seem to be like Baba Yaga."

"What is this politely correct?" Kate asked, not understanding the term.

"Not politely, but politically. Politically correct. This is a collective narrowing of the mind, but we will save that for another discussion. Now it's time to say our prayers and for you to sleep."

"But tell me. What is the lesson?"

Emma smiled. "You are such a clever child to prolong your evening!" She gently patted Kate's hand and said, "In the story there are many lessons."

"I don't know them. Please tell me," Kate pleaded.

"One is that wisdom and kindness can turn the hearts of people, even the King of Winter and the Queen of Summer."

"What else?"

Emma turned to Kate and said, "Sometimes there are wicked people wanting to destroy us. If we are wise, they will end up destroying themselves."

★ ★ ★

For some strange reason, Kate thought about that story and the lessons from it. She felt lost and frightened, speeding along in a flashy car next to a man she hardly knew while being pursued by strangers. What was their intent? Did they want to destroy her?

All she remembered was her grandmother's lesson about wicked people and being wise. But, this was so unreal. How could she be wise?

Where was Emma's counsel? How she longed for and missed her grandmother's strength.

CHAPTER 15

As they headed south on I-95, they began to breath a little easier, as they could no longer see the SUV. Adrenaline was still surging through his veins, but Axel avoided pushing the gas pedal, not needing a speeding ticket. The frantic dash from Kate's apartment unsettled him. He could only imagine what she was feeling.

In reflecting on the two men, he suspected someone from one of the furniture stores had tipped them off. Obviously they were after something, and they didn't find it in what they had stolen. Were they now after Kate to extract information from her?

"We can't go back to your place or to my home until we figure out a few things," he said.

"This is absolutely crazy," she said with a panting breath, turning her head to look behind them.

"Crazy? More like something out of a zombie movie."

"Alluding to horror movies isn't funny, but I agree." She shook her head and then faced him with worried eyes. "Seriously, what now?"

"You might consider calling Detective McGill," he said, seeing how pale she looked.

Kate paused. "I'm not sure."

"Why's that?"

"Can I trust them?"

"Trust *them who?*" he asked.

She stared ahead for a moment and then turned to Axel. "It's just something from my past, so never mind. My concern is that if the police are around and scare off those men, I may never get my things back."

"That's an interesting thought." He liked the logic, although he questioned her mistrust of the police. Did she have something to hide from them? "Okay, I have a safe place where we can work from."

He drove several miles, turned off the freeway, wound into a residential neighborhood and stopped in the driveway of a small house with a two-car garage. After parking the Corvette in the garage next to a gray Honda Civic they went into the house.

Inside was a small living room, with an open kitchen on one side.

Axel said, "There are two bedrooms down the hallway and one bathroom. It's not big but it will do. If you'd rather go to a hotel, then we can do that."

"Is this your place?" She asked.

"No. It belongs to Harry Raintree, my old boss, although the Honda is mine. He stays here when he comes to Miami. It's registered to a company with no direct connection to him. We should be safe here."

She surveyed the room and said, "Staying here is fine, at least for tonight."

He nodded and said, "It's been a long day. Are you hungry?"

"I'm famished and dying of thirst," she replied.

Axel noticed that her eyes were drawn. It was probably a shock for her to flee from those two men, and he could tell that it was taking a toll on her.

He called Harry Raintree to let him know they were at the house and then called a local Chinese restaurant to order a meal. They drove the Honda Civic to the restaurant, picked up the food and brought it back. He didn't want anyone coming to the house, including delivery guys.

They sat at the table in the kitchen and ate in a heavy silence.

Finally he asked, "Why did you choose your profession?" He wanted to avoid a discussion about the men in the SUV, hoping to relax Kate.

She replaced her chopsticks with a fork. "It wasn't my first choice, but my grandmother encouraged me to study economics and finance. Maybe it's like you. You like history, but you take accounting and end up as a private investigator."

He smiled. "For some weird reason history, accounting and being a PI work together for me." He paused, wondering if there was a connection between her work and the theft of her possessions. "What exactly do you do in your work?"

"I'm an analyst. I provide support to portfolio managers."

"Do you think there's anything that connects your work to the burglary? Were you working on anything that might pose a threat to someone?"

Kate paused for a moment, stared at her fork and answered, "Not really, and I never keep anything confidential at home. I don't see any links, but you never know."

Axel nodded. They finished their meal and washed the dishes. If there was no connection between her work and the theft, perhaps there were other relationships to explore. "You said that your family is gone and that you are alone. Do you have any friends that would want something from you?"

"No. Not really. My two closest friends recently moved away from Miami and they wouldn't have any motivation to take furniture and books."

"What about this Chandler?" He kept thinking about the guy with his own jet, feeling dislike, maybe even jealousy. "Would he pull off something like this?"

She glared at him. "Absolutely not. Chandler lives in New York, is independently wealthy and has no need to do something like this. Anyway, he is none of your business."

"Okay, okay," he said, "Tell me something that might give a clue. What about your personal life?"

Kate shook her head. "There's nothing that connects to this crime. I have acquaintances from the office. I go to the Orthodox Church in Miami and am friendly with people there, but for the past few years my world has been nothing but study, work and hanging out with my friends. I know that sounds strange, a young professional without an active social life, but that's a fact."

Mention of the Orthodox Church caught his attention. In America most people were Protestants or Catholic, if they were believers at all. Orthodox Christians were a minority. "Why are you Orthodox?" He asked.

"Why do you need to know?"

He smiled and put a dish towel on a rack. "I'm just curious. You know I'm interested in history."

She took a deep breath and leaned one hand against the kitchen counter. "I never thought about it. My grandmother was from Poland and her family was Orthodox. So, that's where we went to church, although our church here in Florida is a mix of Russians, Serbs, Greeks and other nationalities from Orthodox countries."

Something clicked in Axel's mind. Poland was highly Roman Catholic. It would not be considered an Orthodox country. This was a disconnect. Maybe it didn't mean anything, yet it was a question to be answered. He needed to know more about Kate's family and their background. If she wouldn't disclose it, then he'd use other means. He changed the line of questioning.

"So, you can't think of any friends or acquaintances that might be interested in your things. Could there be an overjealous boyfriend from your past? You know guys can do stupid things."

"There's no one from the past who would steal my things. Stay out of my personal business." Her cheeks turned red.

"I'm just trying to find a connection, that's all." He realized his questions about Chandler had nothing to do with the case. A guy needed to know where he stood. There was a mystery about her that attracted him. At the same time warning bells were going off in his head. He knew he should not get romantic with a client. The big screw-up two years ago could have finished his career. He wouldn't make that mistake again.

"I understand you're trying to find links to the theft, but you won't find anything. As far as Chandler goes, we've been seeing each other and that's enough said," she said, anger rising in her throat.

"Okay, let's leave it there. Just don't forget those two guys in the SUV. They are very real and they want something. We need to know what, but I'll ask no more questions for tonight."

She nodded, lifting her hand from the counter. "Which bedroom is mine?"

"The one on the left. In the cupboard there's a reserve of new toothbrushes and other things you may need. Harry was always prepared for visitors, especially in situations like this."

"I'll need to buy some clothes tomorrow."

"Why don't you first take a look in the closet? It's well stocked, also Harry's doing."

"Thank you." She faced him, their bodies close. With a low voice she asked, "Who do you think those men are?"

"I don't know, but we'll find out."

Her eyes became watery. Axel sensed she was on the edge of breaking down. He desired to take her and hold her and tell her that everything would be alright, but knew he couldn't.

She turned and went to her room.

The lingering sensation of her presence stayed with him as he stood there in the quietness.

CHAPTER 16

Kate went to the bedroom on the left and found it to be simple and clean. She was surprised to find a large, walk-in closet full of shelves with various sizes of clothing, pants, shirts, t-shirts, and underwear, most of it new, still in plastic wrapping. She picked out an extra-large Miami Dolphins t-shirt and put it on.

She went to the bathroom and then got into the double bed. Even though the bed received her like soft arms, she was not able to sleep. The stress of the day had rattled her nerves and it would take time to unwind.

She wanted to call Chandler and tell him about what had happened but didn't want to bother him. He was probably still on his flight to San Francisco. Tomorrow she would call him to give him an update and seek his advice.

Her mind spun from one thing to another: replaying events, the break-in of her apartment, the slow progress of Detective McGill, the frustrating day with Axel Bjorg, and then the horror of the two men in the SUV. She concluded that the thieves were after something specific, and not just breaking into a random residence. But what? Why did the thieves only take her personal possessions? Was it to search them in more detail, as Axel had suggested?

She reflected on the stolen furniture, the two dressers and the bookshelf. They had come from her grandmother. She thought of her grandmother's mistrust of people in authority, especially of government officials and the police. It made sense that Emma would have inherited suspicion toward authority from growing up in a communist country.

Time and time again Emma had warned, "Don't trust the police."

That's why Kate didn't want to leave things entirely to the police, nor seek Detective McGill's protection. That's why she had jumped so quickly to seek help from a private investigator. In reality, she didn't have anything against Detective McGill, so her reaction must have come straight from the teaching from her grandmother.

She thought about Emma and how careful she was about giving out information. Her grandmother often said in amazement, "America is a strange place. If you start talking with someone on a bus or airplane, within a few minutes they have told you their entire life's story."

Her grandmother never revealed anything personal to a stranger. She was cautious about every movement, like a cat surveying the street before stepping outside. Emma never shopped at the same store two times in a row and she didn't keep all her funds in one bank, "in case one bank goes bankrupt."

Kate knew she carried some of her grandmother's characteristics. She had to, having been influenced by her for so many years. She wondered again if her attitudes toward men and the inability to open up and be free around them also came from this.

Kate realized it was strange that Emma never changed after so many years of being in America. She came as a young woman and then met John Miller. They got married and had a son, Kate's father. She should have adapted, but she never did. She kept her Eastern European ways and her foreign accent was always present.

Kate sighed and turned over. Sleep still wasn't coming, so she let her thoughts drift toward the second email from her grandmother. The emails had come on successive Mondays, the first one two weeks ago on her twenty-sixth birthday and the second one a week later, when she was in New York.

She got her laptop, turned it on, opened the second email from her grandmother and re-read it.

Dear Kate,

This is the second email I am sending you. I hope the first one wasn't too much of a shock, and I hope you had time to absorb it before I flood you with too much information.

I know that my sickness happened very fast and we didn't have an opportunity to talk about a lot of things. Above everything I want you to know that I always loved you and wanted the best for you. I know you didn't have an easy childhood, being raised by two elderly women. We probably frustrated you, but I am thankful for your respect and love.

I loved our times together, especially in the kitchen. It gave opportunity for us to work together and to openly share with each other. Please remember that a meal is more than nourishment for the body. It is nourishment for the soul. It is a time for families to unite. Preparing a meal is a creative act of love.

In coming to America I found many new and wonderful foods that we did not have in communist Poland, where we had practically nothing. It was a delight to use the cookbooks in America where Aunt Clara and I made so many discoveries. I hope you can find those discoveries in the cookbooks, especially the old Betty Crocker Cookbook I gave you.

Do you remember the meal we had on your twenty-first birthday? You must find that recipe in the Betty Crocker Cookbook. It will bring back so many wonderful memories and perhaps some surprises.

On another note, I hope you enjoy the few pieces of furniture I left for you. They come from special places, which you will learn more about some day. They are messages from the past.

I send my deepest love and with more to come,
Grandma Emma

She thought back to memories of two crotchety, but loving, old women, the smells of the kitchen, textures and colors of flour, eggs, salt, pasta and sugar.

She deeply longed for them to be here. I need their advice. I'm lost without them. If only they knew how alone and angry I feel to be in such a situation.

She read the email for a third time. Finding discoveries in the cookbooks and surprises? What on earth could that mean?

When Kate had first read the email in her New York hotel room, she wondered why her grandmother had waited three years to send it, although it perfectly fit Emma's character. Emma and Aunt Clara had played chess day and night, and life for them was like a chess game where moves were planned far in advance.

Kate knew that Emma had a purpose with these emails. She was trying to communicate something extremely important.

When Kate opened the email in her hotel room she wanted to head straight back to Miami and find the recipe that was mentioned. But for the life of her she couldn't remember what meal they had on her twenty-first birthday.

Then, when she flew back to Miami and found the cookbook missing, she was devastated. Knowing there was something important in that cookbook, she felt uncertain about her future.

Kate turned off the laptop, put it on the floor and settled back into the soft bed. She felt the quietness of the house. Knowing that Axel was in the room across the hall gave her reassurance from the anxiety she was experiencing. There was something about him that she found attractive. He was smart and strong, and she felt safe to be with him.

She was a fool to have fired him so impulsively, but it seemed right at the time. Now she was grateful he had continued to help her, especially saving her from those two men.

In spite of this, she would remain cautious about sharing things with him, having well learned that lesson from her grandmother. "Only give away information with interest." But, she had to wonder if the lesson was right for this situation.

Somehow her mind could not get away from him, this Dr. Axel Bjorg. What a strange name. She was curious to know more about him.

Tomorrow the search would start anew. Since reading Emma's message again she was more determined than ever to find her things, especially the Betty Crocker Cookbook. Yet the thought of those two men in the dark SUV terrified her. It seemed like hours before she fell asleep.

CHAPTER 17

Kate woke up to light coming through the curtains. A glance at her watch on the nightstand next to the bed told her it was eight thirty. She was upset she had slept so long.

They should already be on the road pursuing their investigations. Axel had not mentioned a specific plan of action, but she wondered if they really needed to visit the rest of the stores on the list. While he seemed competent for some things, she wondered if they were wasting time.

In spite of this, her perspective of Axel had changed after they escaped those two horrific men. Throughout that ordeal Axel was calm and seemed in control, and that gave her comfort.

Chandler also was calm and in control, although in a different way. She couldn't articulate in what way that was. Chandler was refined and at ease among the wealthy and powerful. He radiated assurance, and women turned their heads when he walked into a room. He was a man who commanded power, yet there was also a soft and caring side to him that made communication easy.

With Axel there was something raw yet fun. He had a quickness of mind and energy. She disliked the way he challenged her. Or did she? She understood that he was seeking information which might help solve the case, but he went about it in such an unnerving way. Somehow every conversation with him became an argument, and Kate found it infuriating.

She knew he wanted to know more about her grandmother, but she wasn't quite ready to share that information with him yet, especially the two emails. Anyway, it was uncertain they were connected to the burglary. Above everything, she needed to keep him focused on finding her things and not be meddling into family history.

She got up, took a shower, washed her hair and went into the walk-in closet to check out the clothing options. There was not much in her size. She tried on several pairs of pants until she found a new pair of jeans, tight but comfortable. She picked out a blue, short-sleeved men's shirt. She buttoned it to the top and didn't tuck it in.

It felt strange to be wearing this clothing. Her grandmother and Aunt Clara were against women wearing jeans. They had always said, "Real women don't wear men's clothing. That's how it was in *the old country* and that's why women in America are so confused." Kate had always laughed at that.

The smell of coffee brewing pulled her from her thoughts. She followed the scent to the kitchen, where Axel was fixing breakfast. He wore an apron and had a large spoon in his hand. An opened bag of flour, some eggs and a mixing bowl sat on the work counter behind him.

She was surprised when her heart fluttered, but something about the sight of him like this made Kate want to go to him. She fought the feeling, and leaned instead on the kitchen doorframe.

He smiled, his eyes moving up and down. "Good morning. Looks like you found some elegant clothing."

"That's quite a collection in that closet," she remarked.

"Yeah, that's Harry Raintree. He used this as a place to keep clients when they were in trouble, a kind of safe house. He was prepared."

"Well, I'm thankful, but are the jeans and shirt appropriate for what we need to do today?"

Axel laughed. "You should know that in Miami anything goes. Don't worry, you pass the test."

She blushed and smiled slightly. His approval was positive and she appreciated that he didn't overdo it.

He asked, "Did you sleep okay?"

"It took a while."

"Hopefully you're rested because we're likely to have a busy day. That is, if I'm still working for you." He smiled.

"Yeah, actually, I'm really sorry about that."

"You mean for firing me?"

A twinge of guilt flickered in her eyes, and then she laughed. "Yes, I guess I was a bit quick on the trigger. You saved me and, honestly, I need your help."

"So, can we start afresh?"

She smiled. "Thank you for being gracious about it. What's the plan?"

"I'm not sure how many of the stores on the list will be open on Sunday. Usually these are small mom and pop operations and they don't have the staff to stay open all week. And, now that those two men appeared, we should shift course. Yesterday my hope was that our visits to the stores would bring something out of the woodwork, but I didn't expect what happened. Whatever we do, we need to be careful."

"So what do we do?"

"This morning I made a call to one of my contacts. We'll go visit him." Axel turned up the heat on the stove and put a griddle on top of the burner.

"Who is he? Hopefully not like Buck Bryer."

He laughed. "No one is like Buck. As I told you before, I have various friends who help in various ways. Some were inherited from Harry Raintree and others I found on my own. Occasionally I need protection, so I call some ex-army guys who run a security company. Or, sometimes I need access to hard-to-find information, so I use people who are good at researching databases."

Kate smiled, "You mean like hackers."

Axel smiled back. "Well, maybe some of them cross the line, but there's so much information freely available on the internet, if you know where to find it. I don't ask too many questions about their methods."

"Whom did you call?"

"A friend. He is looking up the license plate number of the SUV from yesterday. Maybe it will give a lead. But, first let's have some breakfast. Pancakes?"

She nodded, feeling her stomach rumbling. "That would be great."

He poured batter in small portions onto the hot griddle and when they began to bubble he turned them over.

"Do you like to cook?" She asked.

Axel smiled. "When I have the time, but it's no fun to cook for yourself. And you?"

"Besides analyzing portfolios and enjoying art history, cooking is one of the things I'm good at."

"Where did you learn it?" He asked.

She hesitated. "Growing up I spent a lot of time in the kitchen with my grandmother and Aunt Clara."

"Is that why the stolen cookbooks are so important?"

She paused again. "Yes, I think so." She thought about telling him about Emma's emails and that one recipe had a 'message', whatever that meant, but decided against it.

With his back to her he flipped a pancake on the stove and asked, "Is one of the cookbooks more important than the others?"

"The Betty Crocker Cookbook." She wondered why she answered so quickly. Was it really vital that he knew her priorities?

He turned around and faced her, expressing amusement. "Why don't you just go out and buy a new cookbook? It'd be less expensive than hiring me, but definitely less fun." He stacked the pancakes on two plates and put more batter on the griddle.

She saw him pause in his movement and become serious. His eyes felt like lasers. She raised her hand to try and hide the flash of heat rising up her neck. "My grandmother's copy is special. It's full of notes and scribbles. It's personal and sentimental to me."

Axel nodded, but for a split second his eyes drifted into space and he seemed deep in thought, and she noticed that he slowly placed the two plates on the kitchen table where he had already put forks, knives and two glasses of orange juice. He poured coffee into two cups, took a small pitcher of warm syrup from the microwave and butter from the fridge.

Her culinary mind spilled forth her words before she could filter them, "Has that butter been around since your friend Harry Raintree was last here?

He grinned. "While you were slumbering I went to the store and bought the ingredients. Everything's fresh." He sat down and said, "Dig in."

She took a bite of the pancakes. They were perfect. In no time at all she had eaten her stack, and he served her a couple more.

When she was finished she sipped her coffee and said, "That was wonderful. I guess I was hungry."

Axel chuckled and asked, "So the cook passes the test?"

"With a top score."

"I'm pleased. You have to know I'm also good at boiled eggs and grilled hot dogs."

She laughed. "Then we won't go hungry."

He quickly cleared the table while she sipped her coffee. She liked his movements, efficient, controlled and manly.

When they had tidied up and placed all the dirty dishes into the dishwasher, he sat down with a fresh cup of coffee and said, "Now if you're okay with it, I'd like to ask you a question."

She became still, wondering what he wanted to know. "Okay."

He glanced down at the clean table, wrapped his fingers around the warm coffee mug, looked her in the eyes and said, "Kate, why don't you tell me just a little bit of what you are holding back? It might shed some light on what we are trying to do."

Her cheeks became red. With agony she pondered what to tell him.

★ ★ ★

She had, at first, decided not to reveal anything about her personal life, but once she opened up it was like a dam broke inside her.

She described growing up in the large house in Palm Beach with two strict but caring elderly women. She shared about being homeschooled and the difficulty of having an endless stream of private teachers coming and going. She told him about the summer trips to Europe and other places around the world. She explained how homeschooling gave flexibility for travel, and how they went to the Bahamas several times a year on short or extended getaways. Happy souvenirs churned through her memory along with some difficult ones.

She wondered if she should stop there, but pouring this out to him was cathartic somehow. It made her feel lighter.

She described her mysterious grandmother who kept things to herself, and of her continual flow of proverbs and riddles. During the trips to Europe, Emma would disappear for days at a time and then rarely tell where she had been.

Sometimes they visited art galleries and Emma bought paintings of unknown European artists or reproductions of famous artists, everything from the Renaissance to the Expressionists. They brought them home and hung them in the many rooms in their spacious home in Palm Beach.

Kate loved those paintings. Several times Emma had teasingly said, "I bought them for you, because of your obsession with art. But honestly, they brighten up the home."

Kate was grateful for this and constantly admired these reproductions from the old masters, a wonderful mix of colors and shapes. Each painting reflected world-views and philosophies of the times in which they were created. Kate found them fascinating.

Emma's main hobby was the ongoing chess games with Aunt Clara. They laughed and friendly mocked each other when one or the other won a game, and they would immediately start another one.

The other hobby was cooking, trying every recipe imaginable, whether it was French, Italian, Chinese or Mexican. Their favorites were the traditional cuisine of Eastern Europe, which tied them back to their origins.

In describing this to Axel, Kate had a flashback to a kitchen engulfed with laughter, a warm glow and the sweet smell of yeast and cinnamon.

Kate appreciated that Axel remained quiet during her rambling exposition, with only a clarifying question here and there, but she still felt slightly uneasy to be revealing so much about herself in such detail, especially to a man. As the words poured out of her mouth her better judgment fought against her, knowing it's best to carefully drip out information to ensure self-survival. She was doing the opposite and suddenly felt more exposed than if she had undressed in front of him.

She was tormented as to whether or not she should tell him about the emails, but she finally went into the bedroom, got her laptop and came back to the kitchen table. She opened the laptop, read out loud the two emails, and then looked at Axel uncertainly. She felt relieved to have opened up and shared buried feelings, but had she done the right thing? Well, it was too late and she couldn't turn back time. Now she could only hope he wouldn't use this information against her somehow.

"Thank you for sharing all that," he quietly said. "You certainly had a different upbringing than most American kids."

She nodded. "Believe me, it was different, but Emma and Clara loved me, and that made all the difference. They were always there for me. Many kids don't get that kind of love."

Axel nodded. "Yes, I agree." He paused, raised his coffee mug to his lips, took a sip and put it back on the table. "There's one thing I don't get. Why did she wait three years before sending the emails?"

"No idea. The one thing for sure is that my grandmother always had a strategy and she never revealed it, as mysterious as that may sound." Not having real answers gave her a feeling of emptiness.

"You said she was a chess player and I'm assuming that carried over into the rest of her life." He scratched his chin. "I find it interesting how she phrased her emails. She speaks in generalities, yet throws in specifics like the meal on your twenty-first birthday. Do you have any idea what she was trying to tell you?"

"Not a clue in the world, other than directing me to the cookbook." Again, the internal void hit her.

"In her second email message she said there is more to come."

"I know, but when?" Her voice trembled.

"It looks like she releases these things every Monday. Maybe there will be another one tomorrow?"

"Do you think these emails have anything to do with the burglary?" She asked.

"It's something to consider. You got the first email two Monday's ago, which didn't have many specifics in it. Then last Monday she mentioned the 'messages' in the furniture and the one recipe in the Betty Crocker Cookbook, which is kind of weird. That might simply be a sentimental reminder of the good times you had or... Maybe it's something more."

"I know. It's just strange that the burglary happened in conjunction with the emails. And they hit my apartment just when I was gone."

"Indeed it seems like someone was watching you. If they were tapping your telephone, perhaps they were reading your emails, too."

A feeling of horror came over Kate. "How would that be possible?"

"In today's world it's easy for some people. This morning we'll visit a friend who knows about these things and maybe he can help. We better hit the road. Bring your laptop, but first let's get some protection."

"Protection?"

His face lit up. "Follow me."

She went with him into his bedroom, a wave of anxiety rushing over her. The violation she felt from the break-in had now become even worse. Was it possible that someone had pried into her life in a deeper way than she imagined?

Axel went to a bookshelf and swung it open. There was a metal door behind it with a keypad. He tapped in a code and moved the handle. As he did, the door opened to another walk-in closet, but this one didn't have clothing. Along one wall there was an arsenal of guns. On shelves on the opposite wall were various electronic gadgets and cameras, some with long telephoto lenses.

Axel took a large utility bag and began to put items in it. He took down a long shotgun from some hooks on the wall and said, "This is a Mossberg pump, twelve-gauge. It sends a serious message."

Kate was shocked. Her grandmother always claimed that guns were evil things. "Do we really need that?" she gasped.

"Who knows? Hopefully not, but it's best to be prepared."

"And, you know how to use that?"

"You don't need any skill with the shotgun. Just point it in a general direction and pull the trigger. Bam! Even you could do it. After a shot you pump it like this." He slid a lever on the bottom of the gun and a shotgun shell popped into the chamber. "Try it, but don't pull the trigger."

He handed it to her. She was horrified. The shotgun was heavy. Quickly, she passed it back to him. "No thank you," she said.

Axel raised his eyebrows, and then turned, selected a couple more guns and showed them to her. "This one's a Glock pistol and this one is an Intratec TEC-9. It's a semiautomatic handgun. Harry and I took it off a street thug. It's old and they don't make them anymore, but it does the job."

The TEC-9 was an ugly gun with a long magazine. The sight of it made her cringe. "I don't like this," she exclaimed.

He stared at her. "Do you remember those two goons from yesterday? They looked seriously bad-news. We don't know their intentions, so it's better safe than sorry."

She hesitated. "I really don't like this."

Axel's face tightened. "I'm not a guy that resorts to violence, but Harry taught me to be prepared."

He took the bag, walked out of the closet and she followed. He locked the closet door and swung the bookshelf back in place. As they went to the garage, Kate wondered if this was getting out of hand and if she should talk with Chandler.

Axel put the bag in the trunk of the Honda Civic and they drove away.

CHAPTER 18

Driving into downtown Miami, Axel's brain was racing. Kate had shared a lot and he needed to process it. Her grandmother sounded eccentric, even wacky, but he didn't want to pre-judge. Florida was loaded with people like that. Maybe he was one of them and he and the old lady would have gotten along just fine.

He strongly suspected there was a connection between the emails and the burglary. If anyone could find out it would be Tommy Holmgren.

He parked the Honda in front of Tommy's place, a small building with an old store front. The large window on the street-side was painted black and covered by an iron grid. It served as Tommy's office and home.

They went to the front door and Axel pushed the doorbell. He pointed up to a surveillance camera aimed down at them and said, "Tommy's cautious."

"What does he do?" Kate asked.

"Officially, high-end contract programming. Unofficially he makes his real money doing research."

"Research?"

Axel grinned. "I guess it has a number of names."

The door opened and Tommy greeted them. "Hey, Axel, come in," he said.

After introductions were made, Tommy led them into something that was a combination of a living room and a computer center. Several computers and monitors lined one wall, and a large screen television attached to another wall.

Axel and Kate sat on a couch that faced the TV while Tommy took a lounge chair on the side.

"Did you find anything?" Axel asked. Earlier in the morning he had called Tommy and given him the license number of the SUV from the day before.

"Sure did. The car is registered to a company called Sable Limited, which seems to be a shell company using an address here in Miami. It's owned by an offshore company called Innokenti Holding registered in Cyprus."

"Cyprus? That's weird." Axel noted.

"I know. It's bizarre. Most of the offshore companies we deal with are registered in places like the Cayman Islands, Panama or the British Virgin Islands. It's unusual to see Cyprus popping up."

"First time I've seen that one," Axel said. "But it makes sense, since Cyprus is an offshore banking center used mainly by Europeans, and Cyprus banks hold tons of money from Eastern Europe." Axel looked at Tommy and asked, "What does Innokenti mean?"

Kate spoke up. "It's Russian for 'innocent.' It's a name given to boys."

Tommy raised his eyebrows. "That's pretty good. How did you know that?"

She smiled. "I took some Russian."

Axel asked, "Do we know who's behind Innokenti Holding?"

Tommy replied, "Not a clue in the world. That information would be held in a safe in some law office in Cyprus."

"What about this Sable Limited? Did you find out anything about them?" The link between Sable Limited and Innokenti Holding raised his curiosity.

"Nothing. Only who registered the company. It's a law firm here in downtown Miami called the Orlov Law Group."

"Did you find out anything about them?"

"I haven't had time. So far it seems they deal in corporate matters and some litigation, at least that's all I could find from their website, which doesn't tell much. They also have an office in New York. I need to do more research." Tommy handed a piece of paper to Axel. "Here's their address."

Axel noticed that Kate seemed deep in thought. He asked, "Do you know that law firm?"

"There's something familiar about it. I feel like I remember my grandmother mentioning someone named Orlov, maybe a lawyer."

"Did she use his services?"

"I don't know. She rarely involved me in her legal and financial affairs."

"Okay," Axel said. "Maybe we better visit Mr. Orlov to find out what he knows about Sable Limited and who's behind it."

"You mean those two men?"

"Either that or who they are working for." Axel turned to Tommy and said, "Maybe there's something else you could investigate."

"What's that?" Tommy asked.

Axel explained about the burglary and the possibility of Kate's phone being tapped. He then told him about the emails without telling him what was in them. "Would it be possible to know if anyone was reading her emails?"

Tommy said, "There are several ways it could be done. I just need the details of Kate's email account."

Kate gave him her email address and password.

"It will take time to research this," Tommy stated. "Can you call me in a couple of hours?"

Axel nodded, they left Tommy's place and went back to the Honda Civic.

Axel glanced at Kate. She seemed tense and lost in thought.

"Any ideas?" he asked.

"Ah . . . I'm not sure. Maybe we should check out the Orlov Group?"

"That's what I was thinking. It's Sunday, but lawyers often work odd hours, unless they're out on the golf course while they bill their clients. At least we can see where their office is located."

The Orlov connection aroused his curiosity. They needed a closer look.

CHAPTER 19

They walked toward the New World Tower, a thirty-story office building in the Miami central business district. Kate had passed by the modern building many times. Wesson Securities was two blocks away.

She felt anxiety as they approached the building. So much had happened in the past few days. It was already deeply troubling to be violated through robbery and being followed, but discovering that the dark SUV might somehow be connected to a law firm with a name that sounded familiar added fuel to the fire.

Walking next to Axel gave her a feeling of security, but she was still alarmed to know he was carrying a gun. She hoped he wouldn't have to use it. She glanced at him. He appeared calm but focused. She wanted to hold his arm and let that confidence flow from him to her. Yet, she knew so little about him other than he had an undergraduate degree in accounting and a doctorate in history. And, he had worked for some character called Harry Raintree. Where was Axel from? To add further complication to her emotional torment, she had to admit she was attracted to him.

She realized her emotions were supercharged, and deducted that any feelings for Axel were nothing more than a reaction to what was happening. It would be wonderful if the visit to the Orlov Law Group would bring an end to this drama and she could then get on with her life. But that was probably wishful thinking.

As they approached the front door of the building Axel asked, "How are you doing?"

She looked at him. It was such a simple question, but it unnerved her to find an answer. "It could be better. All of this is getting to me," she said.

He replied, "I understand. You've had the rug pulled out from under you."

She nodded. "I'm scared. I thought it was a simple break-in to my apartment and would just be a matter of finding some low level thieves to recover my things. But, now it just doesn't make sense to link an SUV back to a lawyer with a name mentioned by my grandmother. It causes me question if I want to continue with this."

"Do you?" He asked, his eyes on her.

She peered up at the building and her body tensed. She whispered, "Yes, I want the cookbook," wondering if she would regret this.

Axel stopped in front of the door, reached out and gently held her arm. "Then let's find it."

★ ★ ★

They entered a large lobby and walked across the shiny marble floor until they came to a wall listing all the companies in the building. The Orlov Law Group was on the twenty-ninth floor, close to the top.

Kate's heart pounded as the elevator ascended.

The elevator doors opened and they stepped into a hallway. Directly in front of them was a wide walnut door with a nameplate that read: 'Orlov Law Group'.

Kate followed Axel to the door. He put his hand on a shiny brass handle and pushed it. She expected it to be locked, but it opened.

They walked into an area with a reception desk on the opposite side. A woman sat behind the desk going through a stack of papers. She looked up at them, frowned, and asked, "Can I be help to you?" She had a strong Eastern European accent.

Axel responded, "We know it's a long shot to come here on a Sunday, but would it be possible to speak with Mr. Orlov, if he's in?"

"Who are you?" She asked staring at them with cold, suspicious eyes.

"I'm Axel Bjorg and this is Kate Miller. It's possible that Ms. Miller's grandmother was a client of Mr. Orlov."

"Just moment," Her foreign accent was rich and silky.

She got up and walked away down a long corridor leaving Axel and Kate standing by her desk. The woman was wearing a tight dress that fit a slender figure. Kate guessed her six-inch heels were Gucci. The receptionist's accent reminded her of her grandmother and Aunt Clara.

In a few minutes the woman came back and said, "He may see you but not very long. It is busy day." She motioned with her hand. "Come."

They followed her down the corridor where there were glass walls and offices on either side. People at their desks appeared busy and concentrated. They passed a conference room with a long wooden table and reached an office different than the others. It had a wooden door and solid walls.

The receptionist knocked two raps, opened the door and said, "You may enter."

They went into a surprisingly large office that made the other office spaces seem miniature. On one side were luxurious green couches and on the other was an oak desk polished to perfection. Behind it sat a man with a round face and deep gray eyes.

He rose, smiled and said, "Hello, I'm Nicolai Orlov. Helena told me you asked to meet. How can I be of help?"

Kate spoke. "Thank you for seeing us on such short notice. I'm trying to tie up some loose ends concerning my grandmother. This is probably a long shot, but I'm wondering if you did some legal work for her?"

"Your grandmother?"

"Oh . . . sorry. Emma Miller. She died three years ago. My name is Kate Miller and this is Dr. Axel Bjorg."

Kate turned to Axel who nodded.

Orlov looked at them with piercing eyes, hesitated and said, "Please have a seat." He pointed to one of the couches.

They went to the couch and sat down, Kate and Axel on one and Orlov facing them on the other. Orlov was a man of medium height and stocky build, like a middle-weight prize fighter. He wore a black suit, a white shirt and a red tie. His shoes were shiny black. His skin was red and ruddy and he had a full head of curly hair turning from black to silver.

Kate guessed he was between fifty to sixty years old. She felt uneasy because of her tight jeans and man's shirt and wished she had worn one of her business combinations.

Orlov said, "I'm sorry, but I don't have much time. Our entire staff is here today preparing for an important case."

"Thank you for any time you can give," Kate said. "I'm wondering if you could tell us if the name Emma Miller means anything to you."

Orlov remained quiet for a moment. He glanced out the large windows at the expanse of Biscayne Bay then stared back at them. He said, "Not really. Was she from Miami?"

"No. Palm Beach, but I recall her mentioning the name Orlov."

Orlov glanced out the window again. "Emma Miller, you said?"

"Yes."

He shook his head. "I don't know that name but even if we did legal work for her I couldn't tell you, because of client-lawyer privilege."

"Even if she was my grandmother?" Kate asked.

"That's correct. We don't reveal details about our clients."

Axel had been quiet and asked, "So you have had no information on Emma Miller?"

"No, I have nothing to tell you." Orlov affirmed.

Axel asked. "There's something else. We are wondering if you know of a company called Sable Limited."

Orlov's face shifted. "Sable? It doesn't ring a bell."

"That's interesting because it seems the Orlov Law Group handled their incorporation."

Orlov glared. "We do hundreds of company setups but I don't recollect this one."

"Your name is on the registration papers."

"It may have been one of our junior associates who did the paper work. I normally don't get involved in company formations." Orlov ran a finger through his thick hair above his ear. He stood and said, "I apologize but there is much work to complete. To be honest, I don't know what Sable Limited has to do with your Emma Miller so I think our time can be used more productively." He walked back over to his desk

Axel and Kate stood.

Axel spoke. "It's a company titled Sable Limited. Their legal address is the same as the Orlov Law Group and they own a dark SUV. It turns out the parent company of Sable is a company registered in Cyprus called Innokenti Holding. Do you know them?"

Orlov slowly turned, his eyes icy blue. "I have no idea what you are talking about and am unable to disclose further information, thereby evoking client-lawyer privilege, if this Sable Limited even exists." He paused, glanced at the papers on his desk and then with a cold voice said, "As I said, I have important work to do. If you have further questions then please see Helene about scheduling a meeting. She can tell you our fees."

Orlov quickly went to the door of his office, opened it and said, "Have a good day."

Kate thanked him for his time and walked ahead of Axel out the door.

Once outside the building Kate stood with her hands on her hips, faced Alex and said, "You challenged him too hard."

Axel grinned. "Not really. He's a thick-skinned lawyer and a lying bastard, sorry. He wasn't going to disclose anything to us anyway. I just called his hand. Now it's up to him to make the next move. If nothing happens, then we can assume Orlov is not directly involved with the men in the SUV. But, my gut feel is that he's definitely connected."

"Even so, I don't like conflict."

"Don't worry about it. Lawyers thrive on conflict, like feasting vultures."

She took a deep breath. "What do we do next?"

"I have an idea. Maybe we should shift gears and explore something different. The meal mentioned in your grandmother's email intrigues me, the one on your twenty-first birthday. Why did your grandmother mention it? This might sound crazy, but I suggest we find a bookstore and buy a Betty Crocker Cookbook. It won't be your grandmother's cookbook, but it might trigger your memory about the meal. Your mysterious grandmother was trying to communicate something, and I'm thinking you're as curious as I am to figure out what."

CHAPTER 20

Axel parked the car in front of a large bookstore and said, "Why don't you go inside and see if you can find a Betty Crocker Cookbook? Let me call Tommy to see if he found anything about your email being hacked." He needed a moment to speak to Tommy alone to make a special request.

"I'm not sure it's the right thing to do. My grandmother's cookbook was old and full of scribbles."

"We have to start somewhere. Let's try and trigger the memory of the meal on your twenty-first birthday."

Kate hesitated and said, "Okay. It might be worth a try." She got out of the car and headed toward the bookstore.

Axel took out his cell phone and quickly scanned the parking lot before dialing. Everything was clear. Then, his eyes drifted back to Kate.

She unnerved him, even caused him to doubt himself. Wasn't he able to take on a female client without falling for her? He had vowed it would never happen again.

Now he felt that vow was under threat as he watched Kate disappear into the store.

What did he really know about her? *Can you fall in love with a person you don't really know?* He couldn't help but hope that maybe once the case was finished they could date and then see if there was something deeper. But, of course rich-boy Chandler needed to be out of the way and that wouldn't be easy. She seemed attracted by the guy and who could blame her?

He dialed a number and after three rings Tommy answered.

Axel asked, "Did you discover anything about Kate's email?"

"I did. Somebody went into her email system and changed the parameters. All messages are being copied and forwarded to another email account."

"That means they'd have seen the emails from her grandmother."

"Without a doubt."

Axel now understood. Someone had read what Emma said about keeping the cookbooks safe, as well at the strange bit about 'messages' in the furniture. He said, "Thanks Tommy. That's a great help. Is it possible to find out the location of the computer receiving her emails?"

"I'm working on it but need more time. I'll call you back."

"Thanks," Axel replied. "There's one more thing where I could use your help."

"Sure, what is it?"

"Could you research Kate's family, especially her grandmother and grandfather, Emma and John Miller? Also, find out anything about a plane crash in the Everglades twenty-three years ago where four people died. Kate would have been three years old. The plane was carrying Kate's parents, her grandfather and the pilot. She said they were never found. I'd like to know the purpose of their trip."

"Okay, I'll jump on it and get back to you when I have something."

"Thanks, I appreciate it, and keep digging into Orlov."

"Will do," Tommy said. "Oh yeah, I reset the email parameters, so no more forwarding, and changed Kate's password to something more secure." He gave it to Axel.

They hung up and Axel waited for Kate. The fact that someone had been reading her emails and potentially listening to her telephone calls worried him. It meant someone had more information than he had thought and chances are there was an ugly purpose behind this.

Indeed he needed to find out more about Kate Miller and her mysterious, well-off Orthodox grandmother who originated from Poland. Obviously the wealth didn't come with her from the Communist Soviet Union, so it must have come from John Miller. Who was he, and why did Kate seem to know so little about him? He surveyed the parking lot again. Something wasn't making sense.

You better forget your Caribbean vacation, he said to himself.

CHAPTER 21

In the past: Kate's twenty-first birthday.

Kate walked through the front door of her grandmother's house into a large entrance. Welcoming smells from the kitchen filtered into the room. Her grandmother had asked her to come home for the weekend, for a happy occasion, to celebrate Kate's twenty-first birthday.

It had been a month since she had been home. She had been unable to do so earlier because of weeks of exams and essay assignments. The major in Economics was getting to her and she was glad for the weekend break.

"I'm home," she happily cried out, her voice echoing off the wall. The immensity of the entrance room never ceased to amaze her. It would be an empty, almost frightening space if it were not for the colorful paintings on the walls, reproductions of Picasso, Matisse and several lesser-known artists. A large, red Persian rug filled much of the room.

A moment later the door to the kitchen opened and her grandmother charged through it, rushed to Kate and hugged her with surprising strength for such a small, spindly woman.

"Welcome home, my little one," her grandmother said. She was a head smaller than Kate.

A minute later Aunt Clara came through the kitchen door, a large smile breaking the wrinkles on her face. "Oh Kate, we have missed you so much."

Aunt Clara walked with her cane and Kate sensed something had changed. Clara's feet shuffled, like the sounds of a woodworker sanding furniture, and she was hunched over more than ever. Age had caught up with her. She was ninety-one, eight years older than Emma, but seemed to be of a different generation.

Aunt Clara looked at Kate and commanded, "Come to the kitchen. You must drink and eat. The school is not feeding you well. You are pale and, what is the word? Skinny. We have real food for you."

Kate laughed. Emma and Clara were always concerned that she wasn't eating enough. She figured it was a holdover from their childhood when there was a constant question of where the next meal would come from. In actuality, the meals at her school were good, so much so that she had gained a few pounds. As a result, a local fitness center had become part of her daily routine.

Kate went into the kitchen and there was a glass of apple juice and three cookies on a small plate.

They sat with her and watched her eat, asking her about her school, how the economics studies were going, if she was getting 'tens' on her grades – it was always a 'ten' and never an 'A'.

"Yes, grandmother, I am getting straight A's." They didn't know how hard she worked with endless evenings and weekends spent in the school library.

Now, to be in the kitchen with them was a delight, memories of her childhood flooding through her. The smell of something cooking on the stove brought back a plethora of recollections: salads, main dishes, desserts, all prepared with fun and love.

The smell of slow-cooked onions, beef and paprika touched her senses and made her hungry, but it also brought back remembrances of conversations, opinions, stories and proverbs from the old country.

This formed the basis of who she was; it wasn't textbooks that made a person's character, but something different. In her case, her identity had been influenced by the history and loving input of two elderly women.

Kate eventually called their attention 'helicopter parenting'. It meant that the two women hovered around her, asking for status reports, encouraging her, and constantly challenging her to do better.

She helped set the table and Clara said an Orthodox prayer before the meal.

Lord, have mercy;
Lord, have mercy;
Lord, have mercy;
O Christ our God, bless the food, drink, and fellowship of Thy servants, for Thou art holy always, now and ever and unto ages of ages. Amen

They all made the sign of the cross, and then Kate ate with delight. No one made Hungarian goulash better than her grandmother, of course with Aunt Clara's incessant coaching.

Her grandmother opened a bottle of French Bordeaux wine and put three crystal glasses on the table, filling each one slightly more than half full. Kate had been taught that this was the proper way to present wine rather than filling a glass to the top of the rim "like the barbarian Americans do."

Her grandmother motioned toward the wine and said, "Now you are legal for this, but I question who came up with that arbitrary rule of twenty-one years old to drink wine? Why do these politicians want to spoil a good meal? They want absolute power over people. Don't they know that wine is a blessing from God?"

During the meal Aunt Clara dozed off several times. Occasionally her head dropped to her chest, mouth open. This was something new. Kate hadn't seen it before.

Her grandmother took advantage of one of those cat naps to whisper, "She sleeps more than in the past, but she deserves it. She's ninety-one. At least her brain isn't fried like an egg."

Kate laughed. "Yes, she's pretty sharp for her age."

Emma raised a bony finger and swung it in the air. "You should believe it. She is much beyond the young people of your age who are brain dead with their iPads and their hopeless music and narrow-minded culture. Those foolish ones prepare for all ways of government manipulation. Believe me, I lived through that and it comes again."

Kate sensed the conversation was drifting into one of Emma's political lectures on out-of-control government. Hoping to divert that topic, Kate smiled and said, "I agree. Aunt Clara is way beyond most people in my school."

Emma softened her voice even more. "That is not about why I wish to talk to you this evening. There is something more serious."

That surprised Kate. What could be more serious to her grandmother than oppressive governments and corrupt officials? "What is it?" Kate asked.

Emma looked at Clara and back at Kate. "As you can see, we are getting older. We have seen the hand of God with us throughout this life, yet I sense it is time to move on."

This struck Kate. "No, what are you talking about? You are both doing just fine."

"Yes, and not yes." Emma said. "Our minds are able, but our bodies are becoming worn out. But, that's not what I want to say. Before it is too late I want you to know we have done our best for you, even though it may not always seem so. Now, how can I say? We want to pass over the baton, but we are doubtful."

"What does that mean?" Kate asked, feeling uneasy, wondering where her grandmother was going.

"You have matured greatly, but I feel your mind is still chasing the dreams of artists and their histories. These things are interesting, but before doing so I ask you to take on a different responsibility."

"Grandmother, I don't want to be President of the United States." They had this discussion before. It always ended with an admonition that "you need a degree and experience in order to get a job." And that "people with degrees in Art History have difficulty finding work."

Emma raised her wrinkled hands. "My little one, you have much promise in front of you, but you are not ready."

"What do you mean?"

"You are now twenty-one and have done well academically, but you are not yet ready."

"Ready for what?"

"For life and for all that is coming."

"What?"

"You must be patient with me. I merely want to remind you of our agreement. You will remember it, please?"

"You mean about getting an MBA or degree in Finance and then getting a job?"

Emma nodded her head. "That is all. It is important."

Kate was frustrated that her grandmother demanded specifics, like those in their *agreement*, yet Emma was vague and mysterious about other things. It was a lifelong pattern, something Kate rebelled against many times, but her grandmother could not be changed. So, she ended up accepting the agreement, both trusting her grandmother's judgment while knowing there was plenty of time to follow her passions.

Aunt Clara's head popped up and she said, "What agreement?"

"It's nothing," Emma stated.

Without a further word, Clara slid her chair back, stood up, leaned on her cane and walked over to the end of the kitchen counter where there was a chessboard. She took a piece, moved it and said, "White queen takes black knight. Check mate!"

Emma stayed silent for a moment and then heartily laughed. "I never saw that coming. Maybe I was too focused on making the meal."

"You're losing your touch. I'll prove it in the next game." Clara shuffled back to the kitchen table and sat down.

After two large portions of Hungarian goulash served with sweet and sour red cabbage and thick homemade bread, Kate was stuffed. Yet, Aunt Clara insisted on another small serving, "To get real food into your body rather than that artificial Jell-O they serve at your school."

Kate barely managed to finish her meal.

When the plates were cleared and put in the dishwasher, Emma went into the pantry next to the kitchen, stayed there for a couple of minutes and then appeared with a chocolate cake with twenty-one lighted candles. At that moment Aunt Clara perked up from another short nap and began singing "Happy birthday to you …"

After Kate made a wish and blew out the candles, they gave her one birthday present, a habit from their childhood, when children were lucky to receive anything on their birthdays and at Christmas. It was small, wrapped in red paper with a delicate white ribbon. She opened it with expectation and found an elegant Rolex watch.

"It's beautiful. Too much," Kate exclaimed, mouth wide open, realizing it cost a fortune.

"I got it last summer when we were in Geneva," Emma said. "Why buy ten watches during your life when one good one will do?"

"Thank you," was all Kate could say, knowing Emma's fanaticism for quality and her disgust of the American throw-away culture. She embraced and kissed each woman.

The evening ended with laughter. Kate relaxed for two days around the house before thanking them again and heading back to school. She had plenty of hard work ahead, but the weekend break and time in her grandmother's kitchen gave her the motivation to face her studies.

At the same time she worried about Aunt Clara's health, and she carried lingering questions about those vaguely defined *responsibilities to come*.

★ ★ ★

Kate's worries about Aunt Clara were well-founded. Three months later her aunt peacefully died and was received into the arms of her glorious God.

CHAPTER 22

Present day

In the bookstore, Kate bought a new Betty Crocker Cookbook and rushed to the car, eager to look through it. Would this trigger the memory of the meal on her twenty-first birthday?

In the front seat of the Honda Civic, she opened the cookbook and ran her hand across the first page. "It just doesn't feel right," she said. "It's too new. My grandmother's cookbook was old and worn, with oil spots, flour between the pages and scribbles everywhere. And, there are recipes here that I don't recognize."

"Just try," Axel said.

They sat for five minutes while Kate turned the pages. She stopped on one page and said softly, "I remember. It's that one." Her eyes became moist.

Axel looked at the recipe, raised his eyebrows and exclaimed, "Hungarian goulash? Why that?"

Kate chuckled. "I know. It sounds basic, but for special occasions we always had something from *the old country*, as my grandmother called it. For Christmas and Easter we had blini and creamed herrings. For birthdays we prepared other Eastern European specialties, including goulash."

"Hey, my mother makes blini, small thin pancakes served with sour cream and sometimes caviar!"

"Really?? We always had it with caviar, and creamed herring on the side," Kate laughed.

"Exactly! Except that's not Polish. It's Russian."

"Even so, that was our tradition." She sighed, "I miss it."

Axel stared at the Hungarian goulash recipe. "So, what does this tell you?"

She shook her head and said, "I don't know. It just brings back good memories. My grandmother liked the Betty Crocker recipes, but she often tinkered with them, saying they needed a little help. People's preferences differ and I guess she was always trying to add in the special tastes from her childhood."

Kate watched Axel as he contemplated her words, his fingers slowly moved across his chin.

He said, "How's this for an idea? You said you like to cook, so how about it?"

"What, you want me to make goulash?" Kate asked.

"Yeah, we can go through the recipe together. Maybe it will tell us something. I propose that we go to a grocery store then head back to the house and cook it. Maybe that experience will trigger some memories. For now I've got nothing else to go on."

Kate raised her eyebrows and teased, "So, *I'm* paying for you as a private investigator while *you* get a free meal?"

Axel flashed a broad smile. "This is Sunday. Let's call it a free day with no charges. Why don't we just relax, enjoy the meal and look for clues?"

Kate liked the idea. Indeed, she needed some down time. Also, cooking goulash would make her feel connected to Emma and Aunt Clara.

And, maybe this would be an opportunity to get to know this Dr. Axel Bjorg a bit better.

★ ★ ★

Nikolai Orlov called his brother in New York.

"Da," his brother answered.

"Leonid, we have a problem. Somehow she found out about Sable Limited and Innokenti Holding."

"What?" Leonid asked.

"She came to my office along with that private investigator."

"This is not good. When was this?"

"Today. They just showed up here. It seems the PI tracked the license number of one of our vehicles to Sable Limited and then connected that to the Orlov Law Group."

"This is unfortunate. I thought we were getting close, especially with the emails from the old babushka. Since they were scheduled on the last two Mondays, maybe there will be another one tomorrow."

"We will see," Nicolai replied.

"Was anything found in the items taken from the girl's apartment?" Leonid asked.

"Not yet. We suspect a secret message is somehow in the furniture, but where, we don't know. That was mentioned in the babushka's email and it was the first thing the young woman went after. We have dismantled the shelves and cupboard but found nothing."

"This is very important. You must keep looking."

"I know, Leonid. There is much to gain."

"We are wasting time to search these things. Let's question the girl," Leonid's voice was deep and commanding.

"Be patient. First we need to find her. We are watching her apartment and the private investigator's house, but there has been nothing. I am also hiring an electronics specialist to track her movements."

"It sounds like you could use more resources. What do you think?"

"Yes, it would be helpful."

"I will bring some men and join you tomorrow." Leonid said.

"Tomorrow, already?"

"This is top priority. I will drop everything I am doing. We may be getting close."

"I agree. We should focus only on this until we have our answer," Nicolai stated.

They talked some more on their strategy and then hung up.

Nicolai Orlov had a feeling of satisfaction. It would be good to see his brother. The men Leonid was bringing with him were mindless and brutal, but they obeyed orders. That's all that mattered. The plan was to follow the girl to discover what she is up to, but eventually she would be brought to one of their facilities and questioned. If the private investigator became a problem he would be eliminated.

CHAPTER 23

Kate stood in the kitchen and opened a bag of large yellow onions. Axel sat by the table with a glass of red wine in his hand.

She felt strange to be cooking in front of a man. Her experiences in the kitchen had always been with Emma and Clara. Now having someone watching her movements made her feel like a child taking an exam.

It took a while for her to find the pots and utensils she needed, but she was enjoying being in the kitchen, a welcome reprieve to the stress she had felt over the past days.

"Are you just going to sit there and watch, or are you going to help?" She asked, eyes smiling.

"Watching is quite pleasant," Axel said his grin bringing small wrinkles next to his blue eyes.

She handed four onions to him and said, "Here, chop these."

"And bring tears to my eyes?"

"The tears from onions are a sign of joy to come. At least that's what Aunt Clara always said."

Axel took a kitchen knife, peeled the onions and quickly chopped them into small pieces.

"You're pretty good with the knife," she said. "Have you considered being a chef?"

"You're kidding me. Being the occasional assistant chef is good enough."

With a spatula she lifted the onions from the chopping board and added them to the chopped beef cooking in the skillet. She pointed at the open cookbook on the counter. "You see this recipe? It calls for one cup of onions. My grandmother always doubled this. Sometimes she would put as much onions as meat. She said that's the secret for goulash."

"I bet it's delicious that way."

She smiled. "Oh, and one more thing. The recipe calls for two teaspoons of paprika, but if you want excellent goulash it should only be made with real Hungarian paprika."

"Your grandmother's recommendation?"

"Of course." Kate took a teaspoon of paprika and held it to the light, admiring its deep red color, its savory aroma attacking her senses.

"You want some history?" He asked.

"I have a feeling I'm going to get it whether I say yes or not," she smiled.

He grinned back, "Peppers came from the new world and were introduced to Europe by the Spanish. They got to Hungary via the Ottoman Empire."

"You are a real historian," she remarked.

"When you do a PhD in history you learn all kinds of trivia.

"I can imagine. You know, I've actually seen the pepper fields in Hungary. They go on forever."

"No kidding! I envy you. I'd give up being a private investigator to travel the world. There is so much to see and learn," he replied.

"I agree," she said. "Maybe someday."

They left the goulash on the stove to cook, went into the living room with a bottle of wine and sat on opposite ends of a couch.

Axel poured her a glass of wine.

She raised it to his and said, "Santé," and then took a sip.

She said, "We have to wait an hour for the goulash to be ready. Really good goulash should cook for two and a half hours or longer, but one is okay."

"That's fine," Axel said. "There's more wine in the kitchen. We can take all the time we need." He put his glass down and turned to her. "Tell me, does this recipe trigger any memories or thoughts?"

"Not really. It baffles me that Emma would mention something this specific in her email."

"Could there be something about Hungary or Europe? You mentioned that your grandmother would leave you for days at a time on your trips over there. Do you have any idea what she was doing?"

"I never knew. When I asked Aunt Clara she said it was to visit friends or for business or to take care of something. But I never got the details."

Kate felt odd when she said this. She had lived her whole life with her grandmother, yet so many things escaped her about the woman. Kate understood she carried many of her grandmother's characteristics and beliefs, for one absorbs the world-view of the important people in your life. But Axel's question was sobering. She wondered what her grandmother had been up to, and she needed to find out.

She remained silent for a moment, and then shifted the subject. "What about you? Are you from Florida?"

Axel smiled. "I was born in Wisconsin, but when I was nine months old my parents moved to Florida. They were originally from Norway but immigrated to the U.S. just before I was born. So I was conceived in Norway, born in Wisconsin and grew up in Florida. And, I'm Lutheran, like most Scandinavians."

"Is your first name Norwegian? It is unusual."

Axel laughed. "It's not exactly standard American, like Kate Miller. Axel is Norwegian for Absalom, from the Bible, meaning 'my father is peace.' And Bjorg is old Norse. It means 'to help' or 'to rescue.' Simple as that."

Kate smiled. It was nice to put a history to a person. That explained his blondish hair, blue eyes and poster-boy looks. His name was appropriate. She did need help, even to be rescued. "If I may ask, what do your parents do? And do you have any brothers or sisters?"

"My parents are retired and live in Fort Lauderdale. I have a sister,

Elsa, eight years younger than me. She's in graduate school at Miami University, same school as me. Her subject is chemistry. When I was a teenager she was a pain in the butt, but I love her to death."

Kate laughed, thinking of the sister relationship. "I'm envious. Sometimes I wonder what it would be like to have a normal family."

Axel smiled. "Don't be envious. There's no such thing as a normal family. Each one is different."

"I guess so," she replied, yet she pondered what it would be like to have a mother and father and siblings.

They sat for a moment in quietness, and then Axel said, "So, any ideas about why your grandmother referred to your 21st birthday goulash?"

She paused and turned to him. "No. I mean, now I definitely remember the meal and a wonderful weekend with my grandmother and Aunt. But I still don't know why she mentioned this in her email. All I know is that Emma and Aunt Clara were always thinking many moves ahead. I'm convinced there is a meaning behind all of this."

★ ★ ★

They ate the goulash in silence and Kate took that as a good sign. Her grandmother always said that when a man is silent at a meal you know it is touching his soul. Or, was the silence because he was thinking of the case?

They washed the dishes together and, when finished, Kate felt tiredness overtake her. She said, "I think I'll go to bed."

Axel turned to her. "Thank you for that amazing meal. I enjoyed our time."

She nodded. It *had* been a good time and she was surprised how relaxed she had felt in spite of the events over the past days. Time with Axel was different than being with Chandler. With Chandler it was all about the excitement of going to gourmet restaurants, receiving flowers, and experiencing the attention he gave her. He was poles apart from Axel, who was an eclectic mix of complexity and simplicity. Axel was inquisitive and intelligent for sure, but even with a PhD he was someone who was completely at ease with a pair of jeans and a Hawaiian shirt.

She imagined that a trip with Chandler would involve going to nice restaurants, attending parties with jet-set people and sailing on expensive yachts. Axel would probably be content to walk barefoot on a sandy beach, cook fresh fish on a barbecue and silently watch a tropical sunset. The difference between the two was striking.

She said, "Thank you so much for your help and for listening so patiently."

He smiled. "It's my pleasure."

They stood in silence, facing each other. Kate stared into Axel's eyes, grateful he was with her. Something inside her told her to walk away, but she succumbed to an unexplained force and spontaneously went to him, wrapped her arms around him and gave him a hug, their bodies pressing against each other.

His arms slowly came up and wrapped around her back, and she felt herself melting into him, feeling the warmth and closeness of his body. Suddenly his body tightened and he quickly let go and took a step backward. He shifted his weight from one foot to the other and said, "Ah . . . I guess I'll go into the backyard for a bit of fresh air and then head to bed. I'll see you tomorrow."

It troubled her, the way he stepped back. Was it rejection? She picked up the cookbook off the table and said, "I'll keep thinking about this, but we must find the one from my grandmother."

"We'll keep looking," he said absently.

She turned and went to her bedroom, shut the door and sat on the bed, placing the cookbook next to her. Her mind was not on the cookbook. Instead, she savored the feeling of his body next to hers, his strong arms around her. It had been a moment of absolute bliss.

Yet, his sudden retraction from her was perplexing. From the way his eyes clung to her she sensed he was attracted to her, but why had he released her so quickly? He had mentioned another woman but said it was over. Maybe it wasn't.

This was foolish, she thought. *Emotions shouldn't dictate thoughts and actions. These feelings must be repressed.* Her grandmother had been a goal-oriented person and for now that's what she needed to be.

Finding her stolen property was of utmost importance. She needed to uncover the mystery of what her grandmother was trying to communicate. The key had to be in the cookbook.

The attraction she had for Dr. Axel Bjorg had to be put to the side. Then she thought of Chandler and felt guilt. *Wasn't Chandler a better fit for her?*

★ ★ ★

Once in bed she took out her cell phone and called Chandler, knowing San Francisco was four hours behind Miami.

After two rings he answered.

"This is Kate. I hope this isn't a bad time."

"No. Not at all. I've had a busy day and now I'm meeting my clients at a restaurant by the wharf. I've been thinking about you all day. How is it going?"

"It was a strange day, in fact, a strange two days. Some men followed me to my home and I had to escape."

"What?" he exclaimed.

"Yes, it was horrible." She felt her legs shaking as she re-lived the experience, and then she told him about fleeing from the two men with Axel, staying at the safe house in Miami and visiting the Orlov Law Firm.

"That's crazy," he said. "Did you tell the police?"

"No."

"Why not?"

"Ah . . . because too much was happening too fast." She didn't want to tell him about her innate mistrust of authority.

"Kate, I'm worried. Unfortunately I can't leave here until late Tuesday, but I could arrive in Miami on Wednesday. In the meantime I can get people to help you. I'm not sure you should trust this questionable private detective. The two men in the SUV sound dangerous and this Axel Burg may not be equipped to help."

"It's Bjorg, not Burg."

"Whatever. I can at least get you some bodyguards, and I have lawyers to interface with this Orlov character if needed."

Her mind rattled. Chandler was accurately evaluating the seriousness of this. She needed to listen to him. "I appreciate your advice," she said.

"Please let me help. I don't want anything bad to happen to you."

"Thank you, Chandler."

"Why don't you find a safe place for a couple of days away from Bjorg and those strange men? I'll meet up with you on Wednesday and we can work out a plan."

"That's a good idea," she said. "I'll do that tomorrow."

"Thank you. That settles my fears," he said. "Keep your cell phone on and I'll call you a couple of times a day."

"Okay."

"And remember that I love you," he said.

"That means a lot."

They hung up and she felt relief. Chandler was wise in appraising her situation. Did she really need to be running around with Axel doing crazy things like barging into a lawyer's office and cooking Hungarian goulash? He made it all seem so logical at the time, but in retrospect it now seemed ridiculous.

Tomorrow she'd take Chandler's advice by renting a car and going off somewhere for a couple of days. During that time she'd call Detective McGill and push him to work harder on the case.

Undoubtedly, her shaken emotions were impacting her judgment. Tomorrow she would take control.

CHAPTER 24

Axel went outside into the backyard and took several deep breaths. The day had cooled and distant sea breezes flowed across his skin. The hug from Kate was unexpected. She had so naturally come to him. It was a simple act, yet it felt like an attack on his defenses. Should he read anything into this? *Probably not*, he thought.

He understood her fragility because of the robbery and all that had happened since. Still, he sensed an inner strength in her, and he believed her to be someone who could stand up to adversity. The hug may have been nothing more than a sign of appreciation or a need for human closeness. But he couldn't shake the feeling that there was something more behind it.

He was the one who stepped back, even though his inner desire was to take her, give comfort, and kiss her. Yet, the lessons he had learned in the past had provided rules not to engage in romance with clients. It was a difficult standard to maintain, especially with someone like Kate. After all, he was a man and not a saint.

He forced himself to focus on the job at hand. Shaking his head, he shifted his thoughts to the encounter with the lawyer, Nikolai Orlov. There was something hard and disturbing about the man, and he sensed an underlying malevolence. Axel knew he had challenged Orlov by mentioning Sable Limited and Innokenti Holding. Perhaps this would cause Orlov to take action, although Axel was uncertain what that might be.

He sat down in a lounge chair and tried to relax, but the ring of his cell phone startled him. The glanced at the caller ID, pushed the call button, held the phone to his ear and said, "Hi Tommy."

"Where you at, man?" Tommy asked.

"A safe house."

"Is it on West Flagler Street near the Miami River?"

"How did you know?" Axel asked.

"It's easy to track a cell phone, man. What you need to do is turn that thing off when we are done and then go buy a burner phone and only turn it on when you want to call someone. Kate should do the same. If I can find you, then anyone with technical know-how can do the same."

"Good point. I'll tell her. Did you find out anything?"

"I've got an answer to your first question about the location of the email address. I pinged it off a server in Miami using a state of the art application. It was borrowed from the NSA and FBI."

"You don't need to give me the details," Axel said.

"Okay, but it's pretty cool technology."

"And I'm sure I'd understand about one percent of it," Axel stated. "What did your ping tell you?"

"Kate's hacked emails were going to a computer in a warehouse here in Miami, just a few miles from where you are. You got something to write with?"

"Just a second."

Axel walked into the kitchen, found a pen and pad of paper and wrote down the address that Tommy gave.

"Thanks so much," Axel said.

"Are you going there?"

"Only to check it out."

"Do you need help?" Tommy asked.

"I'll just do reconnaissance and will call up our ex-Army friends if needed."

"Be careful."

"Will do."

"As far as the other thing about Kate's family, I'll get back to you."

Axel thanked him, said goodbye, and then turned off his cell phone as suggested by Tommy. He went to the walk-in closet in his bedroom and found a burner phone, one of several Harry Raintree had in a drawer.

Then he picked out a dark shirt, put it on, and put a black balaclava in a small backpack, along with wire cutters, a lock pick, nylon handcuffs and a few other small tools. His Glock pistol was in its holster on his hip.

After getting in the car he drove several miles to the address given by Tommy and waited.

CHAPTER 25

At three o'clock in the morning Axel stood behind several large trash dumpsters surveying a warehouse on the opposite side of the street. He had been there for an hour and a half. The warehouse had one dimly lit lamp above a door. On the opposite side of the building was a loading dock. Next to it was a car with a man sitting in it. During the past hour the man had walked around the building one time.

Axel waited and the man came around the building a second time, exactly one hour since the first time. When the man disappeared around the corner, Axel made his move.

He had two choices. The first was to open the door to the warehouse with a lock pick, but if the building had an alarm it would ruin everything.

The second was to demand the man's assistance.

He chose the second option.

Axel put on the balaclava, hiding his face, and then moved quickly across the street, his rubber-soled shoes making no noise. His dark clothing blended into the night. He moved to the corner of the building, peered around the corner and saw the man moving with tired, slow steps.

Axel quickly moved up behind the man, put his arm around him in a choke hold and began to squeeze. After a few futile attempts to break loose, the man passed out. Axel let go, guided the man to the ground, pulled the nylon handcuffs from his pocket and secured him.

Axel waited a minute and then gently patted the man's cheek.

The man's eyes rolled for a few seconds and he tried to get up. Axel put his hand over the man's mouth and pushed him back to the ground. He pulled the Glock from its holster and pointed it at the man's face.

"You want to live?" Axel asked. Taking the rough approach wasn't pleasant, but Harry Raintree always said to do what was necessary.

The man froze.

"Nod your head if you want to live."

The man nodded his head.

"Tell me your name."

"Uh, my name?"

"Yes."

"It is Radomir." He spoke with an Eastern European accent. What was it about all the Eastern Europeans he was encountering these days?

"Good. Now, Radomir, I need some information and I'm only going to ask one time. Is there an alarm on this building?"

Radomir nodded.

"You're the security man so I'm sure you have access to the building. Let me in without setting off the alarm." He pushed the gun to

Radomir's forehead. "Move now without saying a word or I'll turn your brains into scrambled eggs. You understand?" He had practiced this line, having taken it from some gangster movie.

Radomir stayed still for a moment and then he nodded.

Axel pulled Radomir to his feet. They went around the building walked up some steps to a door beside the loading dock. Radomir punched a code into an electronic keypad next to the door.

They stepped inside and into a dimly lit room. He quickly counted fifteen recent model luxury sports cars. He asked, "Are these stolen cars?"

"I don't know," Radomir answered.

Axel pointed the gun at the man's face. "Tell the truth."

The man nodded and said, "Maybe."

Axel suspected the cars would be exported to other countries. Beyond the cars was an area full of antique furniture, which he guessed had been stolen. Against one wall was a long workbench and at the end of it was an office desk with a computer.

He led Radomir toward the workbench, where he found a roll of duct tape and used it to securely tie the man to a chair. Then he tore off a small strip and covered Radomir's eyes.

"Who owns this place? Axel asked.

"I cannot tell you," Radomir said.

Axel pushed the barrel of the Glock against Radomir's temple. "Who owns it?"

"If I tell you they will kill me."

"And what will happen if you don't tell me?"

"You will kill me?" Radomir asked.

"Good guess. Who owns this place?"

Radomir hesitated. "Some men."

"Some men who?"

"By being here you are in danger."

"What are their names?" Axel asked.

"They are known as the Albanians."

"Do they work for anyone?"

"I don't know. I'm just the night guard."

"Okay, good enough."

Radomir raised his shoulders and said, "If you leave me here like this I am dead man. They will surely kill me for letting you in here."

"Let's try and keep that from happening. Now be quiet," Axel stated.

He went to the workbench and saw long oak boards that seemed like they came from a bookshelf. It had been dismantled. On the floor underneath the workbench was a disorderly pile of textbooks, a photo album and six cookbooks. One was a Betty Crocker Cookbook.

He lifted up the Betty Crocker Cookbook and looked inside. It was exactly as Kate had described it, worn and stained with lots of notes, some written in English and others in Cyrillic characters.

He put the cookbooks and photo album in a wooden box, untied Radomir but left the tape over his eyes and said, "I'm leaving. You are free to go five minutes after you hear the door shut. Do you understand?"

Radomir nodded.

Axel lifted the box, walked outside and heard the door close behind him. Then he disappeared into the darkness of the night.

★ ★ ★

Back at the safe house Axel got into bed. It was 4:30 in the morning. He figured he could get three or four hours sleep. He shut his eyes, still feeling the adrenaline rushing through his body.

He had a great feeling of satisfaction to know the cookbooks and photo album had been recovered. In the morning Kate would need to call Detective McGill to inform him about the warehouse. Then the rest of her things could be restored and returned to her apartment.

He had completed what he was hired to do and now the job was done, but he regretted it. Kate would go back to her job at Wesson Securities and resume her romance with Chandler. He would definitely head off on his vacation to the Caribbean, but he wanted to see her again. The feeling of satisfaction was dampened by a sense of loss.

As his mind raced, he knew there was more to this case than furniture and books, understanding they had been taken for a reason. The emails from Emma added to the mystery. He suspected that Kate would want to continue with this but he wasn't sure. If she did, he would help her. She was getting under his skin, and he didn't want her to slip away.

Tiredness overtook him. He shut his eyes and went to sleep.

CHAPTER 26

At eight o'clock Kate left her bedroom remembering her conversation with Chandler and what she needed to do. She wondered how Axel would react if she told him that she wanted to disappear for a couple of days before Chandler arrived.

The hug with Axel the previous evening had been on impulse and she knew it came from her fragile emotional state. Now she rationalized it as an expression of thankfulness for what Axel had been doing. But, had he been doing enough? She now felt uncomfortable about the visit to the Orlov Law Firm and doubted Axel's judgment.

Letting him talk her into cooking a meal was just as ridiculous. While it had been a pleasurable experience to create a meal in a kitchen, Kate wondered now if Axel had hidden motives in it rather than just to help her trigger memories. Was he trying to seduce her with the conversation, the bottle of wine and his caring inquiries on the couch? Was her hug the result of his manipulations? Yet, he was the one who had broken away from her.

Today she would go away on her own and wait for Chandler to arrive.

She carried the new Betty Crocker Cookbook under her arm. Once she was on her own she would have the opportunity to go through it again, to see if it brought back any special memories that might in some way connect with the emails from Emma. It was so strange that her grandmother had singled out an obscure Hungarian goulash recipe. Now she felt more confused than ever. Being away from Axel meant he would no longer be attempting to probe into her personal life. She had revealed far too much and now that had to stop.

She went into the kitchen and saw Axel beside the counter pouring a cup of coffee. His eyes appeared to be tired and his hair was out of place.

With a large grin he lifted the cup and said, "Good morning. Do you want one?"

"Yes, thank you." She glanced at the kitchen table and then froze. On it were some books . . . her schoolbooks and her photo album, the cookbooks . . . the Betty Crocker Cookbook. She put her hand to her mouth. "I can't believe it. Where, how did you . . .?

"I was up late," he said and then he explained about the events, leaving out the part about manhandling Radomir. "You need to call Detective McGill. The police should get over there as quickly as possible before the Albanians discover what happened. In any case it would take a full day of frenzied work for them to empty that place before the police got there." He handed her a piece of paper with the address of the warehouse.

Kate shook her head in disbelief, went to her bedroom and got her cell phone. She walked back into the kitchen and dialed Detective McGill's number and pushed the speaker button so that Axel could listen in.

It rang and he answered, "McGill."

"Detective McGill, this is Kate Miller. I've got some good news for you."

"It's who?"

"Kate Miller. You were at my apartment a few days ago. The robbery."

"Oh yes. How can I help?"

"I've got good news. We found out where my stolen things are."

"You what?"

"They are in a warehouse run by a criminal gang called the Albanians. There are many stolen things in that warehouse including my bookshelves and dressers." She gave him the address of the warehouse.

"How did you find that out?" he asked.

"Through an informant, in our investigations. Do you remember that I hired a private investigator?"

"Yeah, I remember. I checked into the guy, Axel Bjorg. Two years ago a criminal complaint was filed on him."

"Criminal complaint?" Kate asked. She looked across at Axel and he raised his hands to shoulder level, hands toward the air.

"Some lawyers represented a man in a legal battle with his sister. Bjorg was representing the sister and from what I gather from the wording in the file it was a trumped up charge. The complaint was dropped. What did your PI find?"

Noticing Axel's sheepish grin, she said, "Axel Bjorg went to the warehouse last night and recovered some of my things."

"Are you kidding me" Detective McGill exploded. "That's bad news. Really bad news."

"What do you mean?" She asked.

"We know about the warehouse and the Albanians, but we are after the big fish they work for. I can't go into the details of the investigation but the Albanians work for some very dangerous people. Now the whole thing is blown."

"I didn't mean to make any problems. I just wanted my things."

"This is bigger than your stuff. I told you to stand down."

"I'm sorry but I didn't know about all that."

"Look, I've got to move fast to clean this up. Just stay out of it, okay?"

"Okay, but please get my dresser and bookshelves."

"Gotta go. Bye."

The call went dead.

Kate turned to Axel. "Did we do the right thing?"

Axel grinned. "Observe what's on the table. Your most important things. Eventually you'll get back your jewelry and then the furniture, maybe in pieces, but that can be fixed. It's unfortunate we didn't know about the police investigation, but life isn't always perfect. It's their mess now, not ours."

Kate had mixed emotions and said, "I'm thrilled you recovered my books, but I also feel some guilt for messing up a police operation."

Axel smiled. "Don't worry about the guilt. It seems to me there are more important things."

"What do you mean?"

"You need to make some decisions. The stolen possessions have been found and my job is done. You need to decide whether to walk away and get back to your work at Wesson Securities, or continue on."

She considered this and knew what he meant. "Like find out what my grandmother was trying to tell me in her emails?

"Yes, and if so, do you want me to stay on the case?"

CHAPTER 27

Axel's questions struck Kate like a hammer. Did she really want him to stay on the case? Ten minutes ago she was ready to fire him for a second time and go off on her own. Chandler had given her wise counsel, to dump this seemingly unpredictable private investigator and take up his offer for real professional help. Now, Axel had performed faster than expected. He had been up most of the night working for her. She needed to sort through her next move.

She sat down in a chair by the table, looked at the cookbooks, then reached out and ran her hand across the rough leather cover of the photo album. There was an antique feel to it, different than the plastic photo albums in today's department stores.

She opened the album and saw several photos of Emma and her grandfather, John, when they were young: their marriage in a garden, by a lake, her grandmother with a magnificent smile leaning into her husband. Their clothing was simple and old-fashioned, from another time, another world. The next pages had pictures of her mother and father, and the rest were of her as a baby and a small girl. This was all she had of her parents. A wave of nostalgia filled her. They were simple images on paper, but they were everything.

The past few days had been a nightmare and she had tried to stay brave, but now her nerves were on a precipice. Pushed further, she would crumble. She wanted it to be over but knew it wasn't.

Finding that the two men in the dark SUV were linked to Nicolai

Orlov bothered her, but the worst of it was that he linked back to her grandmother.

She closed the photo album, picked up the Betty Crocker Cookbook and opened it. There were some scribbles on the first page written in pencil, faded with time.

- The vanilla cake it is so American, lacking substance.

Kate chuckled and her eyes filled with tears. This was so like her grandmother. Emma's cake recipes from Poland were full of nuts and fruits, and instead of sickening sweet frosting they were topped with sprinkled brown sugar caramelized to perfection.

While her grandmother criticized some recipes, she liked this cookbook the most. Emma had said, "It's tragic. Those fancy gourmet cookbooks have recipes so complex that the food has lost its soul. A good meal touches the heart of the family. That's what I like about this Betty Crocker. She must have come from the old country and someday I want to meet her."

Kate continued turning pages. On almost every one there were comments, some in pencil and others written with a ballpoint pen. Emma loved to tinker and modify recipes, whether they needed it or not. Sometimes there were notes written in Cyrillic and Kate struggled to translate them.

She flipped through the pages and saw so many familiar recipes. Her chest tightened and an ache filled her throat as a flood of memories came washing through her. There was a recipe for Ambrosia Balls, which were similar to Russian Tea Cakes, except with coconut and orange peel rather than nuts.

The recipe for dumplings had notes at the bottom. Her grandmother called these *knedliki* and instead of cooking them in water she steamed them and then served them with roast pork, or roast goose complemented by sauerkraut.

Page after page she reminisced over the recipes, remembering the sweet aromas rising from the pots and the enjoyable times with Emma and Aunt Clara, their laughter filling the kitchen. Sometimes they joked about their experiences in America. Kate regretted they didn't speak more about their life in Poland, but knew the communist experience was painful for them.

What she understood was that the world of excessive socialism had left its mark on Emma and Clara. As a result, they lived lives of extreme caution, always careful about revealing facts and figures, as though someone was always listening. There was a coded language around the house. Money was called *bread*. The bank was called *the market*. A bank account was called *the box*. Everything had its secret term and sometimes the two older women spoke in whispers.

Emma continually said to be cautious, quoting the proverb, "the fool rushes on, but the wise person considers every turn." Every day she read the newspaper, occasionally finding examples of the government gaining more control over people. She said this was becoming like the Soviet Union where politicians had expensive homes, chauffeured cars, servants, the best private schools for their children and superior health-care not available to the common people.

As they watched the evolution of governments in America and Europe, Emma and Clara related that to their experience as children. They fervently held that one should never trust the government for, "it will take away everything you own, wanting you to be poor!" This was typically followed by a proclamation that, "You can only trust God and family."

Kate understood they were overreacting because of their experience growing up, but being in America was very much different. Their life in Palm Beach was anything but poor. They had a large house on the coast and were surrounded by wealthy people. So there was a gigantic disconnect about poverty created by the government and the way they actually lived. Therefore, their conspiracy theories didn't make sense.

Kate flipped to the page with the recipe for Hungarian goulash. It was full of notes. First she noticed there were ticks next to some of the ingredients,

✔ 2 lbs. beef round steak, cut into 1-inch cubes
   1 cup sliced onion
✔ 1 garlic clove, minced
   1/4 cup ketchup
✔ 2 tablespoons Worcestershire sauce
✔ 1 tablespoon brown sugar
   2 teaspoons salt
   2 teaspoons paprika
   1/2 teaspoon dry mustard
   1 dash red cayenne pepper
   1 1/2 cups water
✔ 2 tablespoons flour

1/4 cup water

✓ 3 cups hot cooked noodles

At the bottom of the page she had scrawled some handwritten notes:

- *Why don't Americans use metric system?*
- *Always use Hungarian paprika!*
- *4 cups onion, not only one!!!!!!!!!!*
- **остерегайтесь гнилых яблок России.**

Kate scanned across the page a second time. Something was strange. On the one hand it was heartwarming to see Emma's writing and the comments. On the other, the ticks were only next to certain ingredients and the note in Cyrillic was confusing. All the written comments were in pencil, but the ticks and Cyrillic text were written with a red pen.

She took her hand away from the cookbook and gazed across the table at Axel where he quietly sat. She considered his second question, "Do you want me to stay on the case?"

She would lose time if she waited two days for Chandler. And, while Chandler knew about finances and investments, Axel had a different skill set, as frustrating and unpredictable as he could be.

Her eyes met his and she said, ""I was really surprised to find my books on the table this morning, and I'm so thankful you found them. But yes, there's so much more to figure out about my grandmother's messages and I don't think I can do it on my own. To answer your question, yes. I need you."

CHAPTER 28

Axel carefully observed Kate's movements. He loved the way her long, feminine fingers turned the pages of the cookbook, delicately tracing across the handwritten notes. Her eyes intensely concentrated on each line, penetrating beyond what was on the page. He watched her through each emotion that surfaced on her face. She looked so vulnerable.

He wanted so badly to take her into his arms and tell her everything would be okay, but his wretched "don't mix business with pleasure" policy held him back. Surely history doesn't always have to repeat itself, right?

She had asked him to continue working on this case and that made him glad. For sure he was intrigued by it, but in honesty he just wanted to be around Kate. He liked her presence, the way she challenged him and the complexity of her personality. Definitely there was more to her case and he would pursue it to the end. He was concerned about the dangers lurking in the background and he didn't want to leave her on her own.

With resolve in his eyes he said, "Let's find out why your things were stolen."

"Where do we go from here?" she asked.

"I watched you going through the cookbook. It touches you in a deep way, doesn't it?"

"Yes," she answered, her eyes becoming red.

"You stopped when you got to the Hungarian goulash recipe. Did it cause you to recall anything or did you sense any hidden message?"

"Not really, but these are strange." She pointed out the red ticks and the writing in Cyrillic.

"Do you know what the Cyrillic means?"

"I'm not that proficient, but I think it means something like *beware of the rotten Russian apples.*"

"What?" Axel asked.

"I know. It's weird but you have to understand Emma and Clara. They often spoke in code. Like, money was *bread* and a bank account was *the box.*"

"So, what are apples?"

"I'm not sure. Most of the time it was people, like a good apple and a bad apple. Or, it could be the government, but that was always *the sour apple*, not the rotten apple."

Axel thought for a moment and asked, "What about The Big Apple, like New York City?"

Kate shook her head. "I don't think so. It says Russian apples and I have no idea what that could mean."

Axel paused. "We don't have much to go on, do we?" He brought his fingers to his chin. "Today is Monday. The previous emails were sent by your grandmother on Mondays, so perhaps there may be another one today."

"Let me check my email," she said, taking her cell phone from her computer bag and hitting a button.

Axel immediately grabbed it from her hand.

"What are you doing?" She cried out.

"Man, I'm stupid. Turn it off right now." He pressed the on/off button. "Why?"

"Tommy. He traced me to this address through my cell phone, some form of GPS tracking, and he said we should keep our cell phones turned off. I'm currently using a burner phone."

"You mean someone could track us here?" She asked, her eyes wide.

"Exactly. If someone is smart enough to access your email account, then certainly they'd have the technology to track a cell phone."

Kate took a deep breath. "Oh no."

"Oh yes, and I'm sorry I didn't tell you sooner but I got focused on going to the warehouse and I didn't want to wake you up."

"This is crazy. What should we do?" She asked.

He thought of the men in the SUV, and of the Albanian gang who might seek revenge for his entry into their warehouse. "Let's get out of here. Go grab your things and take whatever you need from the walk-in closet, shirts or whatever, but do it fast."

Kate ran to the bedroom, took a couple of shirts from the closet, put them in a bag along with a toothbrush, went back to the kitchen and picked up her computer bag. Axel had already put all the books into the wooden box and he carried them under his arm.

They headed out the front door and quickly got into the Honda Civic. He started it and drove down the street. Just as they went through an intersection, Axel saw a dark SUV turning down the road they had just left. It seemed the two men in the SUV didn't notice them, their eyes focused on the houses, probably looking for a house number. Axel suspected they were searching for his red Corvette.

He turned right at the next intersection and accelerated, hoping the SUV would not follow, knowing that the Honda could not outrun them.

CHAPTER 29

Kate could almost taste the fear, her heart like a wild animal beating on a cage. They were lucky to have gotten away before the SUV arrived and were frightened to think of the two men in the dark vehicle. Then she thought of the pistol that Axel carried and the shotgun and sub-machine gun in the trunk of the car. These were not for target practice. She trembled, praying they would not have to use them.

They were heading north on the I-95 and Axel took an off ramp to a diner next to a gas station. He parked between two trucks, which hid the car as they went into the diner.

He said, "They have free wireless here. You can check your email and we can get some breakfast."

They found an empty booth in the back and ordered coffee and two breakfast specials: eggs, bacon and pancakes.

As they waited for their breakfast, Kate took the laptop from her computer bag, turned it on and connected to the internet. Then she went to her email account and tried to log on but without success.

"I can't get in," she exclaimed.

Axel tilted forward and smiled. "Oops. Of course not. That's another thing I forgot to tell you. Tommy said your password was too weak so he reset it to something stronger." He gave her the new password.

She typed it in and felt a great relief when her email account opened. As she scanned through her unread emails, a wave of anticipation shot through her and she exclaimed, "There's an email from my grandmother."

Axel moved around to her side of the booth and they both looked at the computer screen. With nervous hands she opened the email.

My Dearest Kate,

I hope you are well and I send you my deepest love. You were always the most precious thing in my life. Clara and I loved you very much. Now, my regret is that I cannot be part of your life. We must accept that the ways of our Lord are perfect and we can trust Him. Clara and I are now in a heavenly place with the Father, Son and Holy Spirit. Our Orthodox customs and our faith in our Savior the Lord Jesus Christ have always been central and it gives me comfort in the last days of my life. I hope this same belief will be a lifelong foundation for you.

Did you remember the recipe from your twenty-first birthday party? It is important to maintain traditions for special events and for our religious holidays. So many people have no traditions and therefore have no links to the past. Those links give a compass for the future. It is frightening in America to see such a great loss in identity, and I'm afraid that Europe is headed in the same direction, although at a slower pace.

For this, you must know more about your origins. We told you some things about your past, but there is more to know. I wanted to tell you everything when you were younger, but could not. It was important to shelter you from danger. Now you are twenty-six years old and it is time.

Therefore, from the birthday recipe write down the special numbers in the order you find them. Go to the market where we went on your twenty-first birthday and find the physical box waiting for you.

In any case, if my messages are not clear there is a backup plan. Someone will communicate with you in the future. So don't worry if this doesn't work. Please forgive me for my surreptitious ways, but there is a reason and I want to protect you from the rotten apples.

My deepest love,
Grandma Emma

She sat silent for a moment pondering the message, feeling Axel's presence next to her. What she had just read turned her stomach. Now there were specifics that only she could understand. Finding stolen things from her apartment was only a beginning. Emma had laid out a course of action and Kate was suddenly on a new mission.

Axel stated, "Surreptitious is quite a word. What does it mean?"

"Clandestine or sneaky, something like that. This message is so typical of her, everything done with smoke and mirrors, but it makes sense to me."

He said, "I don't see how. It's weird, going to the market and finding a box."

"Not at all," Kate stated. "It's the language we used around our home. Some things were camouflaged. It was how people communicated in the Soviet Union in case anyone was listening. Big brother was always present and feared. And they carried that same fear with them even while living in the United States."

"So, what does it mean?" he asked.

The server came with their breakfast and Axel picked up his fork. Feeling a sense of urgency, Kate said, "No, stop. We need to skip the breakfast and grab a coffee and muffin to go. I'll explain on the way."

★ ★ ★

They paid for their uneaten breakfast and left the diner, walking briskly toward their car. Axel turned to Kate and asked, "I'm not sure why we're doing this, but could I ask you to do something?"

"What's that?"

"Can you turn on your cell phone?"

"What for?" Kate asked, eyes wide.

"For now your phone is of no use and it's more important that we lead those guys away from us."

She turned on her phone and handed it to him. He took it and placed it under some tools in the back of a pickup truck in the parking lot.

She regretted losing it, to not be able to call Chandler, but the thought of those two men in the SUV sent shudders down her spine. She was happy to do whatever it took to shake them.

They got into the car, and she gave directions for Axel to head north.

Keeping one hand on the steering wheel, Axel quickly devoured the muffin and then sipped his coffee. "Where are we going? He asked.

"Palm Beach."

"Why there?"

"It was in the email message from my grandmother."

"You're kidding. I certainly didn't see Palm Beach mentioned."

Kate paused, took a small bite from her muffin, chewed and swallowed it. "In my grandmother's secret code *the market* is a bank and *the box* is a bank account. A *physical box* is a lock-box. There's a bank in Palm Beach where we went on my twenty-first birthday. I drove my grandmother there to deposit some jewelry. At that point she had given me a power of attorney on her account. I assumed she had closed her account when she liquidated her possessions. Evidently she's sending me back."

He glanced at Kate and slightly shook his head. "A surreptitious woman for sure. I like that."

Kate nodded, feeling that the covert nature of her grandmother was excessive. She was angry that she had to go through this. Why hadn't Emma openly revealed her secrets to her own granddaughter? Surely it was more than the belief that a tyrant government was prying into private lives. The Soviet Union was one thing, but why have such fear of the U.S. Government? Definitely the government had the capability to listen in on every telephone call, but why would they want to spy on Emma and Clara, and now her?

Kate was simply a junior portfolio analyst living in a modest apartment in Miami. What government would be interested in that? Emma warned that the evil is still out there today. Surely she meant something different than governments. How did this all fit together with the men in the SUV and the Orlov Law Group?

In any case, Kate would heed her grandmother's warning. If she found information at the bank in Palm Beach it would need to be treated with utmost caution. But, what was it all about?

An hour and fifteen minutes later they crossed Royal Park Bridge to Palm Beach. On Royal Palm Way, Kate instructed Axel to park the car in a lot next to a bank.

They decided that Axel would stay in the car to call Tommy and that it might be easier to deal with bankers if she went on her own.

She got out of the car and entered the bank through a set of sliding glass doors into the main reception area.

Directly in front of her were four tellers behind a long counter. An armed guard was standing against a side wall. Palm Beach had a high concentration of wealthy people and bank security was strong.

She approached one of the tellers and said, "My grandmother had an account and safe deposit box here. I thought she closed her account before she passed away, but I'm not sure."

The teller peered through his glasses with cautious eyes and said, "Just a minute."

Kate waited and in a few minutes a man came to her and introduced himself.

"I'm the manager here," he said. "How may I help you?"

Kate explained, "My grandmother used to bank here but closed her account about three years ago. She may still have a safe deposit box."

"I'm sorry, but that's a private matter between her and the bank," he said. "She will have to come in to open the box."

"She can't," Kate stated. "She died three years ago."

"Oh, I see," he said. "Then we require the official papers of her demise and the executor of her estate needs to contact us."

"I know, but maybe I have a power of attorney on her account or at least on the lock-box."

"May I see your identification?" He asked.

Kate reached into her purse, took out her driver's license and handed it to the bank manager.

"Just a moment," he said and he disappeared down a hallway.

Several minutes later he returned and gave back her driver's license. He was carrying an envelope. He said, "Your grandmother doesn't have a lock-box here."

Before he could finish she said, "What?"

"She doesn't have a lock-box, but you do. Can you please come with me?"

Kate followed him in disbelief as they walked down a hallway. They went through a large metal vault door and then came to another metal door. He opened the envelope, took out a key and said, "You never claimed your key. Please sign here."

She signed a release paper and took the key.

The bank manager said, "Please put your thumb on the pad by the door."

She remembered when she had visited the bank with her grandmother how she had put her thumb on the pad on a fingerprint recognition device. Hopefully it was still in the system.

Kate did as she was instructed and a light turned from red to green. She breathed a sigh of relief.

"Now put your six-digit pin code into the numeric pad."

"Six-digit pin code?" Kate asked.

"Yes, we have a high level of security here, so we need both your fingerprint and a pin code."

Kate felt a rush of anxiety go through her body and then she remembered her grandmother's instructions to use the numbers from the recipe in the Betty Crocker Cookbook, the items with the ticks, 2 lbs beef, 1 garlic clove, etc. She had memorized them.

She entered the numbers, 2, 1, 2, 1, 2, and 3. The large metal door clicked open.

They walked inside and went to one of the lock-boxes. The manager took a key from his pocket and put it in a keyhole. Next to it was another keyhole. He said, "Now you put your key in there."

She did so and he said, "Now turn."

They turned at the same time and the door opened. He stepped away and walked out of the room.

Kate stared at the open door for a moment and then pulled out a large metal box approximately twenty-four inches by twenty-four inches, and placed it on a counter top in a small booth.

After a moment of hesitation she opened the lid.

★ ★ ★

While waiting in the car, Axel took the burner phone from his pocket and called Tommy.

Tommy answered. "Hey Axel."

"Any news?"

"Some. I first investigated the plane crash, starting with articles from the Miami Herald. There's a small article about a crash in the Everglades twenty-three years ago. It didn't get much press."

"Was it Kate's family?" Axel stated.

"No way. They found the plane, a one-seater, and the pilot survived."

"That doesn't make sense. Did you discover anything at all about her family, an airplane crash?"

"Nothing. Not a word anywhere."

Axel thought for a second. "What you're saying is that the crash may not have happened."

"Uh-huh."

"Weird," Axel stated. "A wealthy investor is on a business trip and his airplane goes down and is never found. That news should have been all over the front page."

"I know. Axel, you've got yourself into something hyper-bizarre."

Tommy had a way with words, and he was right. There were big question marks surrounding this case. Axel asked, "What about Emma Miller and her sister Clara? Did you find out anything about them?"

"That's the other strange thing. There are hardly any historical records of an Emma Miller or her sister, at least nothing I can find."

"What about the purchase of their house in Palm Beach? Is there a record of that?"

"I had to do big-time digging on that one."

"You mean you went places you don't belong."

"Something like that."

"What did you find?" Axel asked.

"There's is no purchase in the name of Emma Miller. Through Kate's university records I found the address in Palm Beach where they lived, but the house was registered to a company in Delaware. That company is owned by a company in the Bahamas, which has nominated directors. So, we don't know the real owners."

"Did you find anything on John Miller, Emma's husband? Or on Kate's parents and where Kate's mother was from?"

"Again, nothing. Not a trace. It's like Emma, Clara and young Kate appeared out of nowhere twenty-three years ago. They moved into a house owned by an offshore company. Then, there's not much more, like they lived secret lives."

"What about their passports?" Axel asked. "They traveled to Europe each summer so they would have needed official documentation."

"I looked into their passports. They are legitimate, but their birth certificates are questionable."

"What do you mean?"

"First, all three birth certificates say they were born in the United States. We assume that's not true at least for Emma and Clara because they spoke with foreign accents."

"They could have been born in the U.S. and then grew up in another country," Axel reasoned.

"Naw, I don't think so. I saw digital copies of the birth certificates and suspect them to be well-done forgeries. With those birth certificates they got the passports and with the passports they got drivers licenses and opened bank accounts."

"I'm… ah, spellbound. At least that's the best word that comes to my mind," Axel stated.

"Yeah, more like weird. It's like someone in the passport office slipped up or was paid to do so."

"So, there's no history before that?" Axel asked.

"Believe me, I've never seen anything like it. They appeared out of nowhere."

Axel paused, feeling hollow. For now, he had no way of explaining this, but one thing was sure. Every family had a history. Kate's family was shrouded in mystery and he needed to understand more. He switched gear. "Did you find out anything on Nicolai Orlov?"

"I've just started working on that. Researching Kate's family took time."

"I appreciate it," Axel said. He hesitated whether to open another line of research, but went ahead. "Can I ask something else?"

"More and more," Tommy laughed. "What is it?"

"Kate has this friend called Chandler Harrington. He's a financial advisor with offices all over the place, but operates out of New York. I'd like to know more about him."

"What kind of friend?" Tommy asked.

"A friend. Maybe boyfriend."

"Ah ha. I saw Kate. She's hot. You're checking up on the competition."

Axel grimaced, glad Tommy couldn't see him. "Well, let's just say we are investigating all relationships."

"Yeah, yeah," Tommy mocked. "Okay. Call me at the end of the day and hopefully I'll have something on Orlov. And, I'll investigate this Chandler Harrington, but that will cost you more."

"You're ruthless," Axel said, wondering if he should at least feel remorse for prying into Kate's love life. But, heck no. All's fair in love and war.

They hung up. Axel got out of the car and stretched his long legs. He felt the brightness of the Florida sunshine on his eyes. His head was spinning. The information about Kate's family was totally unexpected.

He reflected on Tommy's statement that Emma, Clara and Kate had appeared out of nowhere. How could that be?

An idea came to him. Maybe they were part of the witness protection program. That explained their secretive behaviors. Did U.S. Marshals give them new identities and set them up in Palm Beach? If that was the case, what had they witnessed and what were they hiding from?

That had to be the explanation.

Yet, it would be highly unusual for the government to put people into an expensive house in Palm Beach. Weren't informants always hidden away in quiet little backwater towns?

Did Kate know anything about this, or did the two elderly women keep this a secret? Most frightening of all, were the two men in the SUV part of the plot to get revenge?

Kate was a baby when that happened, so would not have been a witness. But, gangsters went after the families of informants for revenge, to make examples.

Did that make sense? Would the mob really want revenge because of something that happened over twenty-three years ago?

He considered what they were up against, and fear crept upon him like a cold wind. At the same time, his theory had weaknesses. The break-in and theft of Kate's possessions made no sense. If criminals were going to kill Kate to get revenge, why start by stealing her things? And why did Emma send emails now, three years after her death?

This was confusing, only questions without answers. Indeed this whole ordeal had a sinister feel to it creeping in the background and he imagined the worst for Kate. In spite of the warm sunshine, he felt a cold flash move through his spine.

CHAPTER 30

Kate slowly opened the large metal box and pulled out the square package wrapped in brown paper. Underneath the package were several stacks of hundred dollar bills. There were also five small gold bars and a large manila envelope.

She carefully opened the brown paper package and inside found a painting that had once hung in their home in Palm Beach. Nostalgia filled her when she recognized it a reproduction of Picasso's *Jeune Fille en Couleur,* a wonderful abstract of a young girl in bold expressionist colors. Kate had always loved it.

She analyzed it for a moment, then put it aside and opened the envelope. Inside was a letter from her grandmother and two other papers. There was also a key similar to the one she had just used to open the lock-box and on it was a tag with the words 'physical box' and the number 224.

She picked up the letter and read it.

Dear Kate,

I'm glad you found the safe deposit box. Again, I apologize for revealing information in this way. There is a purpose.

First, I was always reluctant to expose you to certain things from our past. It seemed unfair that you would have to grow up carrying the burden of heavy secrets. Perhaps I was too careful and should have revealed more, but I felt it would be best if you had a certain maturity before passing possessions on to you. This is not to say I didn't trust you when you were younger. I wanted to protect you.

Please be aware that Clara and I faced dangers. Your grandfather predicted the end of the communist Soviet Union, and he invested wisely in preparation. Powerful people became envious of his success, and it led to his destruction. That same evil tyranny is still out there, which is why we have always been cautious.

I've made a provision for you but you must retrieve it in bits and pieces. Investment experts teach diversification. That is what I have done. The clues are in the book that I asked you to preciously guard.

This painting is a start. It is an original, not a reproduction. The other paintings in our home were also originals. Some are here in Florida, whereas others were moved to a secure location overseas. They all belong to you.

One last thing: Please enjoy the recipes in the cookbook and always remember the good times we had.

With all my love,
Grandma Emma

Kate's hands trembled as she put the letter on the table and pulled out the two remaining papers from the envelope. The first was a statement of purchase. The painting had been bought fifteen years ago from a gallery in Paris. The transfer of ownership was to Kate Miller.

The second paper was a certificate stating that the painting was an authentic Picasso.

Kate contemplated the items in front of her, the painting, the letter and supporting documents, the stacks of hundred dollar bills and the five small gold bars. Kate's knees nearly buckled under the bewilderment and shock.

This was unbelievable. Her grandmother said she tried to protect Kate from something evil. Kate wondered what that could be. Emotions raced through her as she recalled Emma's cautiousness. She always assumed it was an overreaction to the political system from which her grandmother had escaped as a teenager.

The letter mentioned her grandfather and how he understood the communist system. How could that be? If John Miller was an American investor, what connection did he have with the Soviet Union?

In the letter Emma said she left other paintings for Kate. Some were in Florida and others were overseas. *How will I find them?* She thought.

Knowing it was an original, Kate's hands shook as she folded the brown paper back around the painting.

She wondered if the painting should be kept in the lock-box or if she should take it with her. Is this what the robbers of her apartment were after? She gingerly placed the painting into her computer bag.

Kate put the letter and supporting documents back into the manila envelope and tucked the envelope next to the painting, along with the two stacks of dollar bills and the gold bars.

She looked around the empty room wishing there was a chair to sit in. Her legs trembled and she doubted they could carry her. Leaning against the wall, she tried to calm herself down and couldn't help but wonder if this was real or a dream. She lifted the brown package and walked out of the bank toward Axel and the car.

More than ever, Kate needed to understand what Emma had kept hidden.

CHAPTER 31

At the security exit at Miami International Airport, Nicolai Orlov waited. Passengers walked by pulling carry-on bags and suitcases. He smiled when he saw a large man come through the exit. It was his younger brother Leonid.

Leonid and Nicolai both resembled their father, stocky, with heavy eyebrows and bold faces. Leonid carried nothing, but just behind him were two muscular men lugging suitcases.

Nicolai waved and smiled.

As Leonid came closer, they gave each other bear hugs and kisses on both cheeks.

"Welcome, brother," Nicolai said.

"It is good to see you," Leonid replied.

"Come, the cars are here. It's best we talk there."

They went outside into the Miami heat where two dark SUVs were waiting.

Nicolai followed his brother into the back seat of the first SUV.

The two large men that accompanied Leonid loaded the suitcases into the back of the second SUV and got into it. Both SUVs left the parking area one behind the other.

As they left the airport, Nicolai spoke. "Thank you for coming. We are short-staffed."

"What's the latest news?" Leonid asked.

"We believe we will soon have her," Nicolai said. "She is staying with the private investigator in a small house in a residential area of Miami. We tracked her cell phone signal to the house. One of our men is waiting there, although there could be a problem. The girl may have known we were following her. Another of my men followed a pickup truck for over an hour and found her cell phone in the back."

"That's not good," Leonid said.

"I agree. Another setback is that the police raided one of our warehouses. It is the one run by the Albanians. Unfortunately it had the girl's furniture and books. We have no way of looking further for clues in those items. It really doesn't matter. An expert went through them in great detail and didn't find anything."

"Was the old woman playing games with us?"

"Obviously," Nicolai replied. "She was notorious for this sort of thing. For so many years we searched for her and could not find her while she was almost on our doorstep."

For over twenty years they had focused their search on countries in Eastern Europe: Hungary, the Czech Republic, Romania and others. It seemed like every year someone identified her in one of those places. There were many rumors that she constantly changed her residence from country to country. Eventually they suspected that she was the source of those rumors, but even so, they had photos of her walking into stores and getting on trains throughout Eastern Europe. Sometimes she looked directly at surveillance cameras as though she wanted to be identified.

"We spent a lot of money trying to find her in Europe," Leonid stated. "Never did we suspect that she was in Florida, and we only found that out almost three years after her death."

"We were lucky to at least find her granddaughter three months ago." Nicolai paused, not wanting to break too much bad news to his brother. "We have another challenge. Our access to the girl's email has now been disabled. Her password was changed. Our computer hacker is working on that."

Leonid frowned. "The emails may have been a diversion. Maybe the old woman knew that someone would be reading her emails and put false information in them."

"I thought of that. It is likely," Nicolai replied. "How many men are you bringing?"

"Three. Those two in the car behind us and one coming in on the next flight."

"That's good. I also have three we can trust. Of course there are many others who work in the gangs we control. They can help if needed, but it's best to keep this to a core group."

"So, what's the plan?"

"We put word out on the street, so we have people watching for the girl everywhere from Miami to Fort Lauderdale. Somewhere she will appear."

Leonid looked out the window and then back at his brother. "When this successfully closes it will be the end of a long journey."

Nicolai faced his brother with grim eyes. "I know, and the beginning of a lucrative future . . . but we must find the girl."

"We will, and she will tell us everything," Leonid said with cold determination.

Nicolai felt sanctification knowing that revenge and payout was coming. Now they must find the girl and make her talk.

★ ★ ★

Axel watched Kate walk across the parking lot. She was carrying a brown package and he wondered what it was. Her face was tight and she stared at the ground. His last conversation with Tommy had raised many questions, but from the look on her face, he knew now was not the time to flood her with them.

Kate opened the back door of the car and put the package and computer bag on the back seat. Then she nervously got into the front seat, her hands shaking when she reached for the seatbelt.

"It appears you found something," he said.

"I did, but the discovery only raises more questions. Can we get out of here?"

"Sure," Axel said. He started the car and asked, "Back to Miami?"

"I'm not sure," she said. "I think we should stay around Palm Beach. Can we find some place to talk?"

"How about a coffee shop?" He suggested.

"I have another idea."

She instructed him to drive north past the Breakers Ocean Golf Course and after traversing several cross streets they turned right, toward the ocean. Toward the end of the street she told him to stop in front of a property with a metal gate. Behind the gate was a long driveway.

He parked the car, and she pointed in the direction of the gate. "That's where I grew up."

"Wow," Axel exclaimed. At the end of the driveway, a large Mediterranean-style house faced the sea. A thick hedge surrounded the property. "You grew up there? How many bedrooms does it have?"

"Five, and there's a separate apartment above the garage where our maid lived."

"Does it have a swimming pool?"

"Yes. It's where I learned to swim."

"Unbelievable," he said. "I don't mean to sound 'judgy,' but what was it like growing up there? It's not like everyone can keep up with the Joneses like you did."

"I know. But it was normal for me. It's all I ever knew. As you can see, it's quite secluded. I was homeschooled and my teachers came each day."

"What about your social life?" He asked.

"I had friends from our church. Some of them had similar upbringings as I did, so we would visit from house to house. When we were teenagers we went to movies and shopping malls in West Palm Beach."

"And boyfriends?" He teased.

Kate smiled. "We were well chaperoned. If there was a party, Aunt Clara or one of my friend's parents were there. As I said before, we were Orthodox and those families carry old world traditions."

Axel looked at the house and tried to imagine what life was like in there with two elderly women caring for a girl. Kate mentioned that her grandmother and aunt had loved her. That's all that mattered. It seems Kate treasured their time in the kitchen and the meals they enjoyed together. How many American families eat a meal together each day?

To Kate and the older women, mealtime was a time of laughter and discussion, where the older women passed on their beliefs and values. But, Axel wondered why they kept secrets from her, unless Kate knew more than she was letting on.

"What's in the package?" He asked.

"A painting left to me by my grandmother."

"What kind of painting?"

"It's an abstract called *Jeune Fille en Couleur,* or 'Young Girl in Color.'" She paused for a moment. "It's a Picasso, an original . . . and it's worth a lot of money."

Axel's eyes went wide. He had recovered art for clients before and he knew the value of paintings. A small painting by Picasso could go for five million dollars and upwards. He said, "That's quite a bit of money wrapped up in brown paper in the back seat."

"Yes, it is. For some reason I didn't want to leave it at the bank. Maybe it's because of the sentimental attachment I feel towards it, something I looked at every day in our house." Her eyes stared through the metal gate. "Or, maybe I was fearful that the men in the SUV would break into the bank and take it."

Axel said, "That would be a tough thing to do, but anything's possible. We need to find a safe place to keep it."

"But where?" She asked.

"We'll find something," he said, his brain racing to find a solution.

They sat for a moment silently observing the house.

Kate spoke. "In my computer bag is an envelope with a letter from my grandmother." She took a deep breath, and then seemed to be lost in her thoughts.

Axel remained quiet, waiting for her to continue.

She spoke softly. "The letter reveals some things I didn't know. She was keeping secrets from me because of dangers. She also says there are also more paintings."

"You mean originals, like the one in the back seat?"

"Yes. I wanted you to see the house to get an idea of what I'm talking about. All the rooms over there had paintings in them. We often visited art galleries on our trips to Europe and my grandmother always brought back what I thought were reproductions. Now it seems they were originals."

"How many bedrooms did you say were in the house?"

"Five."

"Plus a living room and other rooms?" Axel asked.

"Yes. Each one had a number of paintings."

"So that could be ten or more paintings!" he exclaimed.

"More than that. Our walls were covered with art. All this time… I just can't believe they are all originals!"

"Where are they now?" He asked.

"I don't know, but you should read this." She reached into the brown envelope and handed him the letter from Emma.

He read it, then commented, "She said the paintings are spread out, some here in the United States and others kept in a safe place overseas. She was wise." He paused for a moment before continuing, "She also warned about evil tyranny. Could that be those guys in the SUV?"

"I can't think of anything else."

"We should go on that assumption until we find out differently," Axel stated. "She also says the cookbook holds the clues on how to find the paintings."

Kate continued to stare in the direction of the house. "Sometimes she makes me so mad!"

"Your grandmother?"

"Yes! Why did she always have to be so secretive? Why did she have to get me caught up in her chess game of a life?"

"It appears she did it to protect you," he softly stated.

"I know, but still . . . it's not easy." She took a breath. "You don't know how much I miss that house . . . not so much the house but being there with my grandmother and Aunt Clara."

There was a moment of silence before Axel said, "I understand what you're feeling."

He felt her pain, loneliness and anger at being an orphan with a big mystery to solve. It was strange that Emma had not laid out a simple checklist to be followed. The evil men had to be central to this. Following the clues in the cookbook should be their next course of action.

Axel's eyes met Kate's as he said, "We need to find a safe place where we can spend time on that cookbook. That is, if you still want me to continue working with you on this?"

Her green eyes focused on his. She nodded and said, "Of course. I need you, Axel."

* * *

Axel knew that going back to the safe house in Miami would be dangerous, so he drove to West Palm Beach where they found a residence hotel. The hotel room had one bedroom and a living room with a couch that pulled out into a bed. It also had a small kitchen with an open bar to the living room.

It provided an ideal place to spend time going through the Betty Crocker Cookbook to seek clues from Emma. Kate insisted that they cook their dinner at the residence hotel, using a recipe from the cookbook.

They went to a local supermarket, where Axel waited in the car with the Picasso painting while Kate went inside.

He had a mix of thoughts. There was still the unanswered question about the non-existent airplane crash, along with the mystery of the false birth certificates. If U.S. Marshals had put them into the witness protection program, surely Kate would have been aware of it, but she wasn't. Maybe she was still hiding something from him. He would carefully question her once they got back to the hotel.

There was something else picking away at his mind. Earlier she had told him she needed him. The soft intonations of the words sounded like more than a plea for help. Or, was that just wishful thinking on his part?

He flashed back to his vow to treat clients professionally, to not mix romance with business, but he felt himself slipping. He liked her. She was attractive, but he knew that lust shouldn't get in the way of reason. With all the outstanding questions about Kate Miller and her family, he needed a lot of reason right now.

But there was more to it than physical attraction. He carried old-world traditions from a family originating from Norway. He still had aunts, uncles and cousins there and had visited several times. Through this he carried some values similar to Kate. They were American by nationality and culture, but there was something else in the mix. Occasionally she smiled, even in facing this adversity, which is tough to do. He enjoyed that and wished she would laugh and smile more. She definitely was strong-headed and had a quick mind, and he liked that challenge.

He told himself that he was an idiot to fall for someone in such a short amount of time. *What was it, three or four days ago when she walked into the office? You need to get your imaginative brain screwed on straight, ya goofball,* he told himself.

He turned and looked at the package on the back seat, grinned and shook his head. Wrapped in brown paper was an object worth millions of dollars. And, there were more paintings to find, with a lot of mystery behind it all. How had he gotten involved in this? All he had wanted was to head off to a tropical island in the Caribbean and swim in a crystal blue sea.

CHAPTER 32

In the past

"This time I think you mastered it," Emma said to Kate. "It is absolutely delicious, just like *Sabatini's Ristorante* in Rome."

Kate smiled. "They refused to give me the recipe."

Emma laughed. "For them, revealing a recipe is like giving away trade secrets. Don't worry, you have outdone them."

"I'm not sure," Kate stated. "It's still missing a bit more lemon."

"No, my dear. You would kill it with more lemon."

"Still, something isn't right."

Emma lowered her fork to her plate and grinned. "You are suffering from chef's syndrome. A chef is always the biggest critic of his or her cooking. Your *piccata al limone* is absolute perfection and you don't need to change a thing. This cooking would launch a thousand ships."

Kate chuckled. "Very funny. It's, 'the face that launched a thousand ships.'"

Emma raised her hands. "It doesn't matter. This meal will win a man's heart."

"That's old-fashioned," Kate countered. "The man has to win the woman's heart."

"Still, food like this helps. What do you think, Clara?"

Clara sat quiet, concentrating on her meal. She lifted a hand behind her ear. "What are you saying?"

Emma raised her voice. "This food would win a man's heart!"

Clara took a bite, rubbed her tummy and said, "For sure, for sure."

Emma grinned and waved a finger at Kate. "See? You must not forget the old-fashioned ways. They may come in handy when you least expect it."

"That's right," Clara said with a grin. "You must win the heart of a man. We are waiting for our great-grandchildren."

Kate rolled her eyes. "I'm too busy with school for that sort of thing."

Clara turned to Emma and with a twinkle in her eye said, "I guess she's right, but when the time comes, we will be there to choose the right one for her."

"Oh, get off it," Kate laughed. "We are way beyond the Middle Ages."

Clara laughed. "It is only . . . what is the word? To make kidding."

Kate shook her head in wonder. Here was her spinster aunt talking about marriage and children.

Clara said, "No matter what, we have complete confidence that you make good choice, of course with our guide."

"Guidance," Kate corrected.

"Yes, that, and most of all your *piccata al limone* is superb."

Their appreciation of her meal gave Kate much joy, and she loved their back and forth teasing. When it came down to it, the two old women were a lot of fun. And, she was thankful for their trust; although sometimes she had doubts about making the right choices regarding her future.

University was indeed going well. She had finished her general requirements and was now focusing on her major in Economics and minor in Art History. Having been homeschooled, she was academically ahead of the other students, but sometimes she felt socially out of place, especially when she was around the opposite sex. Never having men around the house probably contributed to those feelings.

Now she noticed how male students gawked at her. It made her uncomfortable, yet pleased at the same time. Because of this she was determined to first become more socially at ease around other people. Finding a soul mate would have to wait another day.

And, as far as cooking was concerned, to her it was an art. Choosing her ingredients was a bit like choosing colors for a painting. She did it for the pleasure it provided, not to win the hearts of men.

CHAPTER 33

Present Day

Kate's shoulders were tense as she came to the car, anxious to go through the cookbook. She put the two bags of groceries in the back seat next to the Picasso painting and Axel drove back to the hotel. Once in the room she organized the perishable groceries in the small fridge and the rest on the kitchen counter.

Axel opened the package with the painting, spent a long moment concentrating on it and then re-wrapped the brown paper around it and said, "That's remarkable. Your grandmother had exceptional taste."

"I know," she said. "You should see the others. Now let's try and find her clues."

She went to the sofa and took out Emma's Betty Crocker Cookbook from her computer bag and began going through it page by page. Axel sat next to her.

Her impulse was to rapidly go through it, but knew that Emma was a stickler for detail. Therefore, she took her time scanning each page to not miss anything. Where were the clues?

There were notes on practically every page, many of them comments or modifications to recipes. On one page was a scribble saying, "Kate liked this." It was a recipe for carrot cake with a cream cheese frosting.

Kate smiled and said, "When I was a pre-teen I loved carrot cake, then my favorite became apple pie topped with ice cream. But no matter how hard she tried, my grandmother's apple pie was different than what you find in America. She was much more comfortable with her original recipes but she did the apple pie for me."

"I'm sure it was fabulous," Axel said.

"It was, with an Eastern European twist. I'll make it for you some time." She smiled, trying to remember the subtle changes Emma made to the recipe.

She turned to the next page. It was filled with notes that seemed more like a diary of events, or a to-do list.

Axel said, "Here." He pointed to the bottom of the page. It was the number two surrounded by a circle.

"What is it?" Kate asked.

"It's written in red ink. Do you remember the Hungarian goulash recipe? The important notes were in red and there was a number one with a circle at the bottom of the page. Perhaps this page contains step two."

The page was heavy with scribbles, but one note in blue ink had a red tick in front of it. The scribble said, "Visit the physical box at the vault."

"It seems to be a reminder," Kate said.

"I think it's more like an instruction."

"Yes, you're right," she agreed.

"Do you have any idea what 'the vault' means?"

"My only thought is that in West Palm Beach there is a place with vaults to rent. They are highly secure and they compete with lock-boxes in banks. They provide twenty-four hour access seven days a week. My grandmother used a vault there. Maybe it's still in her name and the key in that envelope may fit a lock-box."

"Let's visit it," he said, "But first could I ask you a question?"

"Sure."

"I've been thinking about your family's background and the secrets Emma seems to have kept from you. I'm curious to know if you've ever wondered about the crash of the airplane, the one with your mother, father and grandfather."

"What do you mean?" Somehow she felt attacked by the question.

"Have you ever looked into it?"

"Why?"

"There's no record of the crash in any newspapers."

"I don't understand."

"If you go back twenty-three years ago in the Miami Herald archives there's nothing mentioned. In fact, there's not a newspaper anywhere that talks about the crash. Are you sure that's how you lost your parents?"

"Of course," Kate answered. She felt the muscles in her neck tighten. Emma had told her the story, but was reluctant to talk about specifics, usually referring to the tragedy rather than the crash. "What are you getting at?"

"Something doesn't fit and I'm trying to understand why. There's no record of the accident. And there's something else."

Kate felt defensive, uneasy that Axel was asking these questions. She didn't like him prying into her family history. "What is the something else?"

"You seem to have appeared out of nowhere."

Her eyes became wide. "What? Out of nowhere? I don't understand."

"The birth certificates of you, Emma and your Aunt Clara may be forgeries."

Kate felt her cheeks burning. This couldn't be true. "You're not serious. What are these accusations?"

"Where did Emma come from?" He pressed on.

"What do you mean?"

"What country did she come from?"

"Poland. I already told you that."

"Then why does her birth certificate say she was born in the United States?"

"What? That's not true."

"The birth certificate she used to get a passport says she was born in the U.S."

"Impossible," Kate stated.

"That's what I'm talking about," Axel said. "And you. Where were you born?"

"Miami."

"Are you sure?" He challenged.

"What are you getting at, Axel?" *Who was he to question where she was born or where her family came from?*

He raised his hands. "I'm sorry. This may be a shock to you, but Tommy did some research and that's what he found. But, let me ask something else."

"No. I don't like these accusations."

"You need to consider something."

"What is it?" She asked.

"When you were growing up do you remember anyone ever coming by to check on you, like government officials."

Kate was quiet for a moment. "No never."

"Do you remember U.S. Marshals meeting with your grandmother?"

"No. My grandmother was extreme on certain things. She didn't like the government and said they couldn't be trusted. She felt the United States was moving in the same direction as the Soviet Union where the government elite took away the wealth of the common citizens. I can't see her collaborating with any government officials."

"That may be. In any case do you think she was hiding from something or somebody?"

Kate thought for a moment. "She was very cautious."

"The question is why?"

"I told you. Because of her background."

"Could it have been more than that?"

She felt uneasy and didn't want to face these questions. "I'd rather not discuss it."

"Okay. Just one more question. Where did that come from?" He pointed at the painting, which was propped against a chair.

"From our house in Palm Beach."

"That's not what I meant. Where did Emma get the money to buy it? And imagine that the other paintings in your house are originals. Where did the funds come from to purchase them? And the stacks of hundred dollar bills and gold bars in that bag. How did she get that fortune?"

"From my grandfather. He was an investor."

"Are you sure? There's no record of him anywhere."

Kate was at a loss. He was asking questions she couldn't answer. She had a Masters in Finance and worked for an investment firm and yet she couldn't answer straightforward questions about the origins of her grandmother's fortune.

She felt aggressed by Axel's questions, and the most frustrating thing was that she didn't have answers.

It was too much. She felt dizzy, stood up and said, "I've had enough." She walked into the bedroom and firmly shut the door.

CHAPTER 34

Axel watched the door close and sighed heavily. He wondered why she took it so hard. These questions needed to be asked. They were so basic. Now he was facing a closed door. Had he gone overboard in his questioning? Why was she so sensitive about this?

It was such a simple question. Why had Kate not considered the origins of her grandmother's wealth? Kate had grown up in a magnificent home surrounded by people with large fortunes. She had gone with her grandmother and aunt each summer to Europe and several times a year to the Bahamas. This was way beyond the means of the average American family.

She believed what her grandmother had told her, that her grandfather was an investor. Perhaps he was, but maybe the fortune had come from other sources.

Since the death of Emma, Kate had believed that the fortune was gone. All that was left was a trust fund that paid Kate a monthly stipend. Now it appeared there was more, much more, a stack of very valuable paintings. Emma's last letter said they were hidden away, both in Florida and in another country. What was the next step in finding them?

Axel stared at the shut door and he wondered how he could get this investigation back on track. Kate was an attractive young woman whose life had been shaken, and each new revelation seemed to add to the intensity of the unsettledness.

He felt these questions about family history were important and needed to find a way to gently pose them.

A few minutes later Kate came out of the room. "I'm sorry," she said, "but I'd rather not talk about my family's background because it's painful. I'm paying you to help me recover the items from my grandmother and that's it. I need your help to do that, but I don't want you snooping into my family's past. And you can tell Tommy to stop doing whatever it is he does."

Axel observed her cat-like eyes penetrating his soul. He liked it. "Okay," he said. "Let's focus on getting your things. I suggest we visit this vault company to see if anything can be found."

As the words came out of his mouth he was more curious than ever. One's history forms a big part of who they are. This case was not only about finding paintings, as valuable as they were. It was also about Kate's background. To know the evil that Emma spoke about could only be discovered by looking into the past.

A sly grin came across Axel's lips. He would tell Tommy to continue doing whatever it is he does.

They left the hotel room and he carried the packaged Picasso painting with one hand and the Betty Crocker Cookbook with the other. Kate had the brown envelope with the key and walked in front of him. He liked the way she made long determined strides, posture straight, her body swaying like a female athlete heading toward an event.

★ ★ ★

Deroy Bell, known to most people as Cold-Cap, stood in his favorite place of commerce, surveying the street. Since most of his clients were upscale, working in businesses in the area, his turf was out of plain sight: a dumpster in an alley off of 9th Street close to the North Dixie Highway. His primary product was hash, but occasionally he sold packets of crack cocaine.

His motorcycle was parked next to him and his merchandise was stored under the dumpster, never in his pockets. If the police were to search him, he would be clean. So far he had stayed off their radar.

Business was good, but Deroy knew he was at the bottom of the supply chain. Real money was made higher up the organization, and his objective was to get to the top. He wasn't sure how that would happen, but he knew opportunity when he saw it.

Across the street, a couple walked toward the front door of that vault company where the rich people kept their valuable stuff. The couple fit the description given to every street level drug dealer in southern Florida. A reward was being offered to anyone who spotted them.

A message had been sent to find a tall, green-eyed, blond woman who looked like a model. She was accompanied by a dude who was maybe six-three or six-four. This had to be them.

Deroy, a.k.a. Cold-Cap, noticed that the guy was carrying a brown package under one arm and under the other it seemed he was carrying a large book. The woman held a brown envelope, and a computer bag weighed on her shoulder. They disappeared into the vault company. and Deroy took out his cell phone and made a call.

★ ★ ★

Kate walked beside Axel, trying to match his pace until he noticed at one point and slowed down. He wore sunglasses, and though his head didn't turn, his eyes moved right and left. She assumed his cautious demeanor was due to the fact that he was carrying a painting worth millions of dollars. She was glad for his presence.

She was uneasy because she had lost her temper back at the hotel room and commanded him to keep out of her private affairs. If he would just focus on recovering the paintings, then everything would be alright.

They were in a business district speckled with small shops, a law firm, a flower store. On the corner was Safe Security Vaults. They entered a double door security system, waiting for the first one to close before the second one opened. A guard was seated behind the reception desk. As they approached him, Kate noticed how he checked her out. He stared and his mouth was slightly open.

She coldly said, "Excuse me, I may have a lock-box here but I can't remember the procedure. It's been some time since I was here."

The guard said, "That's weird."

"What's weird?"

"That you don't know if you have a vault here or not."

"As I said, it was a long time ago."

"What's your name?"

"Kate Miller."

"Just a second." He typed her name into a computer in front of him, leaned toward the computer screen and waited. A moment later he said, "Yeah, you're here. You have an account along with an Emma Miller. Do you have any ID?

Kate gave him her driver's license.

He said, "You're good."

"So how does it work?" Kate asked.

"What do you mean?"

"How do I get into my safety deposit box or lock-box or whatever you call it?"

"Do you have a key?"

"Ah . . . yes. Is this it?" She reached into the brown envelope and took out the key.

The guard made a quick glance and said, "That's the one, box 224, exactly what's on the tag."

From then on the procedure was similar to the bank she had visited earlier in the day.

He led them to a steel grid that opened when he typed in a code, then ushered them into a small room before the grid shut behind them. There were three metal doors to the front, right and left. The guard turned to the one on the left, typed in a code, and the door opened.

They followed him into another room with rows of lock-boxes, larger ones on the bottom and smaller ones on the top. Each box had two keyholes.

The guard went to a bottom lock-box, inserted a key and said, "Put it in there."

Kate put her key in the second hole and they turned their keys at the same time. The door of the lock-box opened, the guard smiled and said, "Just push the button there on the wall next to the door when you want to leave."

He left the room and shut the door behind him.

Like the bank, there was a large metal box inside the lock-box. Kate took it out and put it on a desk in the middle of the room. She hesitated a moment, her heart quickly beating, then lifted a latch on one side of the box. Inside she found a package almost identical in size to the one Axel carried. She carefully opened it and stared. It was another oil painting.

"Wow," Axel said.

She took a deep breath, her eyes scanning the painting. "It's by Henri Matisse," she said. It was a simple garden, somewhat abstract, with bright colors.

"It's beautiful," Axel said.

She explained, "It was from his early works during a period called Fauvism. It's called *Le Jardin de Marseille.*"

"Quite amazing," His eyes were fixed on the painting.

She lifted it up and saw that at the bottom of the metal box was a brown envelope. She set down the painting, took out the envelope, opened it and spilled the contents on the table.

There were three passports: Russian, New Zealander and Bahamian. And, there were two keys on a key ring. The larger key was similar to the one that opened the lock-box, whereas the smaller, flat one looked like a key to the front door of a house.

"Any idea what the keys are for?" he asked.

"I don't know. Maybe another safe deposit box, but why two keys?" She became still for a moment and said, "Something about the smaller one seems familiar, but I'm not sure why."

Axel picked up the Bahamian passport and opened it. Inside was a photo of Kate and the name on the passport was 'Catherine Miller.'

"Weird," said Axel. "Why Catherine and not Kate?"

"I have no idea. Kate is a diminutive of Catherine, but the name on my birth certificate is Kate."

"And why would you have a Bahamian passport?"

Kate shook her head. "I don't know. We went to the Bahamas two or three times a year, always staying in the same house. My grandmother must have had some connections with the Bahamian government. I think the nationality laws in the Bahamas are rather relaxed. If you make an investment of a certain size in the country and if you live there for a certain period of time then it's easy to get a passport."

"Did she own the house or rent it?" Axel asked.

"I don't know."

Kate's mind was spinning as she tried to put the pieces together. Why would her grandmother do such a thing? But then again, when it came to Emma, it made sense. Her grandmother often quoted a verse from the Bible, "A wise man sees the evil and hides himself." It seemed as if Emma was preparing an escape plan but Kate had to wonder . . . escape plan from *what*?

Axel picked up the New Zealand passport, opened it and, again, Kate's picture appeared, but this time with the name Katherine Innocens. "Where does that name come from?" He asked.

"I have no idea. I know it's Latin, but I don't know why it's in my passport."

"This time Katherine is spelled with a 'K.' But, your family name is completely different."

Kate shook her head and felt a rush of heat move up her neck. What game was Emma playing? With each step came another layer of complexity. "The differences in names makes it more difficult to track someone though data bases."

Axel smiled. "It's like in spy movies where someone carries several passports with multiple names. She went through great lengths to give you international mobility."

"It seems so," she agreed.

"What was she hiding from?"

"I have no idea. Something dangerous, but we don't know the specifics."

"Why would she have gotten a New Zealander passport for you?"

"I don't know. We took a trip to New Zealand once, and I know that my grandmother spent some time visiting properties for sale."

"Did she buy something?"

"If she did she didn't tell me." Her head was spinning.

Kate picked up the Russian passport and opened it. Again her photo was inside. Half the information was in Cyrillic and half in roman characters. She took a sharp breath. The name on the passport was Katerina Innokenti.

"This is unreal," she exclaimed. "We have seen that name before."

Axel nodded. "Innokenti Holding, that owns the dark SUV that was following you. So your grandmother *had* to have had some kind of connection to Sable Limited."

Kate's legs felt weak. She put her hand on the table to keep her balance.

Axel asked, "Are you okay?"

She waited a moment. "No. Not really. This is just baffling. I don't know what to say. I'd like to go."

Axel took the Russian passport from her and looked at it. "Well at least Kate, Catherine, Katherine and Katerina are variations of each other. It appears she tried to maintain your identity."

"Are you kidding me?!" she exclaimed. "Now I really wonder who I am!" If anything, her identity had been torn apart.

"What would you like to do with the paintings?" Axel asked.

"I don't know."

"I recommend you keep both of them here in this lock-box as well as the gold bars. We need mobility and shouldn't have to worry about multi-million dollar paintings in the back seat of an old Honda Civic."

Kate nodded. "Okay."

She placed the paintings and small gold bars in the large metal box, put the box into the safe deposit box and shut the door. She took the brown envelope with the two keys, walked to the exit door and pushed the green button.

Two minutes later they were out on the street. Kate noticed that Axel scanned the street as they walked.

She was in a daze. The images of the passports kept flashing through her mind. She was in shock, the name from the Russian passport playing on repeat in her head. *Innokenti. Innokenti. Why am I linked to the company in Cyprus? How am I linked with Innokenti? Were those passports fake or real?* Nothing made sense. Earlier in the day she was angry with Axel because he had been prying into her family history. Maybe he was right to do so. There seemed to be so many things she didn't know about her family and about herself, and she was scared.

Waves of nausea came and went, blurring her vision. She glared at the envelope and suddenly hated those keys, especially the key to lock-box 224. That one key had unraveled her whole life, her identity. *Who am I? Who is Kate Miller? And, who was my beloved grandmother and her sister?*

She felt betrayed and abandoned. With all her remaining strength, she fought back tears.

"Are you okay?" Axel asked, observing her watery eyes.

With clenched teeth she hissed, "I'm fine. Let's go and find the true story behind this mess."

She felt him take her arm and gently lead her to the car, his eyes darting right and left, but mostly on her.

★ ★ ★

Nicolai Orlov put down his telephone and turned to his brother Leonid. "We found the girl," he said.

Leonid grinned. "Where is she?"

"In West Palm Beach about an hour and a half north of here. They went into a company called Safe Security Vaults. It rents safety deposit boxes."

"Who identified her?" Leonid asked.

"A street dealer. My intermediary said he goes by the name of Cold-Cap."

"He's sure it's her?"

"It's not certain, but this Cold-Cap is following them on his motorcycle. I'll send a couple of guys up there to make the identification."

"Hopefully we are getting close." Leonid gave a cold, soulless smile.

"There's one more thing that was mentioned," Nicolai said. "The P.I. who is with her was carrying a large package. When they walked out of the building he didn't have it."

"Left it in a vault?"

"It appears so."

"Do you remember what our investigator discovered after the babushka died, that she was a collector of valuable paintings? They magically disappeared after her death, so maybe that's where they are," Leonid remarked.

"It would make sense."

"We need the girl to get into the vault. It is time to take her." Leonid stated.

"Maybe not yet. I suggest we follow her to see her movements. It might reveal something more."

"Okay, but not for too long."

They were quiet for a moment before Nicolai said, "We are close to getting our long waited revenge."

CHAPTER 35

Back at the residence hotel Kate was still reeling from what she had found in the lock-box. The multiple passports had caused her to question everything about her past and her grandmother. What was Emma doing? She needed time to give her mind a break.

"Shall I order some food?" Axel asked.

"No. I need time to think and cooking something will help." She got out the Betty Crocker Cookbook and went to the page for Veal Scaloppini. On the side she had written her own adaptation of the recipe.

"What can I do?" Axel asked.

"Nothing. Go read a book or turn on the TV. This won't take long."

Indeed, within a few minutes, the wonderful scents of butter and lemon, and the sizzling sounds of seared veal wafted through the suite. Kate went to work preparing a side dish of rice and a small Caesar salad. Axel lounged on the couch with his head back and eyes closed. When the oven door clicked shut he opened his eyes and said, "Sure I can't help?"

"You can go to the fridge and open the bottle of white wine."

While the meal was cooking they sat on high stools at the kitchen counter. Axel served the wine and raised his glass to Kate's. She clicked her glass against his, took a sip and then stared into the glass in silence.

When she finally spoke, her voice was distant and soft, "I feel that my world has turned upside down. One day I believe in one reality only to find out that another exists. Now I wonder what is real."

"I understand. It's like a puzzle with new pieces constantly being added."

She said, "There's something else going through my mind. We had many paintings in our house, which I thought were reproductions. If there's one painting per lock-box, then that's a lot of detective work."

"I was thinking of that. On the surface it seems Emma liked to complicate things, yet she must have had reasons."

"Diversification was a fundamental principle for her."

"But why would she go to such an extreme?" he asked.

"It was her nature to be cautious. In the past I thought it was fear of governments, but maybe it's something else." Yet, nothing made sense. The tension in her shoulders and neck gave testament to the weight of the day, and the pain of it only added to her distress. There was so much new information, and she didn't know how to process it. It might take years to track down paintings in lock-boxes. That would quickly become unbearable.

What she found most shocking were the passports. The only explanation was in knowing Emma's thought processes, that she always had an exit plan.

Kate knew that Emma would have prepared various alternatives to escape danger, but she wandered what that danger was. The Bahamian passport made sense to her, as well as the New Zealander one. But the Russian passport left her perplexed. It seemed odd to Kate that her grandmother held a passport to a country that was once a part of the Soviet Union, which Emma had fled from as a teenager

And then there was the matter of her parents and grandfather. Axel said their birth certificates were fakes and there was no record of the airplane crash of her parents. If that was true, then who was *she*? Where was she born? Who were her parents and her grandfather?

She had told Axel to stay out of her family history, but maybe that was the key to solving this.

She glanced across at Axel sitting next to her. He was kind, with an ability to laugh, but often it seemed he didn't take things seriously. Maybe that was a good thing. Otherwise this experience would be way too heavy to carry. In fact, she felt an attraction to him, but wasn't sure how to respond to him or even take it one step further, if that was even appropriate. No, it would not be appropriate, she decided.

In the midst of all that happened over the past days Axel had a strength and calmness that comforted her. Did she like him because he provided a temporary reprieve from the storm? That was probably the case, and she decided the best thing was to keep her guard up around him. In any case, Chandler would be in Florida in a day or two and she would ask for his help. He was wise and could give an objective perspective.

"I think the meal may be done," he said, awakening her from her thoughts. "At least, it smells that way."

"Ah . . . yes, I guess it is," she said.

She got up from her stool, checked the rice and saw that it was done. "*Bon appétit*," she said, after serving the meal.

Axel took a bite, stopped for a moment and said, "Wow."

She smiled, "Pretty bad, huh?"

"I've never had anything like this. What is it?"

"It's called *Piccata al Limone*, lemon veal."

"Where in the world did you learn to cook like that?"

"This is from one of my favorite restaurants in Italy. They wouldn't give me the recipe so I experimented until I got it right."

He took another fork full. "Wow."

Kate chuckled as she started in on her own plate.

Axel shook his head. "Oh man, this is amazing. It's more than food. It's beyond soul food. You created heaven in a few minutes."

Kate's eyes twinkled while watching Axel focus on the food. It brought back memories of Aunt Clara, how she would concentrate on her meal, especially when the food was special. And she remembered how Clara and Emma claimed that Kate's *Piccata al Limone* would someday win a man's heart. But, is this the man she wanted?

The smell of the food made her think of happy times with Emma and Clara. Then she looked at the cookbook and uneasiness settled back on her like a weight of lead. She was now ensnared by Emma's chess game of life.

CHAPTER 36

Cold-Cap watched the dark SUV come to a stop next to his motorcycle. He was excited to receive the reward and make contact with the higher-ups. Now was his chance to advance in the organization.

Two big, ugly, intimidating guys got out of the SUV and walked up to him. Without any pleasantries one said, "Where is she?" He spoke with some crazy eastern European accent.

Cold-Cap pointed across the street to the residence hotel. "In there along with a dude."

"Are you sure it is her?" The other man asked.

"She fits the description, but it's up to you guys to verify."

"We will wait," the bigger one said. "And you will wait with us."

Cold-Cap didn't like that. He had wanted to meet the higher-ups, but now that he had encountered these guys, his instincts were to get out of there. He didn't know why they wanted the woman or what was going down. Suddenly he didn't want to be involved.

"In the car. Get in the back," the bigger one commanded. Actually both were big, but one was like an NFL lineman, enormous. The other was more like a linebacker.

Cold-Cap wasn't sure of their accent and assumed it was Russian. If so, that was bad news. If they were part of the Russian organized crime ring in Palm Beach… He inwardly shuddered. They were known to be the worst, the most violent group and far more brutal than the South American cartels. The Russians were known to shoot, torture and kill without hesitation. His street buddies stayed away from them.

Cold-Cap went to the SUV and got into the back seat. Once the two brutes were in the front seats he asked, "Who wants her?"

"That is not for you to know," the linebacker said.

"When will I get paid?" Cold-Cap asked.

"When we know it is her," the linebacker responded.

The bigger one turned from his position in the front seat, stared at

Cold-Cap and said, "You wait."

That sent shivers through Cold-Cap's spine. He was used to hard street stares, but this one was nothing but evil and empty. He had the impression a horror movie was unfolding and unfortunately he had become a part of it.

★ ★ ★

Axel was enthralled by the meal, which was a zillion times better than his typical daily sandwich. This woman could cook. She was getting to him. His attraction to her had intensified, and it was getting harder to heed the warning bell that had been ringing in his brain since the day he met her.

The *Piccata al Limone* was a killer. With every bite, he was thinking, *I love this woman, I love this woman.* It really was *that* good. Was he being ridiculous? Sure. Could someone seduce you with a meal? Apparently. She had.

He forced himself to get back to the case, concentrating on the discoveries of the day. The grandmother had gone to great lengths to create new identities, even to get passports. Was there a reason for doing this, or had she just been paranoid? He needed to find answers and he couldn't allow himself to be sidetracked by gourmet meals.

Yet with every taste of the *Piccata al Limone* he felt himself wavering. He'd sell his soul for a meal like this.

After finishing the meal they cleaned the dishes, went into the living area and sat on the couch sipping the last of the wine.

Axel observed Kate, her face heavy and sad, like someone coming from a funeral. "It was a rough day for you," he said.

"Very," she replied. "I'm at a loss. Where do we go from here?"

"I have ideas. We need to figure out what Emma is trying to communicate to you. So let me ask about the Russian passport. It's got to be more than chance that Innokenti was used as a name. We must consider how and why it is connected to the company in Cyprus."

"I know. It keeps going through my mind," she said.

"Do you ever remember that name being used when you were growing up?"

"Well, it's a common first name for boys in Russia, but it can also be a family name. It means 'innocent,' as I said earlier. There was an Orthodox priest who was called St. Innocent. He was a Russian missionary to Alaska."

"So you heard the word?"

"Yes, but I thought my grandmother and Aunt Clara were talking about St. Innocent. Now I'm not so sure. So many of the terms they used were part of their code."

"Do you know how we can find out more about this?" The historian inside him was taking charge.

Kate remained still for a moment and said, "Maybe the priest at our Orthodox church here in West Palm Beach could help. Reverend Levkin. He has been at this church for as long as I can remember."

"Did he know your grandmother well?"

"Yes, of course."

"I suggest we go see him tomorrow," Axel said. He took the cookbook, opened it to a page with recipes for bread and pointed to a small number three circled in red. On the page was a handwritten note: *Make kulich and paskha for Easter. Go to church and see Reverend Levkin.* The note was written in red. "What's kulich and paskha?" He asked.

"Kulich is sweet bread and paskha is a cheese dish, something like cheesecake but without the crust. It's traditional for Easter."

Axel paused and stated. "Evidently she's telling you to go to church. Maybe Reverend Levkin has some background on your family. Oops, maybe I shouldn't say that." He grinned.

She visibly tensed at his suggestion, and Axel waited for her usual berate about prying into her family's history. Instead she sat quietly for a moment and then nodded her head. "Okay, tomorrow let's try and see Reverend Levkin." She turned to him. "What do you think my grandmother was trying to communicate with this?"

He went to another page in the cookbook, pointed and said, "I don't know, but look at that."

At the bottom of the page was the number four written and circled in red. He asked, "What does this page tell you?"

Axel watched Kate glance down the page. It was a recipe for soup.

Kate leaned toward the book, her finger scrolling over the handwritten notes. When she moved, her shoulder brushed against Axel and a wave of desire hit him. He cautioned himself to concentrate on the task at hand.

Her finger stopped when she came to a note with a red tick in front of it. "This is strange," she said.

"What's that?"

"It says to check the big physical box. If that's her code, it means there is something in our home, but it doesn't make sense. I need to think about this."

"You're right. We are both tired and need rest. Tomorrow our minds will be fresher, so let's get some sleep."

"I'm more than tired," she said. "I'm exhausted."

They got up and Kate went to the bathroom while Axel opened the couch in the living area and prepared his bed. When Kate was finished in the bathroom he took his turn.

When he exited the bathroom Kate was standing in the living room. She said, "I want to thank you for all you are doing."

He grinned. "It's my job." He wondered if another hug would be coming.

"I know, but without you I'd still be waiting for Detective McGill. We've made some amazing discoveries."

He laughed. "Get some sleep. Maybe we'll find more tomorrow."

She took three steps toward him and hugged him. For a moment Axel stood there wondering if he should hug back. He couldn't help himself. He put his arms around her and held her. He felt the curves of her body pressing into him. Suddenly he couldn't remember why he was trying so hard to resist her.

She lifted her head and their eyes locked. He bent his head down and met her lips with a long, passionate kiss. He could still taste the sweet lemon on her lips. He pressed more firmly against her, hungry for more.

Kate gasped and stepped back, catching her breath. She released her hold on him, turned and went to her room, shutting the door. Shutting him out.

Axel stood still, wondering what just happened. This went against his tendency toward rationality and logic. But life decisions were not only dictated by the mind. Emotions and desires were often stronger than the mind. That internal combat is what tore him up inside.

Every single inch of his body wanted her. He stood there looking at her bedroom door, wanting to kick it open, to go in and be with her, but it wasn't going to happen.

Instead he faced a night of torment.

★ ★ ★

Kate shut her door, her heart pounding. She wondered what she had just done and cursed herself. Going to him like that was a mistake. They needed to focus on finding the paintings and not get distracted by infatuations.

Now she had complicated things. What was she thinking? What about her relationship with Chandler? She realized with a tinge of guilt that she had completely forgotten about him. A wave of regret followed when she considered she had just betrayed him with that kiss. Chandler had been a gentleman with her, respectful in every way. He was the ideal man, someone every woman would dream of. Yet, kissing Axel had come so naturally.

She felt like she was standing at a crossroads. Axel and Chandler were so different. For some reason wealth didn't impress Axel, whereas with Chandler it seemed a major part of who he was. Axel was more interested in finding answers to mysteries. She liked his inquisitive approach to things. It challenged her thinking. Even though she had been angry with him for looking into her family history, she knew he was right to pursue it.

Yet, she wondered why it bothered her so much. She kept claiming it was because her grandmother had always cautioned her on giving away personal information. But, it was more than that. The truth was, it was painful to talk about her family. Throughout her life she had repressed the painful image of her family in the airplane crash, to the point of denial.

Reason told her that not facing truth was unhealthy, yet something beyond reason was controlling her. A force deep in her psyche drove her into avoidance. It had little to do with teachings from her grandmother. Kate had conditioned herself to be distant to avoid the pain of losing someone else she loved. Now this was working against her, and she knew it.

When Axel asked about her history it created tension, almost trauma. Yet, he was asking the right questions.

A flutter went through her when she recalled the strength of his body and the soft, loving kiss that burned through her being. His touch. Oh, his touch. Just thinking about it made her shiver. She shook her head to free her thoughts of him, of the warmth of his lips on hers. The last few days had been an emotional roller coaster. That had to explain the intensity she was feeling.

She looked at the closed door of her room. If she opened it she knew they would go to a place leading to regret, and she didn't want to face that pain.

Yet, she wanted to be with him. No, it was more than that. She *needed* him, more than she had ever needed anything else.

CHAPTER 37

In the morning, after a fitful night, Kate got up, went to the door of her room and slowly opened it. Axel wasn't in the living room.

There was a note on the kitchen table: *Coffee is made, went for food, hope you slept well. Axel.*

She poured a cup of coffee and sipped it, the heat and caffeine bringing life to her body. Anxiety filled her when she thought about the previous night, knowing she would have to face Axel. She was the one who had initiated the physical contact and the kiss, but he definitely didn't back away from it. Now what would he be thinking?

Kate was worried about how the kiss would impact their working relationship. There were still more paintings to find and most of all she needed to find out about her family.

When she thought about the paintings, she felt anger that Emma had done this to her. Her grandmother should have left a straightforward inheritance. Why did Emma go to such extremes to complicate things? Obviously there was a reason. There always was, but what?

Whatever happened between her and Axel, they needed to concentrate on the primary task, to find the paintings. At the end of the day he was working for her, period. She was the client and he was nothing more than a service provider. Or, was he?

The front door opened, Axel walked in and he smiled. "Good morning. How'd you sleep?"

"Okay," she said, knowing it wasn't true. "How about you?"

"Like a baby."

She held her coffee cup, stared at it and spoke softly. "About last night. I'm sorry I, ah . . . approached you. That was inappropriate."

Axel laughed. "Inappropriate? Sorry to contradict you, but I thought I was the luckiest guy in the world."

Kate looked at him, her eyes burning. "Don't mock me. I apologize, because it should never have happened."

Axel grinned. "I'm not mocking. And I'm not sorry it happened. I shall savor the memory."

"Well, let it be. We need to concentrate on the paintings and that's it."

"Sure, but let me ask, did you feel anything last night?"

"I don't want to talk about it," Kate snapped.

"Fine," he said tersely. "Let's pretend it didn't happen and just get on with business as normal."

"Exactly," Kate stated.

"Okay." Axel took a box of cereal and a quart of milk out of the bag he was carrying and set them on the table. He got two bowls and two spoons and announced, "Breakfast."

They sat at the table and ate in silence as Axel's question reverberated through Kate's mind, *'Did you feel anything last night?'* Of course she did.

Now it was like all of her protective walls were crumbling within her. She needed to get her inner compass back to where it was before, if that was possible. Something in her heart told her the attraction had been there from the beginning, from the first time she saw him with his feet up on his desk at his office. So, it was an illusion to get things back to where they were before because that didn't exist.

It was despicable that she had fallen into this emotional trap at a time when recovering the paintings was of primary importance. And, what about her feelings for Chandler? He would soon be in Florida. His presence would help her recalibrate.

★ ★ ★

Nicolai Orlov held the telephone with his hand over the mouthpiece. He turned to his bother and said, "They are still watching."

"Have they seen the girl?" Leonid asked.

"Not yet. She is in the hotel room and probably using the private detective as a toy."

Leonid smirked. "What shall we do? I am tired of this."

Nicolai felt the same frustration. They had waited too many years to get what was rightfully theirs. From their investigations over the past months, tapping her emails and following her, it was obvious that the girl knew very little. But now, it seemed she was discovering things. That was good. The old witch was a master at hiding truth, even from her own family. At some point the girl would know more and then they'd take action. So why wait? Nicolai said, "I think it is time to question her."

Leonid nodded. "I agree. The sooner the better."

Nicolai released his hand from the mouthpiece and spoke into the phone. "After she leaves the hotel verify what this Cold-Cap says, that she is indeed the one we are looking for. If yes, then follow her and grab her in a place where you will not be seen. And dispose of the man who is with her."

He put the phone down and turned to Leonid. With a tight grin he said, "When we are done with her she will no longer have need of this private detective play thing."

★ ★ ★

Axel checked out of the hotel before they got in the car, and Kate directed him several blocks until they came to St. Catherine's

Orthodox Church.

He drove without speaking, feeling angry that Kate had snubbed him before breakfast. Why didn't she recognize that there was an attraction between them? The kiss from the previous night still lingered on his lips. This morning he had lied to her. He had not slept like a baby.

If she was going to avoid discussing the feelings they had for each other there would be no use in pursuing a relationship. So, it was best to put his feelings to the side and get on with doing his job. He had been through this before and should have learned his lesson.

She could gladly have Mr. Chandler Harrington. She could spend his millions and have a life with him, which he hoped would be long and boring and miserable.

Now he'd could get back to being the old Axel Bjorg, private investigator, the man without a care in the world. It was better that way.

They got out of the car and he picked up the cookbook off the back seat and surveyed the church. It had a square tower on one end and a large dome over the center of the building. Christian crosses were on the top of both the tower and the dome.

The historian in Axel became interested. In his studies he had read about the Orthodox Church. He was intrigued by the fact that the global Orthodox Church was unified in theology despite being composed of several self-governing ecclesiastical bodies. They trace themselves back to St. Paul and the original Apostles, so they had a lot of tradition behind them to support such unity.

"I like it," Axel said.

"Like what?"

"The building and the history it represents."

Her eyes drifted toward the building and she shook her head. "I don't understand."

"Never mind," he said, "It's just the historian speaking. Don't forget that I'm interested in history."

Her head bowed slightly, her eyes shifting from him to the ground.

They walked to the back of the church and Kate knocked on a door. A minute later the door opened revealing an Orthodox priest. He wore a white shirt and jeans and had a long gray beard. A large wooden cross hung around his neck. He held a hammer in his hand. Axel wondered if it was a weapon.

The priest smiled and said, "Kate, it is such a pleasure to see you."

"Thank you Reverend Levkin and it's nice to see you too. I'm wondering if I might talk with you. Oh . . . this is Axel Bjorg, a private investigator who is helping me with some things concerning my grandmother."

Reverend Levkin shifted the hammer from his right hand to his left and shook hands with Axel. He smiled and said, "I was just trying to fix a loose door frame. An Orthodox priest has to be a jack-of-all-trades. Please, come in."

He led them through a foyer and into his office, a room with loaded bookshelves on three sides and stacks of books in every corner. He sat behind his desk. Axel and Kate took chairs in front of the desk.

"I've been expecting you," he said.

"You've what?" Kate asked.

Levkin smiled. "It's about your grandmother."

Kate's eyebrows lifted. "That's why I came to see you, to talk about her. Why have you been expecting me?"

Levkin shifted back in his chair. "Before she passed on to be with the saints, she came to me." He reached into a drawer in his desk and pulled out an envelope, placed it on the desk and put his hands over it. "She gave me this envelope and asked that I might give it to you after your twenty-sixth birthday, which was on the first of this month."

"Yes, it was. What is in the envelope?"

"I don't know. I am merely carrying out the wishes of a dying woman." He peered down at his hands. "She was mysterious, your grandmother." Then Levkin picked up the envelope and handed it to Kate.

She took it, slipped a fingernail under the sealed flap, opened it and took out two sheets of paper. She read one and handed it to Axel.

He scanned the page and said, "It's the deed to a house."

She nodded. "It's the deed to our house in Palm Beach."

He said, "The deed shows the owner as Petersburg Limited, a company with an address in Nassau in the Bahamas."

Kate read the second paper.

My precious Kate,
You own Petersburg Ltd. See the fourth red circle.
With all my love,
Emma

She handed both sheets of paper to Reverend Levkin and asked, "Did you know about this?"

"No. I thought her house was sold. At least, that's what I assumed."

"This is so weird," Kate said.

Axel observed the interchange between Kate and Reverend Levkin.

A question had been forming in his mind. He spoke to Levkin. "May I ask how long you knew Emma Miller?"

Levkin stroked his beard. "Maybe twenty years or a bit more. Emma and Clara moved here when Kate was a little girl."

"Do you know anything about their background, like where they came from?"

"Emma said she was from New York, but I don't know how long she had been in the United States. She was from Poland originally, or at least that's what she said."

"What do you mean?" Kate asked. "She was definitely from Poland."

"Yes, maybe," Levkin replied.

"Why do you say that?" Axel asked.

"First, I don't know how long she was in New York. Her English was not very good when she came here. She took intensive English classes for several years from someone in our congregation."

Kate interjected. "She came to the United States as a teenager."

With kind eyes Levkin said, "Kate, I have doubts. I don't want to speak out of place, but I knew she was hiding something. Yet, I never pried into her private life. So many of the people in our church have unusual backgrounds and it is best that they are able to keep their secrets. My goal has always been to provide a safe and secure environment. Our focus is communion with the Holy Spirit."

"Do you believe she was from Poland?" Axel asked. He saw Kate's eyes tighten.

"Honestly, I'm not sure. Her Russian was perfect and I'm not sure I ever heard her speak Polish with anyone. Of course, in the Soviet days everyone in that region learned to speak Russian as a second language. Perhaps she was just good at it."

Axel asked, "How many Polish Orthodox Christians do you know?"

Levkin smiled. "Few. The majority of people in Poland are Roman Catholic."

"Why was she so devout to the Orthodox faith if she was Polish?"

"Good question. I always thought she had a Russian accent from St. Petersburg."

"Do you think she was from Russia?" Axel asked.

Levkin nodded. "I've always suspected, but we do not pry into a person's background."

Axel said, "I understand. Did you ever wonder where her fortune came from? She lived in an expensive house in Palm Beach."

"Again that's not something I would question. About ten percent of the population of Palm Beach is Russian or Eastern European. Most of them have great wealth and that is accepted. But in our culture we feel it is impolite to meddle into a person's finances. I do know that many of them made their money once the Soviet Union fell apart. Some gained privileges because they were connected in some way to the Soviet regime. Others were just good entrepreneurs who capitalized on the opportunities."

"So you don't know about Emma, where she got her money."

Levkin shook his head. "Honestly, no. We were friends for over twenty years but sometimes I wonder if I really knew her."

Kate sat stiff in her chair. "She came to the U.S. as a teenager and married my grandfather, John Miller. He was an investor. That's where the money came from."

Levkin smiled. "I know. But if I may use an illustration, in the Orthodox faith we live in the divine interaction between Christ and the Church, and there is a great mystery in this. We must remember that in life sometimes what we think is a reality may only be a perception. God has a plan and he will reveal truth in His time, for He is truth."

Kate took a deep breath, and her eyes became watery. "So, everything I think I know about my grandmother may not be true? Have I believed a lie?"

"Not a lie," Levkin stated. "Perhaps it was just a carefully crafted story there to protect you. So many people with our background have suffered much and histories are masked to cover the pain. With Emma and Clara there was definitely something more than what met the eye. The one thing I observed over the years is that they deeply loved you."

Kate whispered, "How can I know the truth?"

Levkin smiled. "I think you are in the process."

They talked a bit more before Axel and Kate left the church office and went to the car.

Axel observed that Kate was lost in thought. He didn't say anything, but he wanted to take her, hold her and tell her that all would be okay. But he couldn't. She had made it clear that their relationship was purely business. But if he was honest with himself, he wished for more.

CHAPTER 38

In the car Axel asked, "Where to now?"

Kate reached into her bag and pulled out the key ring from the brown envelope. "Now I know why one of these keys seemed familiar. It's from our house in Palm Beach. I'd like to go there."

"That note from your grandmother said you own Petersburg Limited and that company owns the house. Has anyone lived there during the past three years?"

"I don't know. I thought it was sold to someone and that they would be living there. I never went back."

"If no one is living there, then who's been looking out for the place? And paying the taxes?"

"I have no idea," she stated.

"Let's find out."

On the drive to Palm Beach, Axel was uneasy. He was thinking about a phone call he had made that morning to Tommy. Besides going out to get cereal and milk he had called Tommy to get an update on Nicolai Orlov.

The Orlov Law Group consisted of two offices, the one in Miami run by Nicolai and one in New York run by his brother Leonid. They were Russian by background but both were born in the United States. For years their father was the Chief Administrator for the embassy of the Soviet Union at the United Nations. He had four sons. After the fall of the Berlin Wall, the father moved back to St. Petersburg along with his oldest and youngest sons, but Nicolai and Leonid stayed in New York. They both got law degrees and started their law firm.

The disconcerting news was that the Orlovs were connected with the Russian Mafia. They had represented Russian Mafia gang members in a number of important trials. Even worse, it was reported that the Orlovs were powerful players in the underworld hierarchy.

Axel had learned about the Russian Mafia in his history studies. They first appeared in the United States in the 1970s when the Soviet Union released a quarter of a million Jews, many of them moving to the United States. The Soviets saw this as an opportunity to send others through that open door. They emptied their jails of some of their most dangerous criminals and many of them ended up in Brighton Beach in New York, also known as Little Odessa.

A second wave showed up after the fall of the Soviet Union where ex-KGB and military personnel could use their skills for illegal crime. They teamed up with the Italian Mafia, but were more violent than the Italians.

The Russian Mafia was in fact a loose affiliation of gangs often ruthlessly competing with each other. One of their specialties was assassinations for hire.

If the Orlovs were indeed part of the Russian Mafia, then they needed to be treated with utmost caution. The underlying question was how they could be connected to Emma Miller.

Axel had asked Tommy to investigate them further. He also asked Tommy to check if there was anyone named Innokenti who might fit into the picture.

They arrived at the house in Palm Beach and Kate opened the main gate with one of the two keys. She used the same key to open the front door. They stepped inside to a large entrance area with a circular staircase going up to a second floor.

"Wow. This is quite a place. How do you feel about being here?" He carried the Betty Crocker Cookbook and shifted it from his right to left hand.

"Strange. It feels empty. All the furniture is gone."

"Is there anything we should be searching for?" Axel asked.

"I don't know, but there must be something. My grandmother definite wouldn't put those two keys in the brown envelope for nothing."

"Could you show me around?" He asked.

"Come." She said, motioning with her hand.

She led him through the different rooms until they came to the kitchen. Kate stopped for a moment, "I have so many memories of this room. It's so weird now that it's empty and the special smells are missing."

Axel put the Betty Crocker Cookbook on the kitchen counter and said, "I can imagine." He knew the room had special meaning and now it was a hole.

Kate stood in silence for a long minute and was disrupted when Axel asked, "What's that door over there?" He pointed to a door at the side of the kitchen.

"It's the pantry."

"Let's go see," he said as he opened the cookbook to the page with the number five circled in red at the bottom. On the page there was a red tick next to a note, *look for stocks in shelves in back of pantry.*

He turned back to the fourth circle, which instructed to check the big physical box at home. "Maybe circles four and five are connected. Perhaps circle five is telling us where to find this *physical box*."

"That could be somewhere in the back of the pantry," she declared.

He went to the door and opened it. Inside was a large room with empty shelves on every wall. Axel walked carefully around the room looking at the shelves. The back shelves were different than the rest. It reminded him of Harry Raintree's safe house, with the secret room just off the bedroom.

He searched carefully around the edges of the shelves and said, "I've found it." He pointed to a small latch, and then lifted it. Something released. The shelves swung out from one side, exposing a concrete wall with a metal door.

They said nothing as Kate took the second key on the key ring and inserted it into the door. The key turned and the thick metal door, like the door of a safe, slowly opened.

They stepped inside, turned on the light switch and saw a large room with metal walls. Stacked on a shelf along one side was a row of large brown packages.

"Paintings?" Axel asked.

"They must be," Kate replied.

After a quick count, Axel said, "Ten."

"This is incredible," Kate muttered. "In two days I find out that I'm the owner of some paintings worth a fortune as well as this expensive house. This is too much to absorb in such a short time."

"I know, but what about the rest? You said there were twenty or more in the house and Emma's note said some of the paintings were in storage outside the country."

"I know. Any ideas on how to find them?"

"Emma seems to have everything carefully planned, dripping out a little information at a time. Has she given us any clues?"

"I have an idea, but let's check these packages first."

They opened two of the paintings, one a Paul Klee and the other a Monet, then repackaged them and put them back on the shelves. After closing the door to the safe room and swinging the shelves back in place, they went to the kitchen.

Axel said, "Let me go back to my question about the house. It appears no one has been living here. It also seems to be in perfect condition. Someone has been cleaning the inside and maintaining the garden. Would you have any idea whom that could be and how they are paid?"

"Not really, but the house seems to be in even better shape than when we lived here."

"I have an idea where to go from here," Axel stated.

"And where would that be?"

"The Bahamas."

"Are you just looking for a reason to go to an exotic beach?" She teased.

He smiled and led her to the kitchen counter where the Betty Crocker Cookbook still sat. Axel opened it to a recipe for roast duck and pointed to the bottom. There was a red circle with the number six inside it.

"I saw this before," he said. "Look at the tick."

Next to the red tick was scribbled, *Vacation, visit Petersburg, Nassau, The Bahamas.*

He said, "Anyone reading this wouldn't get it. I sure didn't at first, but it seems Emma is telling you to visit Petersburg Limited in Nassau. At least, that's my guess."

"You may be right," she agreed.

"Absolutely. At least it's a chance to test your Bahamian passport. If it's fake I'll see you in jail."

"Very funny," she said.

"By the way, that seems to be the last red circle with a number in it."

"Maybe we are coming to the end of this quest," Kate stated.

Axel shook his head. "And maybe not. One thing I've learned about your grandmother is that she did the unexpected. There may be more moves on the table."

"I hope not," Kate sighed.

"Let's figure out how to get to Nassau," he said as he picked up the cookbook.

They headed out the front door of the house, and both faced the door as Kate inserted the key to lock it.

Suddenly, Axel sensed movement to his left and a second later a man appeared out of nowhere. Before they had a chance to react, the man swept in with lightning speed and grabbed Kate from behind.

At the same moment, he felt a pair of powerful arms go around his chest and lift him off the ground. The arms felt like giant unmovable pliers squeezing the air out of him. The cookbook fell from his hands to the ground.

CHAPTER 39

A foul breath came from behind Axel's head as the man's arms squeezed tighter. Axel struggled, arms pinned, unable to reach his Glock pistol that was now pressing into his back.

He quickly realized the two men had come from behind the thick cypress bushes on each side of the front door. It was stupid to have not surveyed the yard before stepping outside. He hoped it would not turn out to be a fatal mistake.

His head spun. He felt like a drowning man with no air in his lungs. Kate had her hands free, scratching wildly at the hands of the other man. The man attempted to avoid her onslaught while trying to gain control.

Axel had one final strategy to counterattack, but he had to move fast before passing out. He tilted his head forward and with a quick, powerful movement he pounded the back of his head into the attacker's nose. The man's nose crunched and his grip was loosened. Axel made a second backward head-butt into the man's face even harder than the first and there was another sickening crunch.

The assailant had amazing strength but his grip was loosened just enough for Axel to free one arm. With his free hand, Axel grabbed the man's right thumb and twisted it backward until it snapped. For a split second the man lost control of his grip.

Axel felt a slight release, so he spun to his right and broke away from the giant brute, losing his balance and slipping forward to the ground. The man charged him, so Axel crashed his shoulder into the attacker's lower legs, causing him to tumble like a heavy bag.

While the man was still on the ground, Axel quickly rose to his feet and stomped his right foot into the man's ribs. He kicked the man again, this time feeling ribs give way and crack like breaking sticks.

With a swift movement Axel quickly reached behind his back, grabbed his Glock and crashed it into the man's head. The man still tried to raise himself. *This guy is a beast!* Axel thought. Axel hit him three more times until the man dropped to the ground and stayed still.

He rapidly turned and saw that the slightly smaller man had now gained control of Kate's arms, though she was still struggling like a cat in a bag. Axel raised his pistol and pointed it at the man's head, "Let her go."

The man was Axel's size, but broad and chunky. He had a four-day beard, a shaved head, and wore a dark shirt that made him look more intimidating. The man slowly released his grip on Kate.

Kate gave out a small whimper and raced to Axel's side.

"Who are you?" Axel barked.

The man smiled and said coldly, "You are a dead man."

"Right now I'd say the opposite. Who are you?"

The man didn't answer but swiftly reached behind his back and drew a pistol. Immediately Axel pulled the trigger of his Glock. There was a loud deafening bang that reverberated through the yard and the man fell backward and dropped his gun to the ground. The shot had gone into the man's shoulder.

The man reached down with his left hand to grab his gun and Axel took a step forward, raised his Glock and clubbed the man on the side of his head. The man fell to his knees, his left hand covering the wound on his right shoulder.

Axel struck the man again in the head and he fell to the ground, motionless.

Kate gasped, "You killed them."

Axel's heart was pounding. "Naw, they'll be okay. They'll just have some serious headaches when they wake."

"But you shot that man!"

"In the shoulder. He may have a hard time to use his arm but he deserves it for what he was doing to you."

"Still . . . I can't believe you actually shot him!"

Axel reached down, picked up the cookbook and took the keys from the front lock. "Check their pockets and then let's get out of here."

They went through the men's pockets and found nothing. The larger man also had a gun under his belt, so they took the two guns and left through the front gate. On the other side of the street a black SUV was parked in front of the Honda Civic.

Through the dark windows Axel saw the figure of a man in the back seat. He raised his Glock and carefully approached the car.

The man didn't move. Axel cautiously opened the back door and saw that he was tied up with duct tape, with a band of tape across his mouth. Axel reached in and removed the tape from the man's mouth. The man winced.

"Ouch, careful!"

Axel stared at him and said, "I've seen you before."

"No way."

"What's your name?"

"Cold-Cap."

"Okay, Cold-Cap. You were in West Palm Beach yesterday standing by a motorcycle. You seemed to have a strong interest in the lady here. What's the story?"

"There's no story, man. These guys kidnapped me. Can you let me go?"

Axel pressed his pistol against Cold-Cap's head. "I just shot one of your friends, so I have no problem putting a hole in your head."

Cold-Cap scrunched his eyes and crouched down. "Don't do that."

"What's the story?"

He began by stuttering. "Aw . . . man . . . I'm in trouble."

"I know. You've got a gun pointed at your head."

"There's a reward out on the street for anyone who identifies your lady. I called it in and then these two guys showed up. I was stupid to get involved in this."

"You bet-cha. Who are the two goons?" Axel asked.

"I don't know. Two huge guys you don't wanna mess with."

"Russians?"

"Yeah, maybe, I dunno . . . I ain't good with accents."

"Who are they working for?"

"I don't know, man." He rocked back and forth as he talked. "They just told me to sit in the back seat and I've been here all night listening to some gibberish language I don't understand. They told me not to ask questions. Then they taped me up before heading for the house."

"Did they talk to anybody since you've been with them?"

"Yeah, they called someone on the phone. I think they were told to follow you, but I didn't hear the voice on the other end."

"Where's the phone?"

Cold-Cap nodded his head forward and said, "In the console between the front seats."

Axel opened the console, took the phone and put it in his pocket. He reached into the glove box and took out the registration papers.

He turned to Kate and said, "We've got to go. Those men may have been waiting for backup."

She nodded and they started toward their car when Cold-Cap cried out, "Hey dude, you can't leave me here!"

Axel turned back and asked, "You got a knife?"

"Yeah, in my front pocket."

Axel reached into Cold-Cap's front pocket and took out the knife, a switchblade. He snapped it open and cut the duct tape off of Cold-Cap's wrists and ankles.

"Thanks, man. My hands were ready to fall off." Cold-Cap shook his hands in the air and wiggled his legs.

"Get out of here," Axel said. "And I'd suggest you leave Florida as quickly as possible. If I understand who these guys are, they wouldn't hesitate a second to rip you to shreds.

"Oh yeah, for sure, I'm outta here. Can you give me a ride to my motorcycle in West Palm Beach?"

"No. Start running."

Cold-Cap didn't hesitate. With wobbly, stiff legs he sprinted down the street.

Using Cold-Cap's knife, Axel cut holes in all four tires of the SUV.

★ ★ ★

They drove south on I-95 toward Miami. Kate's legs were twitching from the trauma of being manhandled. The plan was to stop somewhere on the way to get a wireless connection and make flight reservations to the Bahamas. They also needed to stop at Harry Raintree's safe house to get Axel's passport. Kate would travel on her Bahamian passport.

She felt sick to her stomach, her hands quivering from the aftershock. There was no telling what those men would have done if Axel hadn't been there.

The reality that she was being sought by someone and still didn't know why was starting to settle in. She wondered if it was because of the paintings, knowing now that they were worth a fortune. Any criminal would want to get their hands on them.

She turned and looked at Axel, whose eyes were on the road. He had shown a violent side that surprised her. She should have expected it, part of the package of hiring a private investigator.

Yet, she was worried that he had gone too far. He had coldly shot a man and then smashed his head. The multiple blows were done with precision, purpose. He had ruthlessly kicked the ribs of the other man until they shattered. Then he waved it all off with as little emotion as one would have wiping crumbs from a table.

Up until now, Kate only saw Axel as inquisitive and fun even to the point that his lack of seriousness annoyed her. She couldn't deny his seriousness altogether, though; he had found her books and tracked down her paintings. Yet, this new perspective of him was concerning. She was peaceful by nature and didn't know what to think about his rough side.

She couldn't figure him out and it was driving her crazy.

CHAPTER 40

Halfway to Miami, Axel took an off-ramp and found a restaurant with a wireless connection. They chose a booth and Kate went to the ladies' room.

Axel used this as an opportunity to call Tommy.

"Hey, man," Tommy said.

"Did you find anything on Innokenti?"

"I've been doing massive amounts of translating from Russian to English. Innokenti is a pretty common first name, so it was hard to find people with the surname Innokenti."

"So, did you come up with anything?"

"Yeah. It took a lot of digging. There was an Ivan Innokenti who was an economics professor at the University of St. Petersburg. I'm still trying to find information on him, but it looks like he could be the link you're looking for."

"Is he alive?"

"No, that's the bizarre thing. He was murdered along with his son and daughter-in-law, their bodies riddled with gun shots."

"What?" Axel exclaimed. "When was that?"

"About twenty-four years ago in Saint Petersburg."

"Was Ivan Innokenti married?"

"Yeah. I accessed Russian news archives. It was tough going, because digital records over there don't go back very far in time. It appears Ivan Innokenti's wife disappeared along with her sister and granddaughter. Investigators suspected they were also murdered and then the bodies were hidden."

"That might explain why Emma Miller magically appeared in Palm Beach twenty-three years ago, with a new identity."

"Definitely. By the way, *Ivan* in English is *John*."

"John Miller. Kate's grandfather."

"You got it," Tommy said.

Axel reflected for a moment. "Did you get a name for the granddaughter?" he asked.

"I did. It is Katerina Innokenti."

Axel was dumbfounded. The same name on the Russian passport that Kate was carrying. "Too much. Is there anything else?"

"No, the records are sparse, but I'm still digging."

"Okay, thanks. By the way, could you track down a telephone number for me?"

"Sure."

Axel took out the cell phone he had taken from the SUV and brought up the last number dialed. He gave it to Tommy.

"Just a second," Tommy said.

Axel waited, thinking about the news he had just received. This explained Kate's origins. He wondered why her parents and grandfather had been murdered. If the same people were after Kate now, she was in real danger.

A moment later Tommy said, "The telephone number is for the offices of the Orlov Law Group in Miami."

"No way."

"Where'd you get the number?" Tommy asked.

Axel explained the events of the morning, the struggle with the two men and taking the phone from the SUV.

Tommy said, "There's another thing I found out about the Orlovs, but I'm not sure it's relevant."

"What's that?"

"Ten years ago their father and eldest brother were gunned down in a restaurant in Brighton in New York. It seems a rival Russian Mafia group was responsible, at least from what the newspapers said. There was only one short article on an internal page in the New York Times."

"A bunch of pacifists, aren't they?"

"Yeah, the kind to stay away from," Tommy replied, "You be careful. Those guys are bad news."

"I'm finding that out," Axel stated, still in pain around his rib cage.

They hung up and Axel reflected on their situation. He decided that from here on out they must proceed with utmost caution. Nicolai Orlov had vast resources working for him, from street drug dealers to violent assassins. But this still didn't explain why he was after Kate Miller.

He watched Kate as she returned to her seat and wondered if he should tell her what Tommy had discovered. Her understanding of the death of her grandfather and parents was wrong. It wasn't from an airplane crash. They had been murdered.

How would he break the news? After the trauma of encountering the two goons in Palm Beach, he decided to hold off for the right time and place.

★ ★ ★

They made reservations for a flight to Nassau and booked a hotel. The flight was scheduled for the late afternoon, allowing sufficient time to get to the airport.

Axel drove to Harry Raintree's safe house and parked the car. His passport was in a bag under his bed; it would only take a minute to get it. He opened the front door and they went inside and entered the living room. From behind the door there was movement. Axel turned and found himself looking into the barrel of a handgun.

★ ★ ★

Nicolai turned to his brother Leonid and said, "We have a problem." He had received a call from Palm Beach. Somehow Kate Miller and the private investigator had escaped from his men.

He was bewildered that the girl had gotten away. His men were professionals, skilled in several forms of martial arts. To hear that one private investigator had overcome both of them angered Nicolai.

Even worse, one of their men was shot. To add insult to injury, the tires of the SUV had been punctured. He told Leonid what happened.

"Unbelievable," Leonid said. He slammed his hand on the table. "We can't let this continue."

"I know. We are so close to recovering what is ours. The next time we have them in sight we will take them. The private investigator is dangerous. When we capture him, we will keep him under tight security and question the hell out of him. Then we'll erase him from the face of this earth."

"What if we cannot capture him?" Leonid asked.

"Eliminate him. The quicker the better."

"Agreed," Leonid responded. "And the girl?"

"Something tells me she is very much like her grandmother, a cunning witch. During the past three years we assumed she knew nothing. Now I'm not certain. The information must be extruded from her using every means possible."

CHAPTER 41

The deadly, dark hole of the gun's barrel was large, a .357 Magnum. Cold fear swept through Axel's body. The man was several steps away, allowing no opportunity for either fight or flight. Could this be his last moment on earth? And then he thought of Kate, not wanting any harm to come to her.

The man holding the gun was short, around five-foot-seven, but the striking thing about him was his build. His arms and chest were *massive*, accentuated by a tight black t-shirt. Axel imagined that he must be clocking immeasurable hours in the gym and was probably on steroids. A silver chain hung around his neck and he had a diamond stud earring in his left ear.

The man smiled with unusually large teeth that gave him a comic-book look, a somewhat non-human appearance. Axel decided the man reminded him of a pit-bull. The man stood several steps back from Axel and ordered, "Move into the bedroom." His accent was that of a New Yorker, maybe one from the Bronx.

Axel nodded to Kate and they walked down the hallway into Axel's bedroom.

The man had a roll of duct tape and instructed Kate to tie up Axel with it. She did so, hands trembling. When she was finished, the powerfully built man pushed Kate onto the bed and wrapped the tape around her wrists and ankles.

Axel strained against the tape and growled, "Take your hands off of her, Pit-bull Freak."

The man flashed a ferocious grin and said, "I like that name." He scanned Kate up and down. "With her I'll do whatever I want."

Once they were both restrained, he took out his cell phone and made a call. "I have them tied up," he said into the receiver.

He cocked his head, large veins showing on his neck. A moment later he said, "Okay. I will wait."

He hung up and looked at Kate, "My bosses are coming. They have some questions." A cold smile crept onto his face.

He left the room carrying his pistol in one hand and Axel's Glock in the other. A moment later Axel heard the television being turned on. It sounded like a mid-day soap opera. He could hear emotional voices being broken up by dramatic music. Pit-bull laughed at something.

They sat on the edge of the bed, and after a few moments Axel whispered to Kate, "Can you get your hand into my front pocket?" Their hands were secured behind their backs. "Cold-Cap's switchblade is in my front pocket. See if you can get it."

Kate turned her body and then struggled to get her long fingers into Axel's pocket. After several tries she had the switchblade in her hand.

"Hold it blade side away from you and push the button," he whispered.

She felt the knife until she was sure it was facing the right direction then pushed the button. She jumped when there was a loud metallic snap. They waited, only hearing the noise of the television and Pit-bull laughing in the other room.

Axel turned his back to her and quietly instructed, "Just hold the knife straight out and as steady as you can. Let me move my wrists. That way I'll know what's being cut, the tape or me."

The knife was razor sharp and quickly cut through the tape.

Once his hands were free Axel cut the tape around his ankles and then freed Kate. He stood up and put his index finger vertical to his mouth. Sounds of the soap opera and Pit-bull's laughs continued.

He went into the walk-in closet and opened the gun room. After choosing a nine millimeter pistol for himself, he picked up a twelve-gauge shotgun, walked back into the bedroom and handed it to Kate.

He whispered, "Don't worry about being accurate. Just point it at Pit-bull when he walks through the door. And don't hesitate to pull the trigger if you need to."

She nodded, her eyes wide.

Axel went to the side of the door and yelled out, "Help! Help, there's something wrong with the lady!"

There was a *clump, clump* in the other room before the door opened quickly and Pit-bull stepped inside. He was empty-handed and his face froze when he saw the shotgun aimed at his mammoth chest. He grimaced when he saw Axel beside him with the pistol.

"Move over here and stand still," Axel said. He kept the pistol pointed at the man, took the roll of duct tape off a cupboard and handed it to Kate. "Would you do the honors?"

Kate took the roll from his hand.

"Lie on the floor," he commanded. Pit-bull went to his knees and then stretched out face down on the floor.

Kate put the shotgun on the bed and attempted to pull the man's hands together behind his back, but they couldn't touch because of his massive muscles. She taped each hand individually and then liberally ran tape between them. Then she taped his legs together.

Kate showed a forced smile. "Let's get out of here," she said.

"Absolutely. His bosses are on their way."

Axel took the shotgun off the bed and grabbed his passport. They went to the car and sped down the street.

★ ★ ★

The flight to Nassau was fifty-five minutes and Kate's Bahamian passport was accepted at customs with no hitches. They took a taxi to the address of Petersburg Ltd., the company they hoped would provide some answers. They found the building on West Bay Street close to the First Caribbean International Bank.

The colonial-style building was three stories tall, and next to the front door was a small brass sign that said *Global Management Services*. The door was locked.

Axel said, "This must be a financial services company that administers Petersburg Limited. They probably have hundreds of off-shore companies using this address."

"It's a nice building," Kate said. It was constructed of stone blocks and was freshly painted. There were bars over the small windows on the ground floor.

Axel looked up. "I'm guessing all the windows in this building are bulletproof. It was built for security."

"We need to come back tomorrow morning," Kate said.

Axel nodded.

They walked several blocks and checked into the British Colonial Hotel on Bay Street, a large five-star hotel. Kate had booked a suite on the top floor consisting of an expansive living room and two bedrooms, each with its own bath.

Upon entering the suite Axel said, "Not bad." The view of the Caribbean was magnificent, the last light of the sunset making a golden hue on the horizon.

"I thought it would be best if we had accommodations like this for security. My nerves are shot after all that has happened," she said.

In fact, she felt exhausted. Since employing Axel, it seemed to Kate like each step they made brought trauma in one form or another. Terrible memories flashed through her mind: finding her apartment burgled, encountering the two men in the SUV, finding the paintings and everything leading up to Axel shooting the man at the house in Palm Beach. The muscly maniac waiting for them at Harry Raintree's safe house only added to the distress.

This had become too much to take.

On top of all the trauma were her feelings for Axel. He was a complex man. At times he didn't seem to have a care in the world, yet he had underlying layers, like he was holding something back. He was a strange mix, with his degrees in both accounting and history. He was sharp and inquisitive. But the violence he showed in subduing those two men at the house, and how easily he had pulled the trigger of his gun, unnerved Kate.

Then, Axel had pushed the barrel of his gun into Cold-Cap's head and threatened to blow out his brains. This was a side of Axel that made her feel uneasy, but it also gave her a sense of security, and that's what she needed most. She wondered if in similar circumstances Chandler could give her that same feeling. She had her doubts.

The short note in the envelope from Reverend Levkin said she owned Petersburg Ltd. She wanted Axel with her when they visited Global Management Services in the morning. With his accounting background, he might help her understand how Petersburg Ltd. fit within Emma's scheme of the world.

She looked across the room as he stood in front of the window staring out at the glow of the sunset. He seemed so calm. She wanted to go to him and feel his body against hers, to absorb his strength, but something stopped her.

She said, "I need sleep. I'm exhausted."

"Do you want anything to eat?" He asked.

"Not really. I'll just take some of this." She walked to the table in the center of the room where there was a bowl of fresh fruit. She took an apple and some grapes and went to her room.

★ ★ ★

Alone in her room, Kate stared at the phone on her nightstand and deliberated whether or not to call Chandler. After a moment of hesitation she picked up the phone. She needed to hear his voice.

"Kate, I've been worried about you," he stated. "Did you find a place to hide until I get there?"

"No. It didn't work out that way."

"What do you mean?"

"The private investigator I hired found some important information and one thing led to another. We are still working the case."

"What did you find out?"

"It's too complicated to explain over the telephone. When I see you, I'll tell you everything. When are you flying back to Miami?"

"Unfortunately I got hung up in San Francisco. I'll fly back tomorrow evening and will be there the following morning. That's Thursday morning. Can I come straight to your place?"

"Of course. I really want to see you."

"Me too. Where are you calling from?" He asked.

"Nassau, the Bahamas."

"What? What are you doing there?"

"As I said, it's a long story. We fly back to Miami tomorrow and I'll tell you all about it when I see you on Thursday."

"Where are you staying?"

"A hotel." For some reason she didn't want to let him know where she was staying or that she was in the same suite as Axel. "It's getting late. I'll see you in two days."

"Alright," Chandler said. There was a pause. "Kate, I'm really worried about you and want you to know that I love you."

"Thank you, Chandler. I need to go."

"See you soon," he said.

As soon as she hung up, she felt conflicted. Hearing Chandler's voice was not as comforting as she had expected. He emitted confidence and security. She understood why his investment company was successful. But this conversation only made her feel more lost.

Surely it would be so reassuring to see him in two days, yet she didn't feel the urgency for him she had felt earlier. She told herself it was just the circumstances causing confusion and that when she saw him she would feel his presence and his love. It would bring calm into her tormented life. *Or, would it?*

He had what she needed: confidence, security and love. Isn't that what every woman longed for?

CHAPTER 42

The following morning Kate and Axel had breakfast in the downstairs restaurant and then walked to Global Management Services.

Axel smiled. "I washed my shirt and undies last night. Too many days in the same clothing."

Kate laughed. "I know. I did the same. If we have time after visiting Global Management Services maybe we can do a little shopping. Bay Street has tons of tourist shops."

"It sounds like you know the place."

"We came over here two or three times a year, often staying a week or two. Since I was homeschooled, I had flexibility other children didn't have."

"Somehow you had the financial means to do this."

"I guess so, but when you grow up like that you don't fully realize it. And yet, on the other hand Emma and Clara were extremely frugal and counted their pennies."

"Let me ask, do you still think she was a teenager when she came to the United States?"

Kate looked at him. "After all we've discovered, I think she came as an adult."

"Then what about your grandfather and your parents? What happened to them?"

"I don't know," she said with a heavy sigh.

They reached the front door of Global Management Services and entered a reception area, with an attractive young black woman behind a desk. She wore a blue blouse and long, blue earrings.

"May I help you?" She said with a Bahamian accent.

Kate replied, "My name is Kate Miller. I'm wondering if it is possible to find out about a company that is registered to this address, Petersburg Limited."

The young woman hesitated for a moment and said, "Just a minute." She picked up the phone, dialed a number and said, "A Ms. Kate Miller is here inquiring about a company called Petersburg Limited." She listened and then put the phone down. "Please come with me."

They took an elevator to the third floor and the woman led them to a door. She knocked, opened the door, gestured inside and said, "Please."

They entered a large office. On one end a man was seated behind a modern desk. He was elderly, perhaps in his mid-seventies and had small, round glasses that fit his narrow face. He wore a striped blue tie, green suspenders and a light blue shirt with a white collar. Everything seemed to accentuate his penetrating blue eyes.

He smiled and said, "Kate. I've been waiting for you. Please have a seat."

★ ★ ★

S was surprised to know this man knew her name, yet there was something familiar about him. Did she meet him on one of their many trips to Nassau? She couldn't remember.

"How do you know me?" She asked.

He waited a moment and said, "Your grandmother was a client of mine and I've seen you many times over the years, always from a distance. Please forgive me for calling you by your first name, but I've seen you grow up." He spoke with a British accent.

"My grandmother was a client? For what?" she asked.

He smiled. "I know this may be confusing. My name is Peter Claymore and I manage Global Management Services."

"Do you know Petersburg Limited?" She asked.

"Of course. We administer the company."

"Can you tell me about it?"

"It's your company. At least, you are the beneficiary of the foundation that owns it."

"My company? What does it do?"

He gave a warm smile. "It owns assets."

"Like a house in Palm Beach?"

"Yes, among others."

"Did my grandmother sign over Petersburg Limited to me?"

"No. Not really. You have indirectly owned Petersburg Limited since you were three years old. As I said, you are the beneficiary of a foundation and through that the asset is yours."

"You mean I have owned that house since I was three years old," Kate said, wide-eyed.

"Yes," Claymore confirmed.

"Does the foundation or company hold other assets?" Axel asked.

Claymore's eyes shifted to Axel, his face neutral. "I think it is best if I share that sort of information directly with Ms. Miller. We maintain client confidentiality."

Kate realized she hadn't introduced Axel and said, "This is Axel Bjorg who works for me. I would not have found you without him. He's a private investigator and a forensic accountant and I'm comfortable to share all information with him."

Claymore looked at Kate. "Are you sure?"

"Yes. We'd like to know if Petersburg Limited holds other assets."

Claymore paused a moment and replied. "Yes, it actually does. It owns a large property in New Zealand and the house where Kate stayed when her family came to the Bahamas."

"Unbelievable," Kate exclaimed. "That's a beautiful place."

"Indeed, on the waterfront." Claymore removed his glasses and rubbed the bridge of his nose. "That's how we obtained nationality for you, and for your grandmother and Clara. Twenty-three years ago the Bahamian nationality laws were more lenient than today. And I must tell you that we have carefully maintained those properties over the years."

"You mean I've been a citizen here for twenty-three years?"

"Yes."

She was shocked. "You mentioned a foundation. What is that?"

"Your grandmother set it up years ago. You are the beneficiary."

"And Emma Miller was the settlor?" Axel asked.

Claymore smiled. "You seem to know about financial structures."

"Yes, in fact, I do," Axel said. "As Kate mentioned, I have an accounting background, and in my business, I have come across many kinds of corporate structures, both on- and offshore."

Claymore nodded. "That's good. This can be of help to Kate."

"What's in the foundation?" Axel asked.

"It's a bit complicated, but that's how Mrs. Miller wanted it. The foundation owns eleven different companies including St. Petersburg Limited."

"What?" Kate asked, wondering if she had heard correctly.

"That's correct. These companies are registered around the world. Experienced portfolio managers work on behalf of each company. For instance, the one registered in Hong Kong invests in securities in Asia. The one in Guernsey invests in European assets. The one in Switzerland specializes in gold and other commodities."

"It's too much," Kate exclaimed.

"I understand your surprise, especially if you are learning about this for the first time. It takes some overseeing and I've worried these investments have not had enough of that. Your grandmother instructed me to do nothing until I heard from you, other than to maintain the physical assets and to consolidate financial data from her companies, or, I should say, *your* companies. She said I would be hearing from you once you turned twenty-six years old. That's why I was expecting you."

"Why did she create so many companies?"

"Diversity and security. The various companies don't know about each other. I'm the only one who knows how it all fits together, and of course I'm operating under strict guidelines established by Mrs. Miller."

Claymore opened a file on his desk and handed a paper to Kate. "That's the list of your companies."

She slowly took it from his hand and read it. There were companies registered all over the world, in Asia, Africa, Europe and North and South America.

"The portfolio managers working for these companies need to be visited," Claymore said, "At least that's my opinion."

Kate took a deep breath. "I can't believe it."

"I'd advise you to carefully hide that piece of paper," Claymore stated.

"I understand. Do you know the total value of all these investments?" She asked.

He picked up a printout and looked at it. "In the last consolidation, the total was just over six hundred million United States Dollars. The fortune has grown a lot since Mrs. Miller first deposited it twenty-three years ago."

Kate wondered if this was real. "Did you just say six hundred million?"

Claymore's eyes went from Kate back to the printout. "A bit more."

"This is unbelievable! Are you sure about this?" She felt lightheaded. Not one client at Wesson Securities owned that much.

"Yes, I'm sure about this. But, please remember that doesn't include the value of the original art Mrs. Miller was holding." He smiled. "I'm quite proud that I advised her on a few of those purchases, but for most of the paintings she decided on her own. Perhaps they are worth fifty to a hundred million dollars at this point."

"I've found twelve of the paintings," Kate said. "Do you know where the rest might be?"

"Oh yes, in a vault in a bank in Switzerland that specializes in the storage of works of art. The Swiss are among the best for this sort of thing. It's on your list. There are twenty paintings being held for you by the Swiss."

"I don't know what to say," she exclaimed, and was met with silence.

Then Axel asked, "Do you know where the initial investment funds came from?"

Claymore shook his head. "That was never disclosed. Mrs. Miller just showed up here one day and told me what she wanted to do. The foundation was quickly established and then I assisted her in the transfer of funds into a new bank account. Over time we moved those funds to the eleven companies. Emma said that she and her husband were investors. That was all she told me. In today's world the banks are much more diligent in wanting to know the origin of funds, but not back then."

"So, you don't know where the fortune came from?" Axel asked.

Claymore paused, lowered his voice and said, "Not the starting point; although, as I said, I helped her along the way, particularly with international transfers. It seems all her funds had been quickly consolidated into a bank account in Europe. She asked me to, ah . . . how can I put it? To move the funds in a non-traceable way. As I said, the banking world used to be different."

"But what was the origin?" Axel asked.

"When she contacted me she had already moved the funds from a company bank account to another one in her name. When I took over, I managed the movements to their final destinations. The first account was for a company called Innokenti Holding, but I don't know the origins before that."

"Did you say Innokenti Holding? From Cyprus?" Axel asked.

"That's correct. It was from Cyprus. How did you know?"

"That company still exists," Kate stated.

CHAPTER 43

Peter Claymore took the glasses from his eyes and looked at Kate. "May I make a recommendation? Perhaps it is wise to forget the past. I'm sure Mrs. Miller had reasons for her actions, so I'd prefer not to question them. My advice is that we focus on current structures, as there is much to discuss."

Kate reflected. Claymore was right. Great care had been taken to erase the trail of the money from Innokenti Holding. Now was not the time to try to understand the motivations behind why Emma did this. "Yes, that might be wise," she agreed.

They talked through the morning, yet it was difficult for Kate to concentrate. Peter Claymore and Axel reviewed the eleven companies, going into great detail. She tried to keep up with them but a host of unrelated questions raced through her mind.

She felt nauseated when she thought about the size of the fortune. It was an incredible amount of money. How could she manage such a thing?

Now she realized why Emma had steered her into finance and away from art. Still, they had visited art museums each summer, so her grandmother had been attentive to her needs. Their home had even been filled with beautiful paintings, and Kate now understood it was for her benefit. The reason for the financial orientation was clear. Emma wanted her to gain knowledge before assuming management of the fortune.

Hearing that the funds originated from Innokenti Holding in Cyprus stunned her, realizing this company was now somehow linked to Nikolai Orlov. Was this the reason Orlov sent those awful men after her? It still didn't explain why.

She saw Axel carefully taking notes on a notepad that Peter Claymore had given him. Axel seemed to have an understanding of the details, much more than she did. He was inquisitive and intelligent. She sensed he knew things he wasn't telling her and wondered if he knew more about her family history than he was letting on.

When he had pried into her family's past she had been stubborn and resisted him. Now she doubted that her parents and grandfather were killed in an airplane crash in the Everglades. She even doubted that Emma originated from Poland. She even doubted that her real name was Kate Miller. It wasn't only her apartment that had been robbed, it was her very identity. Her North Star had been ripped from its place in the universe and only confusion remained.

She thought about her grandmother and Aunt Clara. They were two elderly, old-fashioned women, just two old babushkas from Eastern Europe. They collected supermarket coupons, only bought clothing if it was on sale, and drove a modest car. They taught Kate to be frugal. The contradiction was that they traveled freely, stayed in upscale hotels and owned expensive houses.

Kate now knew all their traveling was not only for tourism. The real reason for those trips was to visit their portfolio managers around the world. And when they bought properties and art it was not just for enjoyment, but as an investment. Emma had hidden that from her, and she wondered why this was.

All she knew was that Emma was a master planner, carefully crafting each move, and Kate was part of that strategy. The revelation of the hiding places of the paintings had been done step by step, as well as the mysterious path leading to Peter Claymore. Emma had left cleverly hidden clues in the cookbook in such a way that only Kate would know where they led. Anyone else looking at the cookbook would have been lost.

Emma had been a truly exceptional person, and Kate wondered if there was more mystery to come. *Where did the fortune come from and what was the role of Nicolai Orlov in this? And if my parents were not killed in an airplane crash, what happened to them?* Kate pondered these thoughts and in the midst of them was interrupted.

"May I invite you to lunch?" she heard Peter Claymore say.

"Huh?" Kate answered. "Oh, of course. Thank you very much."

CHAPTER 44

After a wonderful seafood lunch in a restaurant above the clear turquoise ocean, they said good-bye to Peter Claymore and took a taxi to the airport to catch their return flight to Miami.

Once on the plane they spoke with soft voices, never speaking directly about what they had just learned. Kate now understood the reason for her grandmother's secret language and behaviors. One never knew who was listening. In fact, she had taken the list of companies given by Peter Claymore, folded it up as small as possible and placed it in her bra.

Kate looked out the window of the airplane at the vast blue Atlantic Ocean below them and then turned to Axel. "Did you understand everything he was explaining?"

"Most of it," Axel answered. "It's complex and I'm sure you'll need to visit him again. And, you might need to plan some international trips. There are many portfolio managers to visit."

"I know. It is quite a responsibility."

Axel laughed. "One many people would die for."

"I'll need to resign from Wesson Securities."

He chuckled. "Your job description has suddenly changed."

He was right. It had changed. "My life has been turned upside down."

"There's one last thing we need to do and then my work with you is finished," he said with seriousness in his eyes.

"What's that?" She asked, feeling a flash of panic, realizing that Axel would no longer be working for her.

"Call Detective McGill. We need to get Nicolai Orlov out of your life."

She nodded. "Orlov frightens me. He's evil."

"Then call McGill first thing once we're back in Miami."

★ ★ ★

They landed at Miami International Airport and took a shuttle bus to the parking lot where they had left the car. They got in and rolled down the windows to let fresh air in.

Kate's head was spinning. Now that she was back in Miami, she wondered if what she had learned in the Bahamas was real or a dream. She raised her hand, pushed it against her breast and felt the folded piece of paper. It was real.

She understood that the responsibility of managing this fortune was not something to take lightly. That was something learned at Wesson Securities. Their high-net-worth clients carried great weight and now she had more wealth than any of their clients. What rested against her skin was more than ink on paper.

She turned to Axel and said, "Can you give me your cell phone?"

He handed it to her and she called Detective McGill.

"McGill," he answered.

"Detective McGill, this is Kate Miller."

"Who?"

"Kate Miller. My apartment was burgled."

"Oh yes, of course. Some people are not happy with you."

"What do you mean?"

"An enormous amount of police work went down the drain when you went into that warehouse to get your things. It set back our investigation."

"I'm sorry, but I didn't know that at the time. There's something else I need to tell you."

"What's that? I hope you aren't doing any more snooping on your own."

"Well, I'm having problems with someone called Nicolai Orlov and I wanted to tell you about it."

"Who?"

"Nicolai Orlov."

"Oh no. You can't get involved," McGill immediately commanded.

"Why not. He's threatening me."

"What has he done to you?" McGill asked.

"He . . ."

At that moment a hand reached into the car and grabbed her cell phone.

"Hey!" she cried out, and then turned to see a large man standing outside the car, her phone dwarfed by his massive hands. Unmoved by her protest, he raised the cell phone dramatically and crashed it to the ground. Another man stood on the driver's side of the car and held a pistol to Axel's head.

"Get out," the man with the gun commanded.

★ ★ ★

After strong arms yanked them out of the Honda, a white van screeched in behind them. A door on the side of the van opened and they were pushed inside and told to sit down. The two men joined them, pointing guns at Axel and Kate.

"Don't move," one of the men said with an Eastern European accent.

Just as the van accelerated Axel heard his Honda start up. They drove for twenty minutes before the van stopped and the side door slid open.

"Get out," a man said.

Axel felt helpless as he quickly surveyed the surroundings. They were in a courtyard next to a warehouse or industrial building of some kind. Someone was driving his Honda Civic and steered it through large swinging doors and parked it next to the van. The swinging doors shut, making them invisible from the street.

The driver of the Honda Civic got out and opened the trunk. He lifted out Axel's large duffle bag, looked inside and smiled. The man raised the Mossberg shotgun, showed it to the other men and they laughed.

Axel counted five men, each carrying a gun. He recognized two. One was the Brute that had squeezed his ribs at Kate's house in Palm Beach, and the other was Pit-bull Freak from the safe house. One side of the Brute's face was black and blue, a result of the multiple blows received from the butt of Axel's Glock. His nose was swollen, with white tape across it where Axel had head-butted him. His right hand was wrapped in tape as well, and Axel remembered the crunching noise when he had snapped his thumb. The Brute awkwardly carried his gun in his left hand.

Pit-bull peered through a swollen eye, which was most likely from the discipline he received for allowing Kate and Axel to escape. They both had sinister grins on their faces. The smaller goon from Palm Beach wasn't there and Axel hoped the bullet wound to his shoulder had put him out of action for a long time.

With a hollow feeling in his throat, Axel counted the bodies and determined that their escape went against insurmountable odds.

"Get inside," Pit-bull said as he rammed the barrel of his pistol into Axel's ribs.

CHAPTER 45

They were led into the warehouse, which was full of cars and car parts. Kate smelled an odd mix of grease, oil and cleaning solutions. It added to the fright of being surrounded by five men waving guns around.

A question ran through her mind. *How did these men know I would be arriving at Miami International Airport?*

She thought again about the folded list inside her bra. She was determined that whatever happened, she couldn't let them find it. She scanned the room and wondered how they might get out of this, hoping Axel wouldn't do anything to endanger them.

"Nice chop-shop," Axel said to the men.

The Brute raised his arm, tapped his pistol on Axel's head and said, "Shut up."

The men led them through a large sliding door into a smaller room with a couple of sports cars, a red Ferrari and a powder blue Porsche. It was the only door into the room, so it was the only way out.

In an open area and on the side of the cars were three chairs. A young woman was sitting on one of them, bound at her hands and feet with duct tape.

"Oh no," Axel moaned.

Kate saw she was pretty with blond hair and blue eyes.

The young woman cried out, "Axel, what's going on?"

His face turned white. "Elsa, I'm sorry."

Kate felt a flash of jealousy that surprised her. Was this one of Axel's girlfriends?

"Quiet, I said." The large Brute tapped Axel's head with the barrel of his gun, this time harder. It seemed like payback for what Axel had done to him. He pointed at the two chairs and said, "Sit there."

Axel took the chair in the middle between Kate and the young woman, and the five men took up positions in front of them. One of the men carried Axel's bag of weapons. He went to a table to the right of Kate and took everything out of the bag.

She counted the shotgun, the Intratec TEC-9, two pistols and Cold Cap's switchblade. In his strong Eastern European accent the Brute sneered, "This is good arsenal."

Kate saw Axel's eyes shift to the guns on the table. She hoped he didn't have any crazy ideas about being a hero. There was no way he could make it to the table, grab a gun and then shoot the five men without being shot and killed himself.

Axel turned to the young woman and started to say something, "I'm so . . .", when Pit-bull pointed his gun at Axel and fired.

There was a loud boom and Kate's entire body jumped as she put her hands up to her face. Lowering them, she saw that Axel wasn't shot. The bullet had gone into the wall behind them.

Pit-bull said, "I said be quiet, or next time I'll aim lower." His words were nasal, his accent straight from the Bronx.

Axel stared at him with icy eyes and Kate wondered how he could be so controlled when a bullet had just passed his head. Now Axel's body was tensed like a leopard ready to strike.

She heard footsteps and Nicolai Orlov came through the door with a man who was a slightly younger version of him.

Nicolai turned to the other man, smiled and said, "At last."

Kate cried out, "Why are you doing this?"

Nicolai grinned, his face hard. "My, my, aren't we feisty?"

"This is absurd," Kate exclaimed.

"And maybe not." Nicolai raised a hand at the man next to him. "Ms. Miller, this is my brother Leonid. We have been waiting a long time for this meeting."

"Why you doing this?"" she demanded.

"We need information from you, and then you will be free to go."

"Don't believe them," Axel interjected.

Leonid turned to one of the men and ordered, "Take him away and feed him to the alligators."

Two of the men started toward Axel when Kate cried out, "No! Please, what do you want?"

Leonid raised his hand and the two men backed off. He pointed at the Brute and Pit-bull and said, "You two stay here. I think you'll enjoy our interrogation because of your previous history with the girl." He turned to the three remaining men and commanded, "You go outside and guard this place."

The three men left the room and a moment later Kate heard the outer door of the warehouse being shut. There were now four men to worry about: the Brute, Pit-bull and the two Orlovs. The odds were still not in their favor and again she hoped Axel wasn't considering anything impulsive.

She peered to her left past Axel to the pretty young woman who was sitting still, almost stoic, similar to the way Axel was sitting. She wished she could do the same.

Leonid Orlov walked over to the table, looked at the guns and said, "Impressive." He picked up the two pistols, walked back and handed the .22-caliber pistol to Nicolai and took the larger nine millimeter Glock for himself.

Nicolai held the .22 pistol in his right hand and said, "Now, let's get straight to business. Where is our money?"

"What are you talking about?" Kate growled.

"We want the money taken by your grandmother, the old witch."

Kate's eyes narrowed. "Don't speak about her like that."

"I will speak any way I like. Your grandmother took a sizable sum from our family. Tell us where the money is." Nicolai took two steps toward Kate and pressed the pistol against her forehead. "I'll give you to three." He started counting, "One . . . two . . ."

Axel exclaimed, "She took what was hers."

The Orlov brothers stared at him. Nicolai lowered his gun from Kate's forehead and took up his former position. "That's interesting. Tell us what you know."

"It's not your money," Axel blurted out.

"What do you mean?"

"Your father was a partner of Ivan Innokenti, Kate's grandfather, a tiny minority partner. Then he killed her grandfather and parents. He would have done the same to Ivan's wife, Emma and her granddaughter had they not gone into hiding."

Nicolai turned to his brother and smiled. "The private investigator thinks he understands the world."

Kate felt bewilderment and said to Axel. "How do you know this? It can't be true."

"It is."

"When did you find out about this?"

"Over the past couple days, piece by piece. It's what you paid me to do."

"Why didn't you tell me?"

"I tried but you weren't ready to listen. I was waiting for the right time."

"You had plenty of opportunity," she argued.

Nicolai raised his voice, "Stop it. You sound like a bickering married couple. Where's our money?"

Kate said, "I don't know." She feared the folded list could be seen beneath her bra and regretted having it with her.

"What in heaven's name allows you to think it's your money?" Axel asked.

Nicolai said, "It's ours. Our father had shares in Innokenti Holding in Cyprus. Upon the demise of Ivan Innokenti the fortune was to be his, but unknown to him the old witch had fiduciary access to the account. Within one day she emptied everything and disappeared. It was like she had an escape plan already in place. From then on we looked for her. For over twenty years we have been searching for her. She was very evasive."

"And ten years ago, your father was gunned down in Brighton Beach," Axel stated.

Nicolai's face turned red. "They said it was an opposing gang, but we suspected the babushka hired someone. She was that cunning."

Kate's head was spinning. "That can't be. She wouldn't do such a thing."

Nicolai said, "Oh yes. When a mother lion is cornered she will do anything to protect her cubs."

Axel interjected, "You're speculating. Even if she did, it was payback for the murder of her husband, son and daughter-in-law."

"Shut up," exclaimed Leonid.

Kate asked, "What was the origin of this money you are talking about?"

The two brothers glanced at each other and Nicolai spoke. "Our father was an entrepreneur and created Innokenti Holding."

Axel spoke up. "That's not true. Your father was a heartless Soviet bureaucrat. It was Ivan Innokenti who created the company and the fortune behind it. He was an economics professor in St. Petersburg during the Soviet era and he knew that broken system would fall. As a smart investor he bought undervalued assets." He stared at the Orlovs.

"Your father was nothing more than a parasite."

Nicolai was sweating. He grinned, his eyes narrow slits. "Very insightful. You seem to understand everything, quite the historian. It's a pity your unusual capabilities will come to a sudden end. Now, where is the money?" He looked at his brother and nodded to him.

Leonid stepped forward, raised the Glock and shifted it back and forth from Kate to Axel to the young woman. He took another step forward and placed the gun close to the young woman's head. "Now tell us what we need to know. Otherwise Elsa Bjorg will have her pretty face deformed."

"Elsa Bjorg," Kate gasped, turning to Axel. "You're married?"

"She's my sister."

Nikolai said, "Enough. We needed leverage and the sister was a logical choice. Now, I'm counting to three and this time my brother won't stop. Where is the money? One . . . two . . ."

Kate watched Axel's hands shoot out in front of him like a snake striking its prey. He deflected the Glock and with a lightning-fast movement twisted the gun out of Leonid's hand. Axel quickly stood up and spun the younger Orlov around, holding Leonid against him as a shield. He then pointed the gun at the Brute and Pit-bull who were standing to the side of Nicolai.

Surprised at Axel's quick move, the Brute pointed the gun in his left hand clumsily at Axel. He fired it, missed Axel, and Leonid jerked backward.

There was no hesitation from Axel. He fired twice, once at the Brute and then at Pit-bull. Their arms convulsed upward and both fell to the ground, the weapons slipping from their hands.

As this happened, Nicolai stood spellbound, watching his brother fall to floor. Then with a frantic motion he raised the .22 pistol and fired three times. Two shots missed, but one found a mark. Axel staggered before dropping the Glock, lifting his hands to his chest, slumping to his knees and falling face-forward.

Something primal triggered Kate's reflexes as she reached to her right and grabbed the Mossberg twelve-gauge off the table. She remembered Axel's words, "Don't aim. Just point and pull the trigger."

She pointed it toward Nicolai, who was turning the pistol toward her. In a second her finger slipped onto the trigger and she squeezed. The sound was deafening. The gun recoiled with a wallop against her arm and she stumbled backwards as Leonid went to the floor.

The smell of smoke and burnt gunpowder filled the room. It mixed with the fumes of grease, oil and paint, giving an eerie odor to the warehouse.

Kate quickly surveyed the room. Five men were down. Leonid Orlov had been shot by one of his own mindless thugs. The Brute and Pit-bull lay still. Nicolai Orlov was an ugly sight, with a massive wound from the shotgun blast, his upper shoulder and neck a red distortion. Blood poured out from his neck. It was horrid and she quickly turned her eyes away.

By instinct she worked the pump of the shotgun, as Axel had shown her. The spent shell flew out the side and a new shell entered in the chamber.

With one hand she held the gun and with the other took Cold-Cap's switchblade from the table, switched it open and cut the tape from Elsa Bjorg's wrists. Handing the knife to Elsa she said, "Free your feet and then take care of Axel."

She looked to the floor on her left with a hollow feeling in her stomach. Axel's bullet wound seemed to be at his heart, and he wasn't moving.

Adrenaline flowed through her veins. The three guards were still outside. After hearing all the gunshots they would quickly be coming.

Kate went behind the front fender of the Porsche, crouched down and aimed the shotgun at the door, waiting for it to open. Her shoulder throbbed from the first shot of the gun and she wasn't sure it could take another recoil hit like that.

There were clanking noises outside and voices yelling and the sound of feet moving through the larger room. Someone kicked a tool or a piece of metal and a ringing sound echoed through the warehouse.

Then from beyond the door someone yelled, "Police! Drop your weapons."

Kate crouched low behind the car, holding the shotgun steady at the door. Men dressed in protective gear entered the room. She didn't trust them, not knowing if they were really police, until she saw Detective McGill.

With quivering hands she lowered the shotgun to the floor.

CHAPTER 46

Miami-Dade detectives quickly took control of the warehouse and waited for the arrival of crime technicians. The scene was gruesome. The Orlov brothers were pronounced dead, as well as the two men Axel had named the Brute and Pit-bull. Orlov's three guards were arrested.

Kate stood by helplessly when medics wheeled Axel from the building. The flashing lights and siren of the ambulance disappeared in the distance, leaving her with a painful void. Immediately after the ambulance left, she and Elsa were taken to a police station where they recounted events as much as they could. She wasn't sure she coherently answered Detective McGill's questions about what happened. The reality of shooting a man was sinking in, making the world around her spin. Everything was unreal, and it felt like she was living in a horrific nightmare.

Once they were finished at the police station, a police officer drove them to the hospital where Axel had been taken. A nurse informed them the Axel was in surgery, but that it was still too early for any news. Axel had received a serious wound and while the nurse tried to sound hopeful, the prognosis didn't sound good.

Kate and Elsa stayed in the waiting room spending several minutes in silence while they reflected on what the nurse had told them.

Finally, with a said face Elsa said, "I don't know what I'd do without my brother."

"You are close?" Kate asked.

"Very. He has always been there for me."

Kate was unsure what to say of how to comfort Elsa when in fact, she needed comforting. The trauma of the past few days was too much to bear. "I understand," she said. "He is a reflection of your family name, *Bjorg*, to help or to rescue."

Elsa turned to Kate and smiled, "He told you that?"

"Yes."

"My brother, the historian," Elsa stated.

"He is a remarkable man," Kate said in a soft voice.

"I know."

A tear rolled down Elsa's face and Kate reached next to her and they gently held hands while they waited for news. It seemed like an eternity. It gave Kate time to think, especially about what Axel had said at the warehouse.

She eventually let go of Elsa's hand, stood up and went to find a nurse.

Still without a cell phone, she asked the nurse if she could make a call. The nurse led her into a small office with a phone. She called Tommy.

"Tommy, this is Kate," she said.

"Oh man, I'm glad you called. I've been monitoring police radio and there is a bit on the news. How is Axel doing?"

"We don't know yet. I'm at the hospital. It may take some time."

"What happened?" He asked.

"It was horrible," she replied. She gave him a summary of the events at the warehouse.

"Those were freaky-bad guys," he said.

There was a pause, then Kate said, "May I ask you something about the Orlovs and my family background?"

"Go ahead."

"In the warehouse, Axel knew things about my family, things unknown to me. Did you help him get that information?"

"Some of it, then Axel figured out the rest. Ivan Innokenti was an investor from Saint Petersburg in Russia and he was murdered. It seems there was a company involved. The Orlovs were mixed up in this."

It was now clear to Kate why Emma and Clara had fled, eventually ending up in Florida, and why they led such cautious lives.

Tommy went on to tell her more about the Orlov family, their background and network in organized crime. It was then she understood how they knew she was arriving from the Bahamas to Miami International Airport.

The final pieces of this puzzle finally clicked into place, and Kate saw the full picture. Angry at the situation, she put a plan into place.

★ ★ ★

The following morning Kate waited at her apartment. Someone knocked on the front door and she opened it.

Chandler stood there in an impeccable dark blue Seville Row suit, white shirt, and colorful silk tie. He smiled and said, "I just flew in and came straight to your place."

She glanced outside and saw his driver leaning against the fender of a dark sedan. He was a stocky man who appeared to be more like a bodyguard.

With a neutral voice she said, "I'm glad you're here, Chandler. Come in."

Once seated on couches facing each other he remarked, "You look distraught. Are you okay?"

"Absolutely not. I've gone through a terrible time."

"Tell me about it."

"It's been horrible. The men following me were after two valuable paintings." She didn't want to tell him about the other paintings. "It's a long story, but even worse, yesterday those men were killed."

"Only two paintings?"

"The men were killed. Didn't you hear what I just said?"

"Only two paintings? That's all?" Chandler asked.

She realized he was ignoring her question and couldn't care less about the death of these men. The confirmation of his cruel indifference made her nauseated and frightened. "Why do you keep asking about the paintings?" She asked.

"From what you told me it seems the men were after something more," he claimed.

"Like what?"

"Like money."

"Chandler, you don't know what you're talking about."

He paused for a moment, face ashen. "Kate, there has to be more. You don't need to hold anything back. I can help you manage it."

"Why do you assume there is more than the paintings?"

His eyes widened. "Because . . ah, why would anyone break into your apartment and then chase after you for only two paintings?"

"They were misguided idiots, like someone else I know." She stared at him, her green eyes like darts.

With tight lips he whispered, "There has to be more."

"And how can you say that, unless you know something I don't?"

His body tightened. "There's no need to play games with me."

"I'm not the one playing games. I know for a fact you were working with the Orlov brothers."

"That's absurd. Why would you think that?"

"Besides Axel and me, there was only one person who knew we were in the Bahamas. You informed the Orlovs and they sent their thugs to meet us at the airport."

"I've never met these Orlovs. What happened in the Bahamas?"

"Nothing. Going there was a dead end." She stared at him. "And, don't tell me you've never met the Orlovs."

"Ridiculous," he sneered.

"You think so? Did you forget that you're their younger brother? I know your true colors, that your father was married several times and had a number of children. That you moved to the United States from Russia and you took the name of your maternal grandfather, Chandler Harrington. But, I also know your real name, Yury Orlov." The long telephone call with Tommy at the hospital the night before had revealed all of this.

Now she was seething with rage. This man, whom she had started to trust, to give her heart to, had manipulated her and lied. The bitterness of the betrayal filled her throat with acid and it took all her strength to remain composed.

"Have you gone crazy?" he growled.

"Chandler, –or should I say, Yury?– you make me want to puke…"

He forced a long breath, as though a million thoughts were running through his mind. With icy eyes he said, "You know too much." He quickly took his cell phone from his coat pocket, pushed a button and said, "You come now."

Almost immediately the front door opened and Chandler's driver walked through it. He closed the door behind him and stood next to it with arms folded.

"This is Vlad, my driver," Chandler said coldly. "He's versatile in many things. Our conversation is not going as I wished."

Kate glanced at the driver and back at Chandler. "After what I've gone through do you think I'm intimidated by your goon? I have more to say. I now know you are the money handler for the Orlov family and their illicit operations, some might say the financial brains behind everything. That's how you afford the fancy clothing and private jet."

He glanced at his driver then back at her and leered. "You're perceptive, but I'm not sure how you arrive at these conclusions."

"You manage Russian Mafia money. It all goes through you." If she had claws she would rip out his eyes.

"How did you make this assumption?" He let out.

"It's no assumption. I have my means," she asserted.

"You're wrong."

"I'm not." She pointed toward the driver. "I'm sure he is there for a purpose. At least before you let him kill me, be a man for once and speak the truth."

Chandler hissed, "You are smarter than I thought." He looked a Vlad and back at Kate, took a breath and with a proud smile on his face said, "At this point there's no harm in telling you. You see, certain syndicates have, ah . . . unusual competencies, but they lack financial skills. Of course these syndicates are not appreciated by law enforcement, so the question is, how do you reintegrate their questionable funds back into the economy?"

"That's where your skills come in," she stated.

He grinned. "You are perceptive, but I guess I should have expected that from someone working for an investment company. Yes, in fact I have created a highly complex network of companies and accounts.

The FBI would salivate to know about it, but they don't. The key to understanding this maze is done the old-fashioned way, on a notebook in a safe in my office. I run a highly important operation."

"You're so wonderful," she mocked. "Well, your two brothers won't be contributing anymore."

He smiled. "Half-brothers. Overbearing partners who were becoming a liability. Unfortunately for them. Let's see the bright side. Our profits will no longer be split three ways."

"Good for you," she said. "Where do you move the funds?" She needed more information.

He grinned. "You are a curious woman. To be honest, there's no need to move money offshore anymore. There are numerous ways to do it in the United States, under the noses of federal authorities."

Laser eyes fixed on him, she sneered, "You are so clever. I'm ashamed I almost fell for your manipulative romantic advances."

With a heartless smirk he said, "It's inbred that all women are gullible. Give them a fancy meal in an upscale restaurant, use the word *love*, and they sell their souls."

"But, you never really had me," she exclaimed, thinking how she had almost given in to him, how she dreamed he was the perfect man, that they would have an exceptional life together. *How many other women had fallen for the same kind of lies?* It disgusted her to think of his deceptions.

"Oh, no," He replied, white teeth glistening with contempt. "I *did* 'have you,' as you call it. My first objective was achieved. I found out you knew nothing about your grandmother's assets, at least not until you hired that private investigator. That's what I needed to know. But, let's get back to the important second objective. There has to be more than two paintings. Your conniving grandmother had more than that."

"I'm afraid not," she stated.

"Look Kate, I was honest with you. Now be honest with me. Where is your grandmother's fortune?"

"As I said, you are an idiot, exactly like your brothers."

He took a breath, his fists tightening. "At least I have my brothers' money, so I thank you for removing them."

"You're sick," she said.

"Perhaps, but effective." He paused and said. "Kate, I actually like you. Besides being a stunning woman, you are clever. Perhaps you learned this from your grandmother. We could form an interesting relationship, a partnership, to enjoy the fruits of enormous wealth. Would you consider this?"

This new attempt at cold manipulation made her flesh crawl. She peered at him, her face tight. "Chandler, you can take your fruits and stick them up a dark place where your head belongs."

His face became red like an enraged devil. "I don't believe anything you said about the money." Turning to his driver he commanded, "Vlad, it's time to extract the full truth from her, whatever it takes."

With a mean grin, Vlad quickly stepped across the room and grabbed Kate by her left wrist as Chandler leaned across and attempted to put his hand over her mouth. In her struggle against Vlad's tight grip, Chandler's hand slipped. She saw an opportunity, clamped her teeth onto his hand and bit with full force. He howled like a chimpanzee and pulled his hand away.

A second later men in SWAT gear rushed into the living room, dove on Chandler and Vlad and pushed them to the floor. Chandler hopelessly fought back and in the scrimmage, someone's elbow banged into his face causing blood to stream from his nose onto his expensive suit and shirt.

Vlad was wiser and surrendered without a fight. After their hands were cuffed, one of the SWAT team members went to Kate's bathroom, rolled up a small wad of toilet paper and stuffed it into Chandler's bleeding nostril.

As two stocky men escorted Chandler out the front door, he fixed his murderous eyes on Kate.

She saw deep red teeth marks on his hand and stared back at him with a contented gleam. A weight of lead fell from her shoulders when she saw him taken away. Her plan had worked. The conversation with Chandler had been captured on video, every word recorded by the police.

Detective McGill came to Kate's side and said, "Our task force has been after the Orlovs for a long time and Chandler Harrington was on our radar. Now we finally got the financial mastermind. The confession about the notebook in his safe was an amazing piece of information. And, I don't know how you found out that Harrington was a brother of the Orlovs."

She deflected his question, not wanting him to learn about Tommy or anything that might lead to him. "He's vermin," she exclaimed, wiping her lips with her finger. "He tasted like poison."

He grinned. "You were tough with him."

"Nothing like what he deserved."

Detective McGill nodded. "I agree. What I can't figure out is why the Orlovs went through so much trouble to break into your apartment to steal two paintings. They had so much more at play in their own organization."

She raised her eyebrows. "I know. It seems they had the wrong idea or were very foolish."

"Foolish to mess with you," he chuckled. "In any case, it's finished and we're very grateful for what you've done."

After Detective McGill and the other police officers left, she sat down on the couch, the same one she had cried on less than a week before when seeing her apartment in disarray. It had been a roller coaster of events and emotions. How the world had changed in such a short amount of time. She was astonished at what she had accomplished. If only Emma and Clara could see this, they would be proud of her.

CHAPTER 47

The next three days were filled with anxiety as Kate spent hours at the hospital where Axel was in critical condition. On the fourth day she decided to go back to her job at Wesson Securities thinking it would divert her thoughts and provide relief from what she was feeling. But, after two hours of staring at stock charts she realized it was wrong to be there. She stood up and looked at the large office space with endless rows of cubicles, and then made a decision.

She went to the supplies room, found an empty wooden box and back at her desk she put all her personal things in the box. There wasn't much. Then she wrote a letter and went to the office of her boss and knocked on the door.

"Come in." he said. He sat behind his desk and on it were a large pile of papers.

She walked in, stood in front of his desk, and after a moment of hesitation said, "I'm sorry, but I have something to tell you." She handed him the letter.

His face remained still as he read it. When finished, he frowned and said, "This is surprise and I don't get it. Why?"

She hesitated knowing so much had happened, yet she was reluctant to share the details with him. Finally all she could say was, "The robbery of my apartment caused me to think about my future."

"You're quitting because of a silly robbery?"

Her boss didn't know about the events at the warehouse, as the names of Axel, Elsa and herself had not appeared in the news. Detective McGill and his team did this to not endanger them, in case there might be criminal organizations seeking retribution.

"There was more to it," Kate said.

"Well, whatever."

"What do you mean *whatever*? Have you ever been robbed?"

He raised her letter and held it in front of her. "Are you sure about this? You had such a promising future here. Why would you throw it away?"

"I don't feel I'm throwing anything away. It's just that I have other priorities."

Her boss took a deep breath and the muscles in his neck tightened. "You see this stack of paper. Those represent our clients and we have an enormous responsibility to manage their assets. You can't just walk out on them."

"You'll do okay," she said, knowing a reality had not yet sunk in. She had more financial assets than their wealthiest client.

"So, you're sure about this?"

"Yes."

"You know that jobs are hard to find." He looked at her with cold eyes. "And I'm not sure I can give a recommendation if you walk out on me like this."

She felt his intimidation, like blackmail. The employees in the office feared him. She said, "I won't be looking for a job."

"You need to live. What are you going to do?"

She paused, wondered how to reply, and with a slow answer said, "This may sound unusual, but I need to spend time waiting for a friend."

"What? That doesn't make sense."

She smiled. "It makes all the sense in the world. Thank you for everything. I've learned a lot."

She stuck out her hand and he reluctantly shook it, then she turned and went back to her desk and picked up the box. Heading for the exit she had only one thing on her mind . . . to get back to Axel.

★ ★ ★

At the hospital Kate went to the waiting area where she saw Axel's mother Ingrid and Elsa his sister. Around the clock they had taken turns sitting at his bedside. Axel's father had also been part of the visitation rotation. It gave time for Kate to get to know Axel's family and she liked them.

Kate took a seat next to Ingrid, Axel's mother.

"How is he doing"? Kate asked.

Ingrid spoke with a slow, sad voice. "He's the same."

Kate knew what that meant. Axel was in a coma hanging between life and death. The bullet had ricocheted off a rib and passed just next to his heart. It would have been certain death had the bullet come from the more destructive nine millimeter Glock. Nevertheless, damage was done.

"I feel terrible that I brought this on your family, especially Elsa who was dragged into such danger."

Ingrid spoke. "I never liked this private detective business and always worried about him. You cannot be blamed for Axel's decisions." She spoke with a slight Norwegian accent, a lovely sing-song that calmed Kate's heart.

"Thank you for that, but I still feel guilt. You know that Axel is very good at what he does. Without him I would not have found my possessions." She looked across at Elsa who had a slight smile on her face. At the warehouse Elsa had heard things about Kate's past, yet Elsa was keeping it secret. Kate felt she could trust her.

"Was my brother easy to work with?" Elsa asked.

Kate laughed. "He has his ways."

"You mean stubborn and independent? It comes from our ancestors, hard-headed Norwegians."

"I wish you could have met my aunt and grandmother to see that my background is the same. It's no wonder that Axel and I had some conflicts, ah . . . I guess you could call it tug-of-wars. But yes, your brother is a wonderful man."

"So, you like him?" Elsa asked.

Kate glanced at Elsa, blue eyes waiting for an answer. The question unsettled her. Why was she here hour after hour? Why had she quit her job? She took a breath knowing she had fallen for Axel. There was something there that she had never felt for Chandler. Initially the times with Chandler had been exciting, just what she was missing in her routine life. But she never felt Chandler in her heart. With Axel it was very different. He challenged her and stirred her inner being in a way that no other man ever had.

She answered Elsa's question. "Yes, I like him." Her eyes became watery knowing that Axel was in a nearby room fighting for his life.

Ingrid reached next to her and squeezed Kate's hand and said, "We like you too."

They sat together, no one speaking, knowing the gravity of Axel's condition as he fought for his life in a nearby room. Eventually, Elsa and Ingrid went into Axel's room to sit next to him.

After twenty minutes they came out of his room and Elsa said to Kate, "We'll come back in a few hours. Can you stay here?"

"Yes, of course," Kate answered.

Elsa and Ingrid left the waiting room and Kate stood up and she noticed someone coming into the waiting area. It was Detective McGill.

He nodded at Kate and said, "I thought I'd find you here."

"It's been a long four days," she answered.

"How is your private detective doing?" He asked.

"Still the same. Unconscious. The last report was that he has stabilized but still not out of danger."

"I'm sorry to hear that." He paused, and then said, "Well, on another front we have some good news. Chandler Harrington lawyered-up but the FBI went to his office in New York and opened up his safe. Indeed there was a note book with the names of his clients, bank account numbers and much more. As a result, there are a lot of people currently being arrested for some serious crimes. It looks like Mr. Harrington was complicit in paying off some hit jobs, so that's another strike against him. The two Orlov brothers were mixed up in much of this. Of course the recording we made at your apartment only puts a cherry on the cake. He will be extradited to New York and it's certain he's going away for a long time."

"They should sentence him to hell to join his brothers."

McGill smiled. "I'm on your side."

"Do I have anything to worry about?" She asked.

"I don't think so. This thing the Orlovs had for you was a small side show compared to all the other stuff that's on the table."

She took a deep breath. "That's good to know. If you and your team had not come to the warehouse, who knows what would have happened."

"Yeah, that was a break. When you called me from the airport and the call was suddenly discontinued, we took quick action. That warehouse was already under surveillance so when we saw the van pull drive into that courtyard, our team was on the way." His deep eyes looked at her. "I still think it's strange that the Orlovs would make such a deal about two paintings when they had much bigger things at play up in New York."

"I know," she replied.

"I've got some other good news, at least personal good news," he said. "This case got me a promotion and I figured it's time to turn in my badge. Retirement sounds very good."

Kate grinned. "I'm happy for you."

"It never would have happened without you and Axel Bjorg. In the beginning I had doubts about him but he did an great job."

They said good-bye and McGill walked out the door. She suspected he knew there was more to this than two paintings, but sensed he would leave it at that. The justice system was now busy with a web of criminal organizations that spread across the United States.

As she reflected on Candler Harrington and the Orlov brothers, Kate finally understood Emma's reasons for discretion. She decided she would follow her grandmother's ways. Prudence would guide her as no one needed to know about her fortune. Her main desire was to use it for something good, but for now that was secondary. Her main concern was Axel and she wondered how long she would need to wait before getting news either good or bad.

She went into Axel's room and sat in the chair next to his bed. His eyes were shut and he was slowly breathing, his chest moving up and down.

After several minutes of watching him, Kate whispered, "Axel, if you can hear me, this is let you know that I need you."

She sensed movement at the door and turned to see a man standing who had been listening to what she had said. She guessed he was in his late sixties and he was tanned and seemed fit.

He laughed and said, "It's good to know this guy is needed by somebody. I always had my doubts."

Kate was surprised. "Who are you?"

"My name's Harry Raintree."

"I've heard about you," she said.

"And, I've heard about you. Axel called me and said he was at my house with a lovely woman. He said you were a client but he wished it was personal. Now I see why."

"You're kidding."

"Nope." Harry Raintree walked over to the bed and looked down at Axel. "I think he'll make it. He's a fighter and now he knows there's someone who needs him."

Feeling embarrassed, she wasn't sure how to respond, and then said, "I meant it."

He smiled. "He's a good guy. You couldn't do better." He looked at Kate and asked, "Where did the bullet hit him?"

"Left side of his chest, close to his heart."

"Terrible student. I always told him to duck."

Kate laughed and somehow Harry's comment and his presence brought relief from the memory of what happened at the warehouse.

"I read about the Orlov's," he said. In my business I always tried to stay away from violent criminals and taught Axel to do the same, but sometimes it can't be avoided. Is the case closed?"

"He did a remarkable job," she replied.

"That's good."

They remained quiet looking at Axel while Kate realized how little she knew about him. She said, "Tell me about him."

Harry smiled. "From the day he walked into my office as a college student I knew he was someone special. His first job was to look into some spreadsheets of a tricky accountant that was siphoning money from a company. Axel was quick to spot anomalies, which I had overlooked. From there he quickly developed and eventually he took over the business, as you must know."

"But tell me what he is like as a person?" She asked.

Harry chuckled. "An independent thinker, loyal, a good guy."

Harry stayed for half an hour and described adventures he had with Axel. Finally, Harry handed her a business card, and said, "Please keep me updated," and he left.

She sat in the quietness of the hospital room where the only sound was Axel's slow breathing, still unconscious, still hanging on a thread between life and death. She wondered if he'd just quietly stop breathing and sensed the emptiness she would feel in her life.

Then she saw his eyes flicker and they opened and he stared at the ceiling.

She stood up to better see his face.

His head slightly shifted and he looked at her. "Where am I?" He asked, the words coming out groggy and slow.

"In a hospital," she replied.

"That's a beautiful voice," he said. His eyes met hers. "What happened?"

"Do you remember the warehouse and being shot?"

His eyes squinted. "Vaguely. But, if I'm in the hospital, are you a nurse?"

"No, don't you remember me?"

"Ah, not . . . much, but you are beautiful."

"Axel, do you know who I am?" She wondered if he was joking.

"Who is Axel?" He asked.

"It's you."

She waited as he took several deep breaths, then with an unsteady voice he said, "I only remember one thing."

"What's that?"

"Katerina, I . . . I love you."

Surprised, she asked, "You remember me?"

He shut his eyes and went back to sleep.

EPILOGUE

The following morning Kate went to the hospital, walked into Axel's room and her heart fluttered when she saw him sitting up in his bed. A rolling tray was in front of him and his hand shook as he placed a half a glass of juice on it.

His eyes met her's and he smiled. "Wow. It's so nice to see you. They tell me I've been out for five days."

"Five long days," she said. "We've been so worried about you."

"Who is we?" He pushed the tray-table off to the side of his bed.

"Elsa and your mother and father. We have been playing tag-team next to you."

He grinned. "I bet I was a pretty sight, but thank you so much."

She was uncertain what to do, and then she walked over to him and took his hand. "I'd give you a hug, but it might put you back in a coma."

"You're right. My ribs are sore but they tell me I'll recover." He paused. "I'm wondering about something."

"What's that?"

"My last recollection was being in a warehouse, grabbing a gun, and then everything went dark after that. What happened?"

Kate took a deep breath, not wanting to re-live that experience. Then she told him what happened, carefully describing each event including the arrest of Chandler Harrington.

When she was finished he asked, "So Chandler Harrington is a brother of the Orlovs? I never saw that coming."

"He was an evil, manipulative human being, if you even want to call him that."

Axel grinned. "I have to confess something."

"What's that?" She asked.

"I was jealous of the guy."

She patted his hand. "Don't be. I get nauseated just thinking of him."

He took her hand and squeezed it and she felt his strength even though he had been unconscious for so many days.

She waited a moment, and then asked, "Do you remember what you said yesterday?"

"Yesterday?"

"Yes, I was here and you woke up for a minute or two."

"I don't remember, but did I say something goofy?"

"You didn't know who you were."

"Oh come on. You're telling me that Axel Bjorg was suffering amnesia?"

"I guess so."

"Did I say anything else?"

She hesitated and replied, "No, nothing else."

"Are you sure? Did I also say, *Katerina, I love you?*" He said it with a twinkle in his eye.

She laughed. "You're a terrible man!" She wanted to hit him on the chest or arm, but held back.

"It was the drugs messing with my head," he said.

"You think so?"

He waited as though he was struggling to find the right words. "I meant what I said, Kate, I love you."

She looked into his eyes and was sure of herself, more sure than she had ever been. She said, "Axel, I love you too."

★ ★ ★

Seven days later Axel walked out of the hospital and he began a routine of light workouts in the morning and long walks in the afternoon with Kate. That gave them time to talk and to share.

During the time of recovery Axel had time to consider his life. The mental playback of the confrontation at the warehouse drained his emotions. When he thought back to the deadly guns pointed at Kate and Elsa, he was overwhelmed with a feeling of dread. His training in martial arts had paid off and his quick reactions had saved them. But everything had become a blur when the bullet entered his chest, and then everything went dark until that magical moment when he saw the most beautiful image in the world . . . Kate's face. That moment confirmed she was the one.

Over the days of recovery he made a decision concerning his business. In the future he'd limit himself to forensic accounting and stay away from anything that had to do with organized crime. But then again, you never really knew what would walk through the door.

Once back on his feet he spent time with Kate and one weekend he went to her home in Palm Beach. She taught him to cook piroshky and knedliki. He was always amazed how effortlessly she mixed ingredients, like she waved a magic wand and delightful creations flew from the oven. They laughed as he attempted to keep up with her.

The meal was a delightful time of discussion and laughter, yet he was nervous of knowing when to pick the right time for what he had to do. After the dishes were cleared they went into the living room and sat on a soft couch. Several candles burned and gave a glow to the room while soft jazz played from speakers in the background. A plate of Swiss chocolates and two porcelain cups of Arabica coffee were on the table in front of them.

He had an important objective for the evening but wasn't sure of the timing, perhaps to wait until the coffee was finished. Then he thought to himself, *now or never* and he removed a small power blue box from his pocket.

He said, "Kate, there's something I'd like to say." He paused while searching for the right combination of words. "You are the most special person in my life. I love you and it would be the greatest joy to spend my life with you. Will you marry me?" He had a longer speech planned, but totally blew it. Getting down on one knee had also been a consideration, but in the last minute that seemed out of character for a hard-nosed private detective.

He opened the box and presented her with a wedding ring, its large diamond reflecting the candle light.

Kate smiled and her eyes filled with tears. She chuckled and said, "What took you so long? The answer is yes."

He moved closer to her on the couch and they embraced and kissed, lingering, lost in each other's presence.

★ ★ ★

The wedding took place at St. Catherine's Orthodox Church in West Palm Beach and the ceremony was performed by Reverend Levkin. Kate's biggest regret was that Emma and Clara were not there.

They held the wedding reception in the backyard of her house in Palm Beach, and it was a joyful event filled with music, dancing and fun. Late at night, once everyone had left, Axel led her to the front door of the house and said, "I'm a traditional guy."

"You? Traditional?" She laughed.

Without answering he swept her up and carried her through the open door.

In his strong arms she felt a sense of security and as he put her back on her feet she giggled, "That kind of tradition is fun, so keep it coming Dr. Bjorg."

They kissed, and as desire took over, they headed for the bedroom.

Eventually, they rested in each other's arms and drifted into small talk, toggling between teasing and romantic expressions. Kate stared into

Axel's eyes and said, "There's something I wanted to ask you. How did you find out so much about me?"

"You mean you want to talk business at a time like this?" He smiled.

"It's more curiosity than business." She replied.

"Okay, what do you mean, how did I find out about you?"

"You knew my real name before I did. Katerina Innokenti."

"It was Tommy who discovered this and when I heard the name I liked it. Katerina Innokenti, Catherine the Innocent. It has some kind of historical ring." He grinned and said, "Well, you've now got four different names on four passports, so you can take your pick. At least when you travel."

"Very funny. I suppose I could also go by Kate Bjorg?"

"Ah, who cares. At least I've got you, whoever you are?"

"Maybe someday I'll show you the real me." She laughed and lightly punched him on the arm.

"Uh oh. What have I done?" He countered.

She happily thought about the trip they had planned, perhaps the longest honeymoon ever, at least in the distance that they would cover. They planned several months to visit the eleven different portfolio managers around the world. On the trip they would visit art museums for her and historical sites for him. They would see mountains, forests, seas and sunsets, and she looked forward to get to know him better along the way.

Their bags were packed and a taxi was scheduled for the morning.

★ ★ ★

Axel fell asleep and Kate watched him breathe, his muscular chest slowly moving up and down. He was still overcoming the injury, but was ready to travel.

As Kate's eyes became drowsy and exhaustion set in, she looked across the large bedroom to the wall where the Picasso painting was hanging, *Jeune Fille en Couleur.* Underneath it stood the stolen antique dresser, now reconstructed by a specialist woodworker.

On the dresser was a large white Bible given to them by Reverend Levkin. And next to the Bible was Emma's Betty Crocker Cookbook.

Kate slid out of bed, went to the Bible and placed a hand on it. After saying a prayer for Axel and his family, and thanking God for Emma and Clara, she crossed herself three times in the Orthodox tradition.

Then her eyes shifted to the old Betty Crocker Cookbook and she opened it to the last page with handwritten notes.

The first one read, *"The way to man's heart is through his stomach, but our teenager Kate says there are never any men around here. Maybe someday?"* Kate chuckled. That man was now sleeping in her bed. Aunt Clara wasn't able to choose him like she'd always teased, yet Kate was sure her aunt would be pleased.

Below that, Emma had written, *"Sometimes in chess there are tactical errors, but that doesn't mean you will lose the game."* That was a good lesson for life.

The last scribble said, *"Kate, may the Lord fill you with His grace all the days of your life. And remember our happy times in the kitchen."*

She thought of the Hungarian goulash and the other recipes of Emma and Clara, remembering their stories like The Frog Princess, and Baba Yaga and Her Son, and of their teachings from the old country, that "sometimes evil people want to destroy you, but in the end they will destroy themselves." Kate had seen it happen.

She carefully flipped through the pages of the old cookbook and imagined the smells, tastes and laughter from the kitchen. She reflected on Emma's instruction that, *"A meal is more than nourishment for the body. It is nourishment for the soul. It's where families unite. Preparing a meal is a creative act of love."*

She had already started that tradition by teaching Axel how to make ambrosia balls and *Piccata al Limone*. Someday their children would join them and the kitchen table would become a place of laughter and uniting.

She closed the cookbook and ran her fingers across the cover, smooth in places and wrinkly in others, worn by use and time, like Emma and Clara.

They were exceptional women, and more than ever she wanted to be like them.

Kate stepped back from the cookbook, slipped into bed and cuddled next to Axel.

Author's Notes

Where do the ideas for stories come from? This one came from an unusual source.

When I moved to Europe my grandmother gave me her old Betty Crocker Cookbook. For years it had been her go-to reference for pancakes in the morning, apple pie after lunch and many other dishes. As a result it is covered with smudges on the pages and scribbles in the margins, which gives it a unique character.

That cookbook has been with me ever since and it triggers some of my fondest childhood memories, particularly my grandmother's laughter as she lovingly prepared meals for our large family get-togethers. I now realize that her meals linked past traditions to the future. Combined with this, her wise advice in the kitchen transmitted culture and values.

My grandmother has passed-on and I still cherish her favorite recipes. One day I looked at her scribbles in the cookbook and imagined what would happen if they contained secret messages. I also recalled her saying that, "A meal is more than nourishment. It touches the soul." Somehow that sparked the idea for the story in *The COOKBOOK*.

I'm thankful to the Archives Department at General Mills for allowing me to use the image on the book cover. It's a delightful illustration of a woman waving a magic wand and perfect muffins, pies and cakes pop from her oven. This reflects an idealistic time where families enjoyed meals and bonded together. Wouldn't it be wonderful if this could be recreated in the midst of our busy stress-filled lives?

One unique aspect of a meal is that it can facilitate romance. For Axel and Kate, the home cooked dinners allowed them time to relax and get to know each other. And of course Kate's culinary skills won Axel's heart. If you'd like to try Kate's Piccata al Limone, I've included that recipe on my website, as well as most of the other dishes found in *The COOKBOOK*.

Also on my website you'll find a list of discussion questions that may help you, your friends and your Reading Group to see the book (and your own life) in new ways. Just go to http://www.casstell.com/reader-group-questions.html

If you liked *The COOKBOOK*, please tell your friends.

Happy reading,

Cass Tell
www.casstell.com

CPSIA information can be obtained
at www.ICGtesting.com
Printed in the USA
LVOW10s1740050117

519816LV00003B/194/P